The London of Us

by Clare Lydon

custard
books

First Edition June 2018
Published by Custard Books
Copyright © 2018 Clare Lydon
ISBN: 978-1-912019-97-7

Cover Design: Kevin Pruitt
Editor: Laura Kingsley
Copy Editor: Gill Mullins
Typesetting: Adrian McLaughlin

Find out more at: www.clarelydon.co.uk
Follow me on Twitter: @clarelydon
Follow me on Instagram: @clarefic

Also by Clare

London Romance Series
London Calling (Book 1)
This London Love (Book 2)
A Girl Called London (Book 3)
London, Actually (Book 5)
Made In London (Book 6)

Other Novels
The Long Weekend
Nothing To Lose: A Lesbian Romance
Twice In A Lifetime
Once Upon A Princess
You're My Kind

All I Want Series
All I Want For Christmas (Book 1)
All I Want For Valentine's (Book 2)
All I Want For Spring (Book 3)
All I Want For Summer (Book 4)
All I Want For Autumn (Book 5)
All I Want Forever (Book 6)

Boxsets
All I Want Series Boxset, Books 1-3
All I Want Series Boxset, Books 4-6
All I Want Series Boxset, Books 1-6
London Romance Series Boxset, Books 1-3

ACKNOWLEDGEMENTS

As ever with any book, this one wouldn't be in your dainty hands without help from a ton of people. First, thanks to my very early reader and friend HP Munro, who helped to shape this into the book it is — thanks for giving up a precious Monday for me. Also thanks to my early reading team — in no particular order Tammara, Iris, Victoria, Hilary, Susan, Katie & Bev — who always spot errors and give good suggestions. Take a bow, you're all terrific!

As ever, thanks to my editor Laura who nods, sighs and tells me it's good, but could I do even better? (nb: I always can); to Kevin for the truly lush cover (you're a marvel!); to Gill for making my sentences stutter less & hug more; and to Adrian for laying it all out with style and panache. The four of you are integral to everything I do.

A tip of the nib to my wife, Yvonne, who always gives great feedback, as well as being a patient sounding board, a great cook and the most generous person I know. I'm lucky to have her in my life.

Finally, thanks to you for reading. I've invested a lot in the London series, and each book is special to me — I hope you feel the same way, too. Writing Alice's story took me back to my early days of dating, when I wasn't getting the full picture, wondering what was missing. And then I kissed a girl and it all made a hell of a lot more sense.

Expect Becca's story next — I can't wait to write it!

Connect with me:
Twitter: @clarelydon
Facebook: clare.lydon
Instagram: @clarefic
Email: mail@clarelydon.co.uk
Join my VIP Readers' Group: www.clarelydon.co.uk/it-had-to-be-you

It's never too late, especially to be yourself.

Chapter One

I'd had the dream again.

I woke in a flurry of hot sheets and damp skin, trying to ground myself back in reality, rather than my dreams which had become far too vivid recently.

Too late: my heart was banging against my sternum and all I could see was her.

I didn't have to touch myself to know I was wet.

For the past three months, my dreams hadn't held back, telling me everything I needed to know, everything I desperately wanted to ignore.

The sheets next to me were still warm: Jake was up and in the shower, already deep into his daily routine. But today, I had no plans, nowhere to be. It was the middle of July, and this particular Saturday was special because it was day one of the summer holidays, and six weeks with no teaching stretched ahead of me like a long, sandy beach, the sea my day, glittering with excitement. I could either dive in or sit on the edge. It was up to me.

The shower shut off.

I tensed as I heard the curtain being pulled back. In two minutes, Jake would be in here, being perky.

He was a morning person, and I was not.

Scrap that — Jake was a morning person, an afternoon person, and an evening person. Constantly upbeat, always ready with a smile. In the year and a half we'd been together, I could count his down days on one hand.

And even saying 'down days' was a lie.

Jake didn't have down days: he just had marginally less upbeat days.

Unlike me, who was having a cluster of what-the-fuck days of late. On top of all that, I'd got a massive spot on the end of my nose that felt like it had doubled in size overnight. When I peered down, I could see it winking at me, my own face mocking me.

"Morning sleepyhead!" Jake walked into the bedroom from the en suite, steam following him from the doorway.

He never remembered to open the bathroom window.

He walked round the bed and bent to kiss me: I winced as our lips connected, but Jake didn't notice. I was sure he'd be able to taste the hesitation on my breath, but he was oblivious — of the hesitation, and of my spot.

Jake never saw my bad points, only the good.

Lately, it was a habit that was starting to grate.

Seconds later, his head was buried in his wardrobe, and he was pulling out clean shorts and a workout top, slipping them on while I yawned.

Jake was a personal trainer, so this was his office wear.

As his head reappeared out of his top, his curls sprang out, then back. His hair hadn't changed since he was a kid – I'd seen the photos. He was cute then and he was cute now.

It's just, I wasn't sure Jake's brand of cuteness worked for me anymore.

"Morning." I finally managed to get some words out, before stretching my arms above my head, trying to appear relaxed, normal.

Inside, I was anything but.

"What time's your first client?"

"Eight," Jake replied, checking his watch. "So I better get moving. What are your plans till I come get you later?"

I stared at him, his biceps rippling under Lycra. When we'd first started going out, his strength had been one of the things I'd found attractive.

I shrugged. "Nothing big — I'm easing in slowly. Maybe some TV, some tea and crumpets."

"Take it slow," he said, with a grin. "Work up to the bigger goals." He grabbed his work bag, striding over to me. He smelled like musk and honey, his favourite shower gel. "I've got clients till 11, but then I'll come pick you up to go to Ikea." He looked down at my book, watch and rings sitting on the thick, beige carpet. "It's time for the next step in our relationship — proper, grown-up bedside tables with drawers and everything."

He kissed me again, this time leaving his lips inches from mine.

I tried not to flinch, but even that action felt dishonest.

Jake didn't deserve dishonesty.

He really didn't deserve any of this.

"You smell delicious," he added, his smile undimmed, his gaze caressing my skin. "Shame I have to go."

I reached out and touched his stubble, ever-present, along with his chestnut waves.

Beside me, my bedside lamp flickered, and Jake glanced at it.

"Might get you a new lamp, too."

I couldn't wait. "Have a good morning."

One that isn't soaked in life questions and self-doubt.

He gave me a wink, then turned and left the room.

The front door slammed and I relaxed for the first time that morning. I spread my legs in the bed, then my arms, wriggling over to the middle, revelling in the space. It's what I needed more than anything right now.

Space to breathe, space to think.

The school holidays had come at just the right time. Although too much time to think might send me into a tailspin, and I didn't need that.

I wanted to scream at the universe, to ask what was happening to me.

Why couldn't I just carry on with Jake and be happy? Plenty of women would be.

But deep down inside, I knew what was happening.

And her name was Rachel.

Chapter Two

Two months earlier...

"**B**abe, you need to look at the camera as well as Rachel when you're chatting. Remember, you're talking to the audience as well as being Rachel's muse." Jake's head was cocked as he gave me direction from behind the video camera. He needed a haircut, but I'd told him that for the past two weeks and he kept telling me he was too busy.

I nodded. "Okay, I'll try." We'd just done a run-through of this week's cookery section for our YouTube channel, Fit & Tasty, but none of this was easy, with Jake's lens trained on me, and Rachel standing next to me.

It used to be way easier, but recently, not so much.

I was beginning to feel a little uncomfortable around Rachel.

Perhaps uncomfortable was the wrong word.

What was the right word?

Nervous?

Flighty?

And then a word landed on my tongue: *aroused*.

I stalled at my own internal dialogue.

Aroused? Really?

If Rachel knew what I was thinking, she'd die laughing — that much I knew.

Over the past year, we'd become close friends, and I wasn't about to tell her she made me aroused, especially when that seemed preposterous.

Rachel didn't arouse me, she was my friend. And where did that language even come from? Was I turning into a Victorian-era cliché? Would I start wearing Pride And Prejudice-style bonnets soon, wafting my many-layered undergarments as I walked?

I was parking 'aroused'.

I had a boyfriend, after all. Although that fact didn't seem to be the barrier it once was, with my body reacting in all sorts of weird ways every time Rachel was nearby.

Perhaps flustered described it better. That, and tongue-tied, which was the last thing I wanted when Jake was staring at me.

Rachel — the one who was making me flustered, tongue-tied and whatever else — skidded back into the kitchen, breaking my thoughts. Her short, dark hair was styled to perfection, her pale skin carrying just the right amount of make-up for the camera. She'd lost weight since we began filming: I hadn't thought she'd had any to lose, but she'd reacted to seeing herself on-screen, describing herself as a "hefty lump".

It was the last thing I thought she was. With her strong arms and fierce cheekbones, I thought she was exquisite.

And there was another new word I was using when I thought about Rachel.

It was certainly better than aroused.

Rachel's sparkling blue eyes made me think of summer days and endless nights.

Damn, that was new, too.

This time last year, I was just getting to know her, after we'd ended up being left together when our two best friends, Tanya and Sophie, began seeing each other. Within months, we'd become firm friends, fuelled by our love of food — Rachel was a chef, and I just loved to cook and eat. We became once-a-month restaurant buddies, trying out all the new openings around town.

And then, six months ago, Rachel and Jake had decided to team up and create a whole new sideline, dreamed up in this very flat over a meal that my oldest friend Tanya had cooked.

I could still remember the night: Tanya and Sophie on one side of the table, Jake and I down the other, and Rachel presiding over us, getting more excited by the second as the idea was tossed around. Jake wanted to share his personal training secrets, while Rachel wanted to demystify cooking with her flavour-packed recipes — and their YouTube channel, Fit & Tasty, was born.

So, in a way, this was all Tanya's fault. Especially because she then volunteered her flat with its massive kitchen as our

filming base, which meant any excuses we might have had
to stall the launch vanished.

Somewhere along the line, I'd been pulled in front of the
camera and was now a regular feature on Rachel's cooking
segment, as well as being camera operative and video editor.
I'd taught myself video editing as part of my role as Head of
Art & Design at the local college a couple of years previous,
so I was happy to help. It was being in front of the camera
that was tipping me out of my comfort zone.

"Found them!" Rachel said, brandishing solid wooden
salad tongs in her right hand. Over the past few weeks I'd
noticed how long and slim her fingers were, and how they
were covered in scars from encounters with knives and
hot plates — a hazard of being a chef according to her.

Rachel shared a flat ten floors below with Sophie, her
best friend and Tanya's girlfriend — which meant if she
couldn't find what she needed at Tanya's, it was easy for
her to nip downstairs to retrieve it from her own kitchen.

"I still don't understand why you need those tongs,"
Jake said.

I didn't need to glance at Rachel to know she was
giving him a look. "That's why you're the muscle in this
relationship, and I'm the brains."

Jake grinned. "And I have no problem with that."

The relationship between Rachel and Jake warmed my
heart: it was like the cutest brother-sister match-up ever,
without any of the history and family angst. They had the
perfect, goofy, on-screen chemistry.

Rachel and I used to have the perfect on-screen frisson, too, but lately, something had changed and I couldn't quite put my finger on what it was.

She was cooking a delicious yet simple pasta with mozzarella, tomatoes and basil, and her fingers were slick with olive oil as she mixed the ingredients in a glass bowl with her bare hands. The sweet smell of the tomatoes was making my stomach growl: Rachel had bought them from her special supplier and the taste was off-the-charts good, the kitchen smelling like it had just been punched in the face by an Italian.

It really was true what they said: if you started off with the best ingredients, the food was always going to be great. The buffalo mozzarella Rachel was using was so ripe, it was almost walking off the plate. My dad, an Italian by birth and happiest when he was creating in the kitchen, would adore everything Rachel did.

Between the ingredients and the chef, I'd be hard-pushed to envisage a more perfect lunch.

And there I went with my new, weird thoughts again, blood rushing to my cheeks as I processed them.

Maybe 'aroused' wasn't too far off the mark.

Had Jake noticed? I hoped not.

I glanced at Rachel who was washing her hands, oblivious.

I was doing a good job of sitting on my emotions, squashing them down until they couldn't breathe.

"Sorry to be a pain, but can you give me two more

minutes? I need the loo." Rachel dried her hands on Tanya's bright orange tea towel. Then she walked down the hallway, leaving Jake and I alone.

On this fresh May morning, the flat was flooded with buttery sunshine even though the temperature outside was only just clambering into double figures. Tanya's flat, our base for Fit & Tasty, had a wall of glass on one side, which sucked up the sunlight on the 30th floor, making our show look sun-kissed, rich and gorgeous. Her open-plan kitchen and marble-topped island made our cookery segments pop, too, and we were all beyond grateful she'd agreed to let us use it to get the channel up and running.

As soon as the bathroom door shut, Jake walked over to me and my stomach flipped, but not in a good way.

"You seem a little tense today, a bit stilted," he said, reaching out to rub my arm. "Everything okay?"

I nodded, giving him a tight smile, before smoothing out its jagged edges as best I could. "Just a bit tired, that's all."

Tired of all these emotions swirling in the sticky silence. Tired of wondering what the hell was going on in my head.

"You look gorgeous, so just pick it up for the recording," he replied. "Give the camera some love. And remember, I'm behind the camera, and you love me, so it should be easy, right?" He gave me a peck on the lips, before resuming his position.

Not for the first time today, everything that came out of his mouth was an irritant, but I ignored it. Jake was purely directing the shoot as normal but, somehow, it felt like he was intruding on 'us'. An 'us' that only included me and Rachel.

My world view had been tipped on its head and I was struggling to make sense of anything I was thinking or feeling.

Rachel reappeared, her cheeks red, her blue eyes on me like a laser. My heart thudded in my chest as I wriggled out of their grip.

Jake clapped his hands to grab our attention. "Okay, let's take it from the top — I'll get a close-up of you mixing the ingredients in the bowl before panning out for your introduction, okay?"

Rachel nodded, giving me an encouraging glance before resuming her position, hands in the bowl.

"In three, two, one, action."

"Welcome to another episode of Fit & Tasty — emphasis on the Tasty! — with me, your host Rachel Cramer, and my able assistant, Alice Di Santo!"

Rachel spun around to grin at me, and I gave a hesitant wave.

Hi everyone, my name's Alice and I'm having a crisis of confidence and sexuality!

I really hoped my wave didn't convey that.

"Alice goes out with the cameraman, so watch carefully as she gives him a full-on stare every time the camera turns on her," Rachel said, which made my stomach churn and my cheeks flare.

I might go out with him, but it wasn't him that was making my equilibrium wobble and my hands shake.

"Today, we're cooking a really simple pasta dish which is terrific after a big workout session, so make sure you watch one of Jake's Fit videos before you try this tasty dish." Rachel gave the camera a grin, then swivelled on her right foot, remembering her mark for the camera, making sure to keep her head up and smiling as much as she could. After five months of doing this, she was a pro.

"Alice, have you got some mozzarella all chopped and ready to go?"

I stared at her, then at Jake, then back.

Whereas this seemed to be getting easier for Rachel, for me, every shoot seemed to be a trip into ever denser unknown.

* * *

Half an hour later, we were done with our shoot and then it was Jake's turn. He was soon out on Tanya's balcony, pumping his arms as he got into his stride during his latest high-intensity workout. Jake liked to record at least two 20-minute sessions a week, as well as doing daily motivational shout-outs to keep his followers on track, which they loved.

This time, I was behind the camera, with Jake squat-jumping, which had to be one of the most sadistic exercises around.

"So what's going on with Hercules out there?" Rachel

whispered, her arms folded, watching Jake from the balcony door.

My heart rocked as I looked at her, a mix of heat and confusion twisting in my veins.

What was wrong with me? I steadied myself before replying, not trusting myself to do otherwise.

"He's gone into machine mode," I replied, as we both watched.

"He's pretty amazing," Rachel whispered back. "Although I prefer yoga — I do too much heavy lifting at work, so when I get home, I like my workout to be more gentle."

Jake did his final repetition, and then jumped up, bouncing on his toes. "And that's it for today with me your host, Jake Best. Just remember, do your workouts regularly, eat Rachel's food and you'll be a polished diamond in no time!" He grinned as I switched off the camera and gave him a thumbs-up. "And we're done," I told him, giving him a clap. "Good job, you made me exhausted just watching you."

"That's the plan — if you get exhausted watching, you may as well join in, right?" His phone vibrating on Tanya's balcony table interrupted us, and Jake ran over to get it. He rolled his shoulder as he relaxed into conversation, a smile tugging at the corners of his mouth. He was always happiest after a workout, and today was no exception.

I turned to Rachel, gulping as I caught a whiff of her perfume. I had no idea what it was, but I'd smelt it on a woman in the supermarket the other day, and had involuntarily found myself following her to the frozen vegetable aisle before I knew what had happened.

"What perfume do you wear?" I folded my arms across my chest to stop my hands doing anything stupid. My heart was leaping about in my chest. "I've been trying to work it out — it really suits you." It was an effort to speak without tripping over my words.

Rachel's face lit up with one of her gorgeous smiles — her teeth were the straightest thing about her. "It's Ralph Lauren's Romance. I've worn it forever, but I still love it."

I nodded, staring at her perfect skin, inhaling the scent of her again. I could easily get addicted. It was mesmerising, just like her full, glossy lips, so perfect and kissable.

Shit, why was I thinking that?

"Have you got any plans today in the," Rachel checked her watch, "seven hours till we meet to go for dinner?"

Tonight was our monthly restaurant date, just the two of us. It had slowly become my favourite day of every month, when I got to spend a whole evening with Rachel.

"Nothing big. Jake wants to go shopping for new towels and bed linen, but I'm trying to put him off. I can think of so many other things I'd prefer to do." *Plane my shins. Pluck my pubes out one by one. Eat an entire plate of offal.* "How about you?"

"I'm meeting my sister for lunch — she's got a new girlfriend, so that's going to put me to shame, again. My baby sister can get a woman, but I cannot. That's the trouble with having a lesbian sibling — she shows up all my deficiencies. Without her, I'd just be the lesbian sister. Now, I'm the single, lonely lesbian sister."

I had no idea how that could be. I'd already come to the conclusion that lesbians in London were stupid, blind, or both.

If I was single, I'd... Actually, I'd no idea what I'd do.

Besides, I wasn't single, was I?

As if underlining that, my boyfriend walked up to us, a small white towel now wrapped around his neck, his bare muscles on show.

Rachel squeezed one of Jake's biceps, shaking her head as she did. "You are a walking advert for your mantra, sir. I hope you're ready for women and men to swoon when we start getting more views. Especially if you keep doing your routines with your top off."

"I don't think it'll be anywhere near what you'll get when you do your cooking section topless," he said, breaking out his trademark grin.

Rachel let out a cackle of laughter. "If we need the views, I'll consider it," she said, before looking down and grabbing her breasts.

My breath caught in my throat and I concentrated hard on my mouth not falling open.

"Although I'm not very well endowed in that department." She glanced over at me. "Alice, on the other hand..."

I held up the palms of both hands, in tandem with my eyebrows. "I don't think that was in my job description."

Suddenly, an image of Rachel's hands on my breasts flashed through my mind and heat rose in me, starting in my feet and finishing in my hair follicles.

I was rooted to the spot: this was definitely a new thought, too.

I was having an avalanche of them today, and I couldn't quite shuffle my thoughts and reactions into working order, my breathing accelerating and decelerating like a learner driver with a foot twitch.

Rachel gave me a look I couldn't quite pin down. "I'm all for tearing up job descriptions," she whispered, before walking back into the kitchen, shuffling her ingredients on the worktop.

She was all for tearing up job descriptions? What did that mean?

"Anyway, enough boob talk, although perhaps it's something I could work into my script if I try hard enough." Rachel paused, putting a hand on her hip, giving me a look that could stop wars. There she went being all exquisite again.

"Although is that too much of a lesbian stereotype?" she asked.

"Do whatever comes natural," Jake said. "Lesbians like food and exercise, too, right?" He glanced at me, giving me a wink. "We still need to do the intros for this week's show. So you want to do me on the balcony first, Alice, or Rachel in the kitchen?"

And with that, my mind went completely blank.

Chapter Three

Ibit into our main course and savoured the flavours — because they really were like nothing I'd tasted before. Cod with celeriac, black vinegar and caviar, and it was a taste sensation. Coming on the heels of the opener of rhubarb, salted ricotta and buckwheat, it was almost taking my mind off the fact I was sitting opposite Rachel, who looked good enough to eat, too.

When she glanced at me with her intense turquoise stare, I admired her daring gold eye shadow, how it was smeared upwards, like she was in a band, about to go on stage. I ignored the steady uptick of my pulse when I was around her and concentrated on the impressive food.

That, after all, was the reason we were here.

Rachel's friend Adam was the chef at this new venture in Hackney. The restaurant was stylish and cosy, the space formerly a haberdashery store now converted to a ten-table ode to modern British cuisine. Bare wooden tables mixed with shiny cutlery, and the wafer-thin wine glasses shone bright under the low, shaded metallic lighting. Artwork from a local artist adorned the walls, sitting atop bare brick. But for all the skilled design that had gone into this place, the food was the star.

"This is amazing, by the way." I pointed at the cod while a party kicked off in my mouth.

Rachel nodded. "I know — did you see the review in The Observer Food Monthly last week? Adam is on the up. And did you know he knows Jess?"

I furrowed my brow. "Jess who owns the café near you? As in Jess and Lucy?"

Rachel nodded. "Adam used to work in a call centre with her, would you believe? Small world."

I swallowed my food. "They both worked in a call centre and now they're both serving up great food. Makes you think what other talent is hiding in call-centre cubicles, doesn't it?"

I put down my knife and fork as a waitress in jeans and black T-shirt bustled past, carrying the first course to a table nearby. The low hum of other guests' chatter permeated the air, along with satisfied sighs over appreciated food.

"My parents would love this place — I should tell them to come here. My dad would moan about the portion sizes, but he'd appreciate the flavours. He can't help the first part, being Italian. You'll never go hungry in our house."

I smiled as I thought about my dad, who loved nothing more than to recreate Italian classics for an appreciative audience — which me, my mum and my sister Sabrina always were. Dad had become especially insistent since his parents had died in the past five years. It was as if he was trying to invoke their spirit through food, making all Nonna's specialities to keep her flame alive.

"I'd love to meet your dad," she said, her gaze making me wriggle in my seat.

I smiled. "I'll invite you round one weekend, I promise. My dad's Italian dishes are a thing of beauty. Jake and I are going for lunch on Sunday, along with my sister, her husband and their toddler terror, Flavia." I winced as I spoke. Somehow, saying that sentence to Rachel felt wrong. "Dad promised us tiramisu on our family WhatsApp group this week and he makes the *best* tiramisu."

"Like I said, whenever you want to invite me, I'm available."

"I'll let you know when there's an open spot at the table," I lied. There was no way I'd subject her — or me — to that scrutiny.

"So how was lunch today with your sister?"

Rachel's eyelids briefly fluttered shut as she recalled her day. Then the corners of her mouth turned upwards, and, not for the first time, her smile threw a lasso around my heart, tugging on it so tight I could barely breathe. I pressed my feet into the floor to ground myself, and hoped my thoughts weren't seeping through my skin by accident.

"It was the usual. Her telling me to go out there and find a woman, and me rolling my eyes. She's had such a different experience from me and we're not even that far apart in age. She came out at 16, she's always had a girlfriend, and she wouldn't know internal struggle if it bit her on the arse. I took a little more time to come out and was a little more worried about what everyone thought. I'm not sure Becca's ever worried what anyone thought."

Was that what I was experiencing? Internal struggle? Maybe it was.

"Sounds like Becca's had an easy ride so far."

"She has, but that's her own doing. She sees what she wants and she goes for it — I'm a little more cautious." Rachel's gaze was fixed on me as she spoke.

My stomach flip-flopped, and I cleared my throat to cover it up.

"Which is annoying when she's 23, and I'm supposed to be the older, sorted one," Rachel added, before looking away.

"Families are always fun."

She gave me a rueful smile. "But this woman won't last, and I told her so."

I scrunched my face. "And how did she take that?"

"Not well. She told me I needed to get out more and get laid. And she might have a point." Rachel grinned before continuing. "However, this woman won't last because she's not properly out, so this isn't even a case of me playing my mystic psychic card again."

"But I love it when you tell me you're psychic." Rachel's belief in her psychic abilities was legendary — even if they didn't often come true.

She rolled her eyes. "I've had some wins. I told Sophie that when she met someone, it was going to be big — and she and Tanya are."

I raised an eyebrow. "That wasn't very specific though, was it?"

"I've had other successes, too. But anyway: Becca's new girlfriend is your age—"

"—ancient, then."

"—nearly pensionable," Rachel grinned. "And this is her first relationship with a woman."

Coming out at 35: I'd always thought that was ridiculous until now. Like you should have known earlier, surely?

That is, until the many cases of being flustered and tongue-tied around my current dinner partner.

"Is coming out late such a crime?" Did I sound too defensive?

Rachel shook her head. "Of course not — people come out at all ages, I know that. A friend of mine recently came out at my age, 30. But Becca's girlfriend's family don't know, her colleagues don't know and she wants to keep it all quiet for now. I told Becca that's a bad sign, but this has never happened to her before; she's 23, she's invincible. But not being who you truly are ruins relationships. I told her that and she told me to stop being so sanctimonious."

"Sounds like she might have a point."

Rachel frowned. "It's just a bugbear of mine. I've been out with women before who weren't committed. You have to be comfortable in your own skin for relationships to work, otherwise nothing does. But Becca's going to have to find out the hard way."

"Or it might work." Somehow, Rachel being so down on this woman wasn't what I wanted to hear.

"You know what, it might. I'd love to be proved wrong, so let's hope this woman does just that." She sat forward. "And I'm not being cynical, I'm just being honest because I've seen it a million times. But maybe, *just maybe*, this one will work. I'd love it to — I have faith in happy endings. Maybe we'll be going to her and Becca's wedding this time next year."

"I'm coming, too?"

"Yes, because you're on Gwen's side — that's her girlfriend's name. She's Welsh, and a vet." Rachel threw me a resigned smile. "Maybe I'm just jealous because I never meet Welsh vets when I go online. Or perhaps I do just need to get laid."

My head filled with white noise and my teeth clamped together as I processed that gem, tiny frissons of something shooting up my arm and making my shoulders twitch.

I picked up my wine and took a healthy slug.

And then another.

"You'll meet someone soon, I have no doubt. You're a YouTube star, and look at you, you're gorgeous. I mean, what right-minded woman could resist?"

But that right-minded woman was not me.

Because I was straight and in a relationship with Jake.

Check all my social media, ask any of my friends.

Rachel held my gaze as my words danced around my peripheral vision.

For a moment, our eyes locked, and I entertained the fact she could see right through me, see exactly what I was thinking.

But then I snapped out of it, because that was folly.

She was gay, I was straight, and never the twain shall meet.

Rachel sat back, another of her luminous smiles framed perfectly on her face.

Damn those smiles of hers.

"So says the woman who's happily shacked up with a gorgeous man," she said, shaking her head. "Honestly, sometimes I wonder what I'm doing wrong, and how I can fix it." She paused, biting her lip. "Like I was saying to Sophie only the other day, I'd love to meet someone, I really would. Someone like you would be fabulous." She waved her hand at me. "You're beautiful, cultured, and you love food. A lesbian version of you would be great." Another pause. "I've checked you haven't got a sister, right?" She smiled as she finished.

It was all I could do not to offer myself to her then and there, on a plate. "I do, but she's married with a kid." I tried to keep my voice even, my body still. Even though every part of me was shaking from her words.

"Always the way," she said, grinning. "But I don't dwell too much, because where does it get you? I'm still doing my positive affirmations every morning, and I know that soon they're bound to come true."

"Affirmations?"

She nodded, then tucked her chin in, bashful. "It's going to make me sound all hippy-dippy."

I grinned. "I happen to love hippy-dippy. Always remember, I'm an art teacher."

Her laugh coated the air like honey. "I forget sometimes," she said. "At the risk of sounding like a loon, every morning I get up and tell myself I am worthy of love, and I will get a girlfriend this year." She sat back. "But this year is moving fast — it's May and still nothing. But I have faith in my affirmations."

"You should," I said. "If you say something enough times, it's going to come true, right?"

I wondered if I should take up some affirmations as part of my daily routine.

Chapter Four

It was a gorgeous mid-summer morning, nearly the end of June and only two weeks till I broke up for the summer — and if this weather held, I couldn't wait. The A levels were over, my students were finished, so I was spending this Friday morning doing some familial bonding with my sister, Sabrina, walking among the greenery of north London on Primrose Hill. The air was already bone dry, wrapping itself around us as we prepared for high-summer action.

Sabrina had Fridays off work, so she was making use of her free time, bringing her three-year-old daughter Flavia out for a walk with her Aunty Alice. Although right now, Flavia really wasn't taking part in the outing, being fast asleep in her buggy, mouth open and clutching Peppa Pig in her tiny arms.

Sabrina was two years older than me and happily married. She wasn't known for her wisdom, but when it came to relationships, I had to assume she had one up on me.

"You know you and Simon," I said, as we began walking up the incline to the top of hill.

"I do know him, seeing as he's my husband." Sabrina squinted into the sunshine even though she was wearing sunglasses, a few strands of her dark hair caught in one of the arms.

It was only 9am, but already I could feel sweat on my back — today was going to be a scorcher. The pre-glow of sunshine to come hung in the air, but the park was surprisingly clear, just a few stragglers dashing by on their way to work. I loved London in the summer, especially later on when half the population went on holiday and the city cleared out. I especially loved it in the sunshine.

"When did you know?" I winced. I knew how it sounded, and what did I want Sabrina to say, anyway? To tell me the secret to everlasting love? To show me how to stay fully in love with Jake, and not have my head turned by a certain chef?

She had no control over that and, it was turning out, neither did I.

Sure enough, Sabrina stopped pushing the buggy and turned to me.

"When did I know?" she said, her voice rising at the end to show what she thought of my question. "When did I know what? That he should never drink gin because it makes him sob? That he does a very impressive Robbie Williams impersonation?" She narrowed her eyes. "Or when did I know he was the one for me?"

I blushed and nodded, keeping my eyes focused on the

pavement beneath my feet, on the warm air stroking my arms, on the London that was spread out ahead.

Anywhere but Sabrina's face, and the many calculations I knew my sister's mind was already processing.

"Let's see." Sabrina resumed the buggy pushing up the incline, a satisfied smile creasing her face. "It was probably when he bought me flowers when I had toothache. Or perhaps when he bought me a banana holder for my bananas. It's the little things that mean people are keepers." She paused, turning her interested gaze on me. "Are you thinking you might have found your one?"

I *so* wished I could nod and beam at her, tell her that one plus one did equal two.

But I couldn't.

I'd found Jake, but now my heart was washing its hands of him and reaching out for someone else.

Someone new.

Someone completely unexpected.

And that was so scary, sometimes it made me catch my breath.

I shook my head slowly. "Not quite. It's just lately I'm wondering if I *should* know by now. I mean, we've been together a while, should there have been a moment when I knew he was the one for me?"

Sabrina took a moment before she replied. "I think you just know," she said. "I mean, not in a lightning-bolt kind of way, but more of an over-time kind of way. I got together with Simon, we had loads of sex, and when that wore off, you have to think whether or not you're happy with what you're left with. That's the crux of any relationship." She paused. "Only you know the answer, but I'd say what you're left with is pretty good. Jake's kind, considerate, he's got arms of steel and looks hot in a pair of jeans. You could do a lot worse."

I could do a lot worse. But was that reason enough to stay with someone? My head said Jake was the safe bet, but my heart wasn't just having second thoughts; it had drawn a line in the sand and was standing there, arms crossed, pouting.

We reached the top of Primrose Hill and my mind went back to our childhood, when Mum used to bring us both up here to look at London when we visited. Our parents had met here, but moved out when they had us, bringing us up in the Surrey countryside. However, as soon as we'd flown the nest, they'd moved back in. They were Londoners through and through, just as we were now, too.

"Remember when we used to come here when we were kids?" I ran my fingertips along the metal plaque that showed what you could see in the skyline ahead.

Sabrina nodded. "And now we're bringing Flavia. Who looks really interested, by the way." She put her arm around me and squeezed hard. "Who knows, if things do work out with Jake, maybe you'll be bringing your kids up here soon, too. A little springy-haired boy in tight shorts — I can picture it now."

I knew she meant well, but her comments ran through

me like a chill wind, even on this heated morning. I was pretty sure it was what Jake wanted — to settle down, get married and have children. He hadn't come out and said it, but he'd been dropping hints.

Only, every time he did lately, I closed him down, changed the subject.

When I was growing up, meeting a man like Jake, getting married and having kids was all I was focused on. However, now he was here and offering me that future, I wasn't sure I wanted it.

I was on the verge of dumping all my carefully planned dreams because of a new feeling, one that scared the hell out of me and sent me into a tailspin all at the same time.

Feelings for another woman. Feelings I wasn't meant to be having at all.

"I'd love that, you know — a little cousin for Flavia," Sabrina said, as her daughter stirred in her buggy.

We both looked down, but it was a false alarm, the toddler merely moving in her sleep.

"I'm not exactly thinking along the same lines." I sounded vague, which fairly reflected the state of my mind.

"Right!" Sabrina squeezed my arm. "I get it. You want to get married first."

My heart fell into my shoes.

Not quite. "That's not happening any time soon."

I should just tell her, but it wasn't as easy as it sounded. And what would I say?

That Rachel and Jake were on my mind, 24/7, but

it was Rachel who was making my heart boom, not my boyfriend?

"I just think life was a lot easier when we were kids, when Mum and Dad were bringing us here, when we used to race to the top of the hill and collapse, nothing else to worry about later on."

Sabrina scrunched up her face. "You make your life sound terrible. Things aren't that bad, are they? Cheer up, you're on holiday for six weeks soon. I'd love a bit of that!"

"I've just been wondering if there shouldn't be something more, something that makes my life stand out, something that takes my breath away." I paused. "I guess that's it — I want something to take my breath away and I don't have that right now."

Sabrina bit her lip, her knuckles whitening as she gripped the buggy tighter as we made our descent.

"Breathtaking is asking a lot," she said. "Simon took my breath away the other night when he made me a cup of tea without me asking. That's the kind of thing that inspires me." She glanced my way, trying to work me out. "Maybe you should get Jake to give you a personal training session. That'd be sure to take your breath away."

I gave her a tight smile: that was kinda the issue. Jake was lovely, but our relationship had always felt safe. Whereas Rachel was the opposite: every time I saw her, I forgot how to breathe.

Sabrina stopped and glanced at me. "But I thought

everything was going so well. You've got a lovely flat, you like your job, and you've got a great boyfriend — and a new role in a hit food and fitness channel. Who'd have thought you'd be a YouTube star this year?"

"Not me." But the channel was part of my problem.

"That Rachel seems lovely, too, I'd love to meet her. But most of all, I'd love to have her cook for me — does all her food taste as good as it looks?"

"Better," I said, thinking back to the past weekend when Rachel had done wonders with some chicken, mustard and spinach.

"And have you been out at any swanky restaurants lately? You being such good friends really jumps off the screen — your chemistry is a big draw."

She had no idea.

"That's what Jake says," I said, feeling the blood rush to my cheeks. "Along with all the YouTube comments."

"I know, I was reading them the other day. Some people have got some nerve writing what they do — they know you're going out with Jake, yet they want you to get it on with Rachel? It's a food and exercise channel, not Porn Hub."

I shrugged, like I hadn't been reading them incessantly. "Online comments are the province of anonymous keyboard warriors. They can say what they like, they're not going to get caught, are they?"

"It's a bit rich though, isn't it?" She paused. "How does Jake feel about it?"

I shrugged, squirming under such scrutiny. I knew she was asking out of concern, but this was a bit too close to the bone. "You know Jake, he's very chill about stuff generally."

Sabrina glanced my way, and was quiet for a moment. "And is there any truth in the comments?"

I screwed up my face in outrage, but didn't dare look at her, just in case she could see right through me. Make no mistake, my sister had that superpower.

"Of course not, why do you say that?"

But she wasn't about to be thrown off so easily. "You're not sure about Jake, and I've got eyes. Yes, I can see you're good friends, but you've chatted more about Rachel over the past year than you have about any other friend. Nobody else gets as much air time, not even Jake. And Rachel's a lesbian, so—"

"—so we're bound to get it on? Come on, Sabrina, I expect more from you than that." I kicked a stone down the hill and we watched it scuttle off the path, into the fading grass. I knew my outburst was more to do with me than Sabrina, but I wasn't going to tell her that.

She stopped pushing Flavia's buggy as we got to the bottom of the hill, coming to a standstill beside some trees in full bloom — Mum would know what they were called, but I hadn't mastered that art yet.

"I'm not just saying that because Rachel's a lesbian — I know full well that lesbians don't hit on every woman they meet." She put her hands on both hips in punctuation, her stance defensive, her stare direct.

"All I'm saying is that it seems like you might like her. And I get you're defensive, it's a scary thing. But if you do like her, I'd say it's best to tell Jake before anything happens. Because if it does and you're on screen together, I'll be able to tell. And after that, it's only a matter of time before everyone else can, too. And then, I wouldn't want to be in your shoes when the comments start rolling in."

I bit my lip before answering, my thoughts scattered, my brain stuck as if jammed, its warning light flashing.

"You're barking up the wrong tree here, sis." I dug my heels in where they didn't need to be dug. "Yes, I'm questioning things with Jake, but it has nothing to do with Rachel. She's gay and I'm not. End of story."

Sabrina gave me a look I recognised, one that told me she was happy to park it for now, but also, she didn't believe a word coming out of my mouth.

And honestly, I can't say I blamed her.

Chapter Five

Seeing Sabrina had shaken me up, brought my feelings into razor-sharp focus. I'd been fending them off for so long, but I was growing tired. How long could I fight without my feelings striking back? And didn't I owe Jake more than this? He'd been nothing but patient, but even he was beginning to wonder what had changed.

Last night at dinner he'd asked what was wrong, asked me to talk to him, but I hadn't been able to. Mainly because I couldn't. Talking to Sabrina had been the first step. The next step was admitting it to myself, and then taking action. Because what I was doing now wasn't fair to anyone.

To me, to Jake, or to my heart.

I exhaled, pushing my sunglasses up my nose, coming to a stop in the middle of Finsbury Park. The traffic roared by on both sides of the green space, and I settled myself underneath my favourite oak tree, shielded from the late afternoon sun. It was the final week of school, the term winding down to a close. Work stresses were fleeing my mind and now real life was stamping its feet, waiting for some attention.

It'd been waiting for a long while, and as I settled down on the faded, pale yellow grass, I knew this was the perfect place to do a stock-take of my life. Chiefly, of who I was now and what the hell my next step should be.

Because with every day that passed, it was clear I was not the same person I was six months ago. Or even two months ago. Or even yesterday.

It was high time I lifted the lid, became brave.

If I was going to move forward, bravery was everything I needed.

These new feelings had been brewing just under the surface, but I'd been steadfastly ignoring them. And while I was at work, or with anyone else who wasn't Jake or Rachel, I could manage them. It was almost too easy. I was adept at giving the impression that everything was fine. Nobody had caught on, and I was developing an impressive talent for acting.

I was Alice di Santo, the straight girl with the cute boyfriend. I blended in with the crowd.

Everything about me spelt normal, content; I had a boyfriend, I was the norm.

Only, it wasn't true, was it?

And that came flooding out whenever I was around Jake or Rachel. Spilling out of every pore, leaving me in wild panic, questioning everything I'd ever believed about myself: had my whole life been built on a lie? And why was it choosing to announce itself now?

I couldn't carry on as I was: I was hurting myself

and everyone around me. If I kept on without changing anything, one day something would happen and I would shatter into a thousand tiny pieces. And by then, I might be so fractured, it would be impossible to piece myself back together again. I didn't want that to happen.

I wanted to be the best version of me I could possibly be, and I knew there was only one way to do that.

Accept who I was becoming and see what I should do about it.

I chewed on my thoughts and stared up into the pastel blue sky. It was a perfect summer's day, while I was a perfect summery mess.

Yet only I had the power to change things.

But giving up everything I'd always thought was mine to take, and going on a different journey scared the shit out of me. Taking the road less travelled, rather than the road laid out for me since birth.

If I stayed with Jake, I knew every inch of road, every divot. I'd driven down it many times before. If I turned right with Jake by my side, it was the move everyone expected. The option I'd expected forever.

I'd always thought it would be the easiest move, seamless, smooth.

But every time I tried, my heart stalled. Far from being easy, staying with Jake was ringing every warning bell in my body, the clanging growing increasingly loud.

From being the easiest route, suddenly staying with Jake was the route that left me frozen with fear.

Fear of not living a full life, a true life.

A life I really wanted.

But also a life I never expected in a million years.

If I turned left, I didn't know the other road at all. I'd never driven it and my GPS couldn't find it. This road might be paved with gold, but equally, it might be paved with heartbreak and uncertainty.

My head had been telling me to stay on the more certain road, to go where I was expected. But now, even my head was being turned.

Apparently, in my thirties, I was staging a protest.

I'd always been a good girl. I remembered birthdays, flossed most days, I'd got a degree and then a boyfriend.

But now, every time I saw that boyfriend, I clammed up.

And every time I saw the object of my desire, *her*, I clammed up for very different reasons.

I couldn't carry on — I saw that now as brightly as the sun above.

Did that mean I was heading down the road less travelled? Maybe.

Was I scared? Out of my tiny mind.

Was I excited? A petrified excitement that made me want to pee every time I thought about it.

Did I feel like I was alive?

Yes, and the feeling was so huge, it felt like it might swallow me whole.

Chapter Six

As promised, Jake picked me up after his Saturday morning of training, coming out of the shower smelling of musk and honey again, just as he had this morning. He was chirpy, in nesting mode. Jake loved shopping for homeware, whereas I did not.

Despite that, I was doing some of my best acting again, having spent the morning drinking a vat of tea and making concrete decisions.

I couldn't carry on, and with a whole summer ahead of me, I had to change things.

I was going to tell him.

I'd come to that conclusion yesterday, bottled out last night when he didn't get in till late and was tired, so it was going to be tonight. We'd go to Ikea, get the tables he was hell-bent on buying, then come back and I'd sit him down.

It was the right thing to do.

The only thing to do.

But it didn't stop me chewing on my nerves as we sat in the Saturday traffic on the first day of my summer holidays, wishing I was anywhere but here.

Blazing summer days were not supposed to be spent on the North Circular in a microwave-hot car, thinking about how you should split up with your boyfriend.

"I'm still not sure why you want new bedside tables," I said, not for the first time since we left.

"Because I want you to have one — take it as a sign of my ongoing commitment to us."

He was joking, I could tell from the lightness in his voice. But when he said it, he might as well have slapped me.

"We're a couple, and I just thought you might like a say in what you wake up to every morning." He turned his head and I could see my reflection in his black sunglasses. "But maybe I'm wrong, because you seem less than pleased about the prospect." He paused, pressing on the accelerator as the traffic eased forward and a sign to Ikea hoved into view. "If it offends you that much, we don't have to do it."

I shook my head, clenching my toes, staring ahead at the clear blue sky. "No, it's fine. I've just got a lot on my mind." I shrugged. "What to do with my impending summer holidays, that sort of thing."

Like, become a lesbian?

Jake reached across and squeezed my thigh, leaving his hand there as he did.

I tried not to flinch, as an avalanche of guilt and mayhem slid down me.

I didn't want Jake's hand on my leg, on my anywhere. I wanted to scream and I was pretty sure that soon, I would.

"I'm sure you'll think of something." He paused. "And if you don't, we can always give you more work to do for Fit & Tasty. Wait till your students get hold of it, you're going to be more of a superstar than you already are."

I wasn't sure I was prepared for that — a few of my students had already found the channel and had been over-excited about my role in it. And with ratings for the episodes starring Rachel and I going through the roof, it looked like my involvement was only going to increase.

We pulled into the packed Ikea car park half an hour later, and I tried to unlock the tension in my body as I got out of the car, rolling my shoulders as I squinted into the July sunshine.

Jake slammed the door of his black Nissan and walked to the front, holding out his hand to me.

I bit the inside of my cheek and put my hand in his, looking for all the world like just any other couple: care-free, happy, together.

Up ahead, a man and a woman walked hand in hand, the girl leaning in to say something, the guy laughing.

I clung to Jake, searching my mind for something funny to say to him, but it was blank. I couldn't come up with a single gambit, my thoughts a blizzard of emptiness just swirling round and round.

Ikea was its usual cavernous self and stuffier than the car, pointedly reflecting my mood this morning: hot and bothered. It smelt of dust and wood, and the tinny background music did nothing to lift my spirits. All around, couples brandished tape measures, and stressed parents clutched hastily written lists while kids jumped on colourful sofas, the harsh strip-lighting glaring overhead.

Jake led me through the maze of showrooms, stopping to ask my opinion of a few bedside tables along the way. I gave vague opinions and he looked at me like he didn't believe a single word falling from my lips, but he let it go.

We made it through to the warehouse and Jake was bouncing on the balls of his feet, peering at the number he'd keyed into his phone, trying to locate the tables he wanted.

"I can't find it, can you see it on your side?"

I was peering at the lower shelves, but I couldn't see them either. I shook my head.

"I guess we could see if that other one is around here — the one with the thicker handles. Did you like that as much, though?" Jake held my gaze from across the other side of the shelf.

"Yes, you can have a hot dog later, but Mummy has to get her things first," said a woman behind me.

I turned my head, before focusing back on Jake and his expectant face.

Suddenly, it was all too much. I couldn't do this anymore. I couldn't buy a new bedside table with him, because it wasn't going to be my bedside table, was it? This was the first decision Jake was going to have to make on his own, and he needed to know why. Doing anything else would be leading him on, and I didn't want to do that.

I was tired of keeping it all in.

"Jake, we need to talk." I frowned at him through the gap in the shelf. In front of me was a stack of floating shelves, and a woman with red hair elbowed me out the way with some force to get to them. I decided not to remonstrate with her: I had enough on my plate.

He smiled through the gap. "You're taking this table shopping very seriously," he said. "If this is wigging you out too much, we can stop for the day. Although maybe now we're here, it makes more sense to get something. Even if it's just a hot dog." He grinned, but I could see the confusion in his eyes. "You like Ikea hot dogs. I'll even throw in an ice cream afterwards because that's the kind of guy I am. All heart."

"I agree, you are the best boyfriend ever." My heart was thudding in my chest. I was standing on a precipice, ready to jump, but Jake kept holding me back, offering me a safety net. I so wished I wanted to take it, to run into his arms, to let him smooth out my jagged edges, but I didn't. "But you're just not the best boyfriend for me."

There, I'd said it.

I flicked my gaze up and stared across the gap in the shelves, into the eyes of the man I'd been with for the past 18 months.

I didn't want to hurt him, but staying silent was hurting him, too.

Jake frowned.

"Did you hear what I said?" A shiver of dread ran

through me, every hair on my scalp standing on end. Even though this was the right thing to do, it was never going to be easy. At the very least, I needed him to be able to hear me, so I didn't keep having to repeat the words over and over.

Jake nodded, wordless, before looking down and putting his phone in the back pocket of his jeans.

"Why am I not the best boyfriend for you anymore?"

He was still standing on the other side of the shelving unit and, somehow, I couldn't have choreographed this any better if I'd tried. Distance and a physical object between us at this stage was exactly what I wanted. Because if he'd reached out to touch me, if I'd looked into his eyes and seen the hurt up close, it would have been too much.

So this was perfect, even though I knew it wouldn't last.

"It's not you, it's me." Lame, I knew.

"Spare me," he replied, walking around the shelves towards me.

Panic rose swiftly.

I wasn't ready to deal with him yet.

Hell, I was barely ready to deal with myself.

He appeared at my side, his face hardened. "What's going on? Why are you saying this? Talk to me and I'm sure it's something we can fix." He was trying so hard to understand.

I shook my head, the overhead lights seeming brighter than the sun outside. "There's nothing to talk about."

He bit his lip as he stared at me, his face creased with confusion, his grey eyes still the kindest I'd ever known. "I think there is. You can't just tell me out of the blue in Ikea that you don't want me anymore." He paused, the skin around his eyes crinkling. "Is there someone else?"

"No!" I said, my voice punching the air as I shook my head. "No, there's nobody else. This is about me, nothing to do with you." I touched his arm, and it was his turn to flinch. "Jake, you're everything, you're amazing. But this is my stuff, not yours."

He eyed me now as if for the first time, trying to work out my emotional password, to say the right thing. "Look, if this is a freak-out about the tables, we don't have to buy them. Let's get out of here, drive home and we can talk about it there."

I nodded, my emotions icing over. "Yes please to getting out of here."

I turned sharply, nausea bubbling up inside me. I walked blindly, ignoring all the people and the noise, stumbling down the aisle, desperate to get out of Ikea. Out of this relationship.

A small child screamed somewhere behind me, but I didn't turn my head. The waft of hot dogs drifted into my nose as we sidestepped the queues at the checkout, before I lurched outside, the sunshine stifling.

Jake appeared at my side, his smile vanished, his expression crushed.

We walked across the sea of cars in deathly silence,

the heat scorching my skin. It was lunchtime, but today had taken on a timeless quality.

When we arrived at the car, Jake unlocked it remotely with a beep. We got in simultaneously, sitting in the boiling interior without a word, the slamming of our respective doors sealing us from the outside world.

I sat still, not even daring to shrug my handbag into the footwell: all normal actions seemed fraught with meaning, as if doing it would say to Jake I was getting on with my life, so why wasn't he?

But that wasn't true: from the moment I'd told Jake I no longer wanted him to be my boyfriend, everything had changed.

Across from me, Jake raked both his hands through his wavy hair, shaking his head slowly. "Is this really it? Eighteen months together and it's over, just like that? Is there nothing I can say to change your mind? Because I'm struggling here, Alice."

He let out a deep sigh. "I woke up this morning with a girlfriend, and now I don't have one." He shook his head. "I'm having a little trouble getting my head around this." He reached out a hand and put it on my arm. "Explain it to me at least, so I can understand. Otherwise, it's making me doubt everything I thought I knew." He looked at me. "Why am I not enough anymore?"

I swallowed down, selecting my words carefully.

I hated the pain that was filling up the car, stabbing at my skin, my heart.

I reached over and took his hand. I was beyond claustrophobic, but I was trying to keep it under control. "It's not about you, Jake, as much as it's a cliché to say."

He snorted. "It's a total cliché and you know it."

My heart winced as he spoke. "I do, but there's nothing more I can say. I was going to tell you this week, and I should have. But coming here today brought it to a head. I can't buy a bedside table with you, because I won't be the one waking up with it. You need to buy one you like, it can't have anything to do with me."

When I looked over, he was crying, wiping away silent tears from his face.

Which made me a monster.

"Jake, don't cry," I said, helplessly.

He sniffed, wiping away more tears. "What do you want me to do? React with no emotion at all? My girlfriend — who I love very much by the way — has just broken up with me out of the blue. There was me planning our future, but she couldn't even stand the thought of buying a bedside table with me. I'm glad I never presented you with an engagement ring, because who knows what reaction that might have got." He shrugged, banging the steering wheel with his fist.

I jumped, startled.

He turned to me. "There's really nothing I can say? Your mind's made up?"

I took a second, before nodding my head. "I'm so sorry, Jake. I really am."

His shoulders slumped as he turned the key in the ignition, facing forwards. "Not half as sorry as me." His voice was smaller now, defeated. "You coming home or do you want me to drop you off somewhere on the way?"

I hadn't thought that far ahead — this hadn't been my plan today. "I'll come home, pack a bag and get out of your hair for the weekend."

As Jake drove out of the car park, I wasn't sure what I was feeling.

But I'd done it — there was no turning back.

Ready or not, today was the start of a brand-new chapter.

Chapter Seven

I wasn't sure where to go with my weekend suitcase packed, suddenly homeless. Tanya? Probably. My parents? Perhaps. But none of them were perfect. First, I'd have to tell Mum why I'd left Jake, and that would be painful. She loved him and I couldn't take the disappointed look on her face as she realised her daughter had let him slip through her fingers.

And then, wait till she heard the reason.

I wasn't sure quite how my parents might react to the fact their youngest daughter was questioning her sexuality, but I guessed I'd find out soon enough.

My friend Tanya was the obvious choice, but Tanya went out with Sophie, who also happened to be Rachel's flatmate. Plus, Rachel lived in Tanya's block, too. Yes, I'd left my boyfriend and was facing up to the fact I wasn't quite as straight as I thought, but I wasn't sure I was ready to come face to face with the reason for my life crisis. And what if Rachel had no feelings for me at all?

More to the point, what if she did?

It was one thing to fancy a woman; it was quite another

to go any further, to even consider the prospect of more. Kissing her? Getting naked with her?

I shuddered as the thought of kissing Rachel barrelled through me, catching me unaware and nearly making me topple down the Tube stairs.

I took a deep breath as I clutched the metal railing leading down to the Northern Line.

This was completely my doing and I had to take responsibility for it and face up to whatever it entailed. But first, I had to figure out where I was going to sleep tonight.

I made a decision and, annoying everyone coming down the stairs behind me, turned and rushed back up into the afternoon sunshine around Finsbury Park tube, the torn streets and scruffy air safe and familiar.

I hit the number and waited.

Sabrina answered after two rings. "Hey little sis, how's you?"

That question was nearly my undoing, but I managed to hold it together. "Okay," I croaked.

"No you're not," Sabrina replied. "What's up?"

"I've left Jake." Now I'd told someone else, it made it that bit more real.

"Shit the bed! I know you said you were questioning things, but this is a whole different ballgame." Sabrina's voice spelt surprise.

"Yeah, well now I'm homeless, so I was wondering — could I come and stay this weekend? And perhaps a little longer?"

Sabrina let out a long sigh. "Have you forgotten we're having our extension done, starting on Monday?"

I clicked my tongue against the roof of my mouth. "I had." Shit, there went my safety net.

"So ordinarily, I would say of course you can. But what with me, Simon and Flavia all cramming in upstairs for the next few months, it's probably not the best thing to do. Unless you want to see family life at its absolute worst, and I don't want to put you off any future family plans you might have." She paused. "But anyway, enough of my extension. I take it this was your decision after what you were saying the other day?"

I let out a croaky cough. "It was — I've fallen out of love with him, and I couldn't carry on."

"I didn't realise it was that serious." Sabrina cleared her throat. "Are you okay?"

It was the first time anyone had asked, but I couldn't decipher my feelings, lying like confetti on the floor of my mind.

"I'm good — a little shaken, a little lost, but I'll survive."

There was a pause on the other end of the line. "You could ask the parents, they've got a spare room."

I winced. "I know, but then they're going to want to know the circumstances and, *you know*."

"You make it sound very mysterious."

"Not mysterious, just... well, what we were talking about the other day might have something to do with my reasons, and I'm not sure I'm ready to tell Mum just yet."

Another long pause. "Rachel?"

I coughed before replying, but my voice was still strangled. "Yes," I said, my heart booming in my chest. If there was one word in the English language that was having a crazy affect on me at the moment, it was Rachel.

"Goddit," Sabrina replied, not sounding one bit surprised. "But I think Mum would be fine. She has met a lesbian in her time and never reacted badly."

"Yes, but I'm her daughter, which makes it different." I knew enough coming out stories to know that much.

"What about staying with Tanya — doesn't she have a fancy pad? Assuming it is Rachel who's thrown your sexuality into the air, and not Tanya. Because that would be very messy."

I coughed again. "No, I am not in love with Tanya, and yes, she was my next port of call. She has a spare room, plus she'd be thrilled someone could be there for her dog."

"Then you're sorted, so long as she's not having any building work done, too." Sabrina paused. "But Alice?"

"Yeah?"

"Have you said anything to Rachel yet?"

Every muscle in my spine tightened. "No," I replied.

"Then give it a little time. You don't want to come running out of a relationship and fall sobbing into her arms. It's not a good look."

"I've been coming to terms with this for the past six months, maybe longer. I didn't just decide this weekend."

"Six months?" Sabrina's voice had gone up two decibels. "I'll park that for now. Just remember, it's all new to Rachel, too."

She had a good point. "I'm not going to rush over there and throw myself at her. Give me some credit."

"You're making rash decisions, so I need to double-check." Sabrina paused. "You want to meet for a drink later? Simon's out now, but when he's back he can sit with Flavia."

"Maybe, I'll let you know. If I end up at Tanya's, it might be tricky."

"Okay, text me. But if not tonight, one night soon, yes? Especially because there's so much to talk about."

"Promise. And good luck with the building work."

"Good luck with your rebuilding work."

"Thanks, I might need it."

Chapter Eight

Tanya buzzed me up to her apartment, and when I stepped out of the lift on the 30th floor, she pulled me into a hug, eyeing one of her oldest friends with a mix of concern and curiosity.

When I stepped inside, her chocolate-and-black King Charles Spaniel, Delilah, began to bark, her tail wagging, running over to jump up at me.

"Hey Delilah, how are you, girl?"

I bent down to pet her, glad Delilah was there to take my mind off the memory that was pressing into my very core, threatening to overtake me: the previous week I'd been here filming the latest Fit & Tasty video with Rachel. Then, I'd stood beside her, asking questions while she chopped onions and garlic. I'd spent the whole time trying not to get too close, not to shiver on camera, not to transmit my feelings to everyone watching.

Beyond leaving Jake and my growing attraction to Rachel, what the hell was going to happen with Fit & Tasty when the shit properly hit the fan? I had no idea. Would Rachel and I keep working together? Would I be able to keep my feelings under wraps? And what about Jake and Rachel?

Rachel didn't even know this rock had struck their business yet, possibly threatening to take it under.

But I couldn't think about that.

Today, it was enough to just put one foot in front of the other and breathe.

Tanya took my case through to the spare room, before coming back to the open-plan living space and walking over to the kitchen, leaning on her white island and eyeing me with curiosity. I didn't blame her — it wasn't every day she got a call like this one from her best friend.

"Nice spot, by the way."

I touched the end of my nose and grimaced. "Thanks for pointing it out."

"You're welcome," she said. "Is this a tea and coffee moment, or a something-stronger moment?" She straightened up and walked over to where the kettle sat on the kitchen counter.

"It's a 'fuck me, I've just blown up my life' moment." I raised both eyebrows and blew out a long breath.

Tanya gave me a grimace. "Beer, then?"

"Beer sounds perfect."

Tanya waved me out to the balcony, accessed via her giant glass doors. "Go ahead, I'll bring them out."

I sat down on one of her black outdoor chairs and took in a lungful of air, which always seemed far fresher this high up, even in the badlands of Woolwich. Tanya's flat was one of my very favourite places, and I still recalled the day Jake and I had moved her in.

Jake. I gulped at the memory of his tears, his crumpled face as I'd packed my bag and walked out the door. It was one of the hardest things I'd ever had to do, because he'd done nothing wrong.

"So," Tanya said, sweeping her shoulder-length chestnut hair out of her eyes, and crossing her tanned right leg over her left.

Her denim shorts and red T-shirt showed off her wiry, athletic frame well, the same frame that had made her a star athlete during our university years together. Tanya had been the goal-grabbing centre forward on the women's football team, as well as a swashbuckling all-rounder in the cricket.

"Catch me up. Last time I saw you, you were happily living with Jake. Now, two weeks later you turn up on my doorstep telling me you've left him. What gives? Did he cheat?"

"Why does everyone always assume that?"

"Because it's normally true."

I sighed. "No, neither of us cheated."

Tanya nodded her head. "Okaaaay," she said. "If no cheating has gone on, what's the story? Because otherwise, none of this makes sense. You and Jake were good together."

I cleared my throat. "First of all, is Sophie here?" I turned my head towards the flat, expecting Sophie to burst through the balcony doors at any moment. I had a lot of time for Tanya's girlfriend, but she was far too closely linked to Rachel for comfort.

Tanya shook her head. "She's got a ton of dog walks today, so she won't be back for a bit."

"Good."

Tanya looked confused. "Why is that good?"

I winced. "It's just... complicated." I leaned forward. "Is it okay to stay here for a bit? I mean, as in live here, not just stay for a beer."

Tanya gave me a firm nod. "Course it is."

"Thanks, that's one thing I can tick off my list." I sat back and crossed my legs.

Tanya scrunched up her face, assessing the situation. "So are you going to fill me in? Tell me just why you've blown up your life this fair Saturday?" She glanced up at the clear blue skies. "Lovely day for it, by the way." She moved her sunglasses up her nose and turned her face to the sunshine.

I glanced upwards, then, blinded, closed my eyes. "I left my fucking sunglasses at the flat, along with half my life."

Tanya got up.

"Where are you going?" I asked, alarmed. Sudden movements and me didn't mix today.

"To get you some sunglasses."

I smiled: I loved Tanya, my platonic soulmate. Yes, my biological family had been my first port of call, but Tanya was my chosen family, along with my other friends. My logical family, as Armistead Maupin put it so well.

"Thank you," I said, slipping the shades onto my face, glad to be able to hide away from the world as much as possible. "I don't quite know how to explain."

"Start with a single word."

I stared at Tanya.

We'd known each other for 20 years, and our running joke was that I looked more like a lesbian than Tanya ever did. Tanya had long, glossy hair, power suits, a stellar career. Whereas I dressed in jeans, had more chequered shirts in my wardrobe than was strictly necessary, and taught art.

That I was now tumbling towards a self-fulfilling prophecy wasn't lost on me. Maybe this was all Tanya's fault in the first place by constantly telling me I was a lesbian: my subconscious had heard it enough times, and now it was acting on it.

"I blame you," I blurted, shaking my head with a smile.

"Right — what have I done?"

"You kept telling me I'm gay."

Tanya raised an eyebrow. "And now you are?"

"Well, not yet, but I'm thinking about it."

Tanya took a swig of her beer, before frowning. "Let's back up for a minute," she said, circling with her fingers. "You think you might be gay?"

I put my head in my hands. Was I completely gay, or was this a Rachel-shaped explosion? "I don't fucking know!"

There was a beat before Tanya asked the next question. "And I'm assuming this has something to do with a certain other lesbian who lives in this block? And I'm counting out myself and Sophie by the way, just in case you were wondering."

I dragged my hands away from my face, my mouth creeping open. "Am I that obvious? Does everyone know?" I put my hands back over my face. "Oh god, I can't stay here if she knows." Did Rachel know? Did Sophie know? Had the whole lesbian world been wondering when I might come to this logical conclusion?

I ground my teeth together. "Does she know?"

Tanya leaned over and put a soothing hand on my arm. It helped, bringing me back to the here and now, making me look up at her and listen, rather than letting my thoughts spiral out of control.

"I don't think so," Tanya said.

"Then how do you?"

She shrugged, narrowing her eyes. "I know you, remember? I know the signs. I know what you do when you're flirting with guys because I've seen it before."

"What do I do?" I sat up, my interest piqued.

"You blush, you stutter, you swish your hair in a particular way, you get very touchy." Tanya paused. "I've watched your YouTube videos, and it struck me when I saw the most recent ones. It was just... *there*, on screen. I mean, don't get me wrong, you could just come off as being great friends, because you are, but it made me wonder."

I pulled my knees together, my thoughts running round and round in my head. "Have you mentioned this to Sophie?"

Tanya winced.

"Oh god, Sophie knows?" Tanya knowing was one thing, but Sophie knowing? Rachel's flatmate and best friend?!

"It's not just me who noticed it, Alice. She commented on your on-screen chemistry, too. And then I thought, is there something more to it?"

"Has Rachel said anything to her? About me, I mean?"

Tanya shook her head. "She's not likely to, is she? You're living with her co-star, remember, and you're straight. She's not going to waste her time mooning over something she knows full well she can't have. You're simply not an option."

I flung my head back quickly, making Delilah bark at the sudden movement. I reached down and petted her.

"It's such a mess, but when I realised I had feelings for her, I couldn't carry on with Jake." I paused, lifting up my sunglasses. "Would you believe I broke up with him in Ikea?"

"Ikea can do strange things to you," Tanya said with a sad smile. "Poor Jake — how did he take it?"

"How do you think? He wanted to buy bedside tables with me and all the while I was thinking..." I blushed, an image of Rachel popping into my mind that was far from platonic. "Well, my thoughts of late are best left unbroadcast." I took another swig of my beer, then looked out at the river, twinkling below in the late afternoon sun.

"You think I'm of any interest to Rachel?"

Tanya took a moment to answer. "I do."

I let out a strangled groan. "There's a *but* coming, isn't there?"

"Just that you need to get yourself together before you even *go* there. This is big, and you're fragile at the moment. You need to be measured, not go charging in. For your sake, for Rachel's and for Jake's. There's a lot at stake here, a lot of people's feelings."

"I know that, I'm not stupid." I steadied my breathing. "I wasn't planning on going down there and jumping her. I've got all these feelings, but I've got no idea what to do with them. I mean, what does 'jump her' even mean?"

Tanya let out a throaty laugh. "Oh shit, you've got so much to learn. Promise me this — when you do sleep with your first woman, will you call me after to tell me about it?"

I rolled my eyes. "I will not. And like I told Sabrina earlier, I might be bisexual and not lesbian, so I'm not ruling out sleeping with men ever again."

"We live in a modern world, you can be whoever you want to be," Tanya said, before smiling. "But right now, the thought of sleeping with Rachel is more appealing than sleeping with a man?"

"It's all I can fucking think about." It was the very thought that had been crashing into my every waking moment for the past few months, making me sweat guilt at an alarming rate. "But this is such a mess — I haven't just hurt Jake, I've tipped my life upside down and their business together." I paused. "What am I going to do?"

"You're not going to worry about it just yet." Tanya leaned over and patted my leg. "For now, the sun is shining, the sky is blue, you have your health and the woman you fancy has the hots for you." She paused. "Shit, that was almost a poem, wasn't it?"

I sat up. "She likes me, too?" My skin tingled with anticipation.

A gurgled laugh bubbled up from Tanya. "She hasn't told me that, but like I said, I watched your videos. And let's just say, the chemistry, the touching, the hair flicks? It's a two-way street. Now you just have to tell her you're available and open to it, without breaking Jake's heart in two."

"I'm not sure I'm going to be able to do that."

I didn't want to break anybody's heart, but I'd started the process and it was always going to have casualties; that was just the nature of relationships. There were winners and losers, and I still wasn't sure which I was. Jake might feel like he's a loser now, but in the end, he was better off without me. I took another swig of my beer.

"What am I going to do about Rachel and Jake? They work together, things are really just taking off for them. I've already buggered up Jake's personal life, I don't want to be responsible for his work life falling apart, too."

Tanya gave me a measured look. "All very noble of you, but how exactly are you planning to do that? You've just told me you've got feelings for Rachel, and if something does happen, you're bound to run into Jake."

"I know," I replied, head firmly back in my hands. "And please stop talking about me sleeping with Rachel like it's a given. Like it's the most obvious thing in the world."

"I've watched your YouTube channel, remember?" Tanya raised a single eyebrow.

"So you keep saying," I said. "Whatever happens, I do not want to fuck things up for Jake totally. If I can't be the woman of his dreams, I certainly don't want to turn into the nightmare ex-girlfriend, the benchmark to measure all others by."

And if I wanted to do that, I had to take things slowly, and if anything did happen with Rachel, let Jake know.

Resolved, I sat up straight. "Can I ask you a favour?"

"Your face tells me I'm not going to like it."

"Can you not talk to Sophie about this, at least for a little while please?"

Tanya screwed up her face at that. "We don't keep secrets from each other, you know that. I'm working on her to move in with me, and she's hesitant. I don't want to give her any opportunity to doubt me."

I held up a hand. "I know that, but for me, your best friend — and it won't be forever, I promise. Just until the dust has settled, until life has calmed down a little. A couple of weeks, tops."

"But Sophie's going to know you're living here, that you split up with Jake."

"I'm not asking you to hide that, that would be stupid," I replied. "But can you just not tell her the reasons? She's too close to Rachel."

Tanya gave me a look.

"What does that face say?"

"It says I don't think it's going to be as easy as that. Sophie lives with Rachel. Rachel lives in this building. And Fit & Tasty uses this flat as their filming base. So avoiding the pair of them isn't going to be easy."

"It is if I know when they're filming and I get out of the flat."

"You're not carrying on with the channel?" Tanya's voice was laced with surprise.

"Not right now, I can't." That part was just too difficult to even focus on, so it was best shelved until further notice.

"But you know Rachel will come up to see how you are. You're friends, after all." She took a swig of her beer, never taking her eyes off me.

I sucked on my top lip. Even the thought of seeing Rachel was making my heart beat like crazy. "I know we'll run into each other, it's inevitable. And when we do, I'll deal with it." I said that last bit with utter conviction, even though my body was telling me anything but. "I just don't want her to know the reasons behind my break-up with Jake. Not right away."

"Obviously."

"So you'll keep quiet for now? For me?"

Tanya eyed me before slowly nodding her head. "If Sophie asks, I'll just tell her things weren't working out for you and Jake, nothing more."

"Thank you." I gazed at my best friend, then shook my head. "How can life get so complicated, so quickly?"

Tanya smiled. "It happens. Look at me — I remember when Gran died and I first thought about taking Delilah. I didn't think I could do it. Stupid, really: Delilah was gran's dog, so I worked it out.

"Same with you. This is huge right now, making the step, changing your life. It's going to be bumpy and painful, but in the end, it'll be worth it, wherever you end up. You'll find somewhere new to live, and you'll get a girlfriend if that's what you want."

Tanya sat forward, taking my hand in hers. "But go after what you want, Alice, because life's short. Don't live your life in the shadows just because you don't want to hurt Jake. That's not how it works. Now you've made such a drastic change, you owe it to yourself to follow through."

I stared at her long and hard before I nodded. "I know you're right, but I just need a little time."

"Don't take too long, because if this is who you really are, you've already wasted long enough."

Chapter Nine

The following morning and I'd slept surprisingly well. Over the past few months, I'd got used to waking up and staring at the ceiling while Jake snored softly beside me. But now, Jake was no more, and perhaps my conscience was clearer because last night, laying in Tanya's spare bed, I'd dropped off to sleep with ease, just as I'd heard Sophie's voice in the lounge.

Tanya's girlfriend had given us time alone, but she'd come up to sleep when Tanya had texted her saying the coast was clear. It was only a matter of time before Sophie moved in officially, seeing as she was here most nights anyway. Tanya had even given her a drawer, which had made me smile.

Sophie had a drawer: that was commitment.

I thought of my drawers full of stuff at our flat — *Jake's flat* — and wondered how he was feeling today. I rolled over and picked up my phone from the bedside table. Should I send him a text? Was that a bit callous when I'd just walked out on him the day before? Perhaps. I dropped the phone on the duvet and it didn't make a sound.

Rachel drifted into my mind, and her affirmations. Right at this moment, if she was in, she was only ten floors below me — and that made my stomach wobble. Was she lying in bed, staring at her ceiling, thinking of me, too?

Of course she wasn't.

She was probably in front of her mirror, doing her affirmations, the thought of which made me smile.

Perhaps I should do some affirmations to get my new life going. But what should they be?

I frowned as I tried to come up with some.

"I will make Rachel interested in me."

Nope, that still needed more work. How about: "I am deserving of love and am open to it being from a woman."

Not bad.

I stared at the ceiling, still brilliant white, seeing as Tanya had the whole flat redecorated recently. The spare room walls were the colour of martini olives, and the room was spacious, too, with a king-sized bed, wardrobe with chunky handles, and a multi-coloured chest of drawers that had no doubt cost more than a week of my teaching salary. Tanya was a corporate lawyer, after all, so money was no object. Even her spare room, most people's dumping ground, reflected her perfectly: cool, calm, expensive.

A pressing on my bladder meant I had to get up, so I hopped out of bed and flung on some shorts, before making my way down the hall to the bathroom, all cool grey tiles, shiny mirrors and hotel chic. One day, when my life was sorted, I'd own a bathroom like this.

The ping of the front doorbell interrupted my thoughts and my heart picked up speed. Who was at the door? Jake, come to plead with me to change my mind? I washed my hands and gave myself a stern look in the mirror, my heart thudding in my chest, my hazel eyes still red from sleep.

It was probably just someone for Tanya. A parcel, perhaps.

I heard voices and gulped, swallowing down my fears. I strained my ears but couldn't make out a man's voice in the mix, just a dull rumble of sound. Knowing I couldn't hide in the bathroom forever, I took a deep breath and stepped out into the hallway, walking towards the lounge.

And that's when I recognised one of the voices and stopped walking. Could I swivel on one foot and make it back to my bedroom cocoon before anyone realised? I was going to give it a damn good try.

However, as I turned, I came face to face with a bed-headed Tanya, towering over me as usual, arms outstretched for a hug.

I couldn't do anything else except fall into it.

"You lost?" Tanya squeezed me tight as she spoke.

"Kinda," I replied, alarm bleeding from me as if my whole body was an open wound.

Tanya took my hand in hers, not heeding my non-verbal signals as she pulled me towards the lounge and near-certain catastrophe. I began to resist Tanya's pull, but she always had been that bit stronger than me.

"Sophie's been and got pastries from the café, so it's

a Sunday morning on the balcony in the sunshine. We thought it'd be the perfect way to start the day and your fresh start, put you in a good mood."

"But—" I wanted to dig my heels in, put the brakes on, but everything was happening on super fast-forward and I didn't appear to have a say.

"—No buts, you're not hiding in your room all day feeling sorry for yourself. Today is the start of the rest of your life, and we need to start it right. With strong coffee and Jess's delicious pain au chocolat and pain aux raisins. Am I right?"

She gave me a grin and tugged me, off balance, down the rest of the hallway and into the lounge.

It was only when Tanya saw we had another visitor that she flashed me a panicked look; the very same one that had been on my face for the past few seconds.

Because the extra visitor was Rachel, standing in the kitchen beside Sophie, her black hair artfully swept to one side, in a pair of Abercrombie & Finch baby blue jogging bottoms, a white V-necked T-shirt hugging her slim, pale frame.

I swayed and colour bled into my vision, mainly blood red and deathly black: was this where I passed out?

I tried to recall my recent affirmations, but they seemed to have deserted me.

Tanya squeezed my hand, before turning to address Sophie, currently standing by her large white kitchen island.

"Hey!" Tanya said, a jaunt in her voice I was sure

she'd added just for me. "I wasn't expecting company, I would have put my posh shorts on."

Sophie looked up with a smile, her blonde hair newly cut, licking her fingers as she finished placing the pastries on a large oval plate. "Rachel's hardly company," she replied. "I just realised we were out of jam, so I texted her to say if she brought some up, she could share breakfast with us."

Rachel grinned. "And I didn't have a better offer this morning, so I said yes."

This, at least, told me one thing: Tanya hadn't blabbed, otherwise Sophie would never have done this. I was relieved to know I could trust my friend to keep a secret, even if this was my ultimate nightmare, meeting Rachel on day two of singledom. Or was it day one? After all, this time yesterday, I still had a boyfriend.

"I wasn't expecting to see you, though," Rachel added, smiling at me. "Did you have one too many on Tanya's balcony last night?"

I should have known staying here was going to be too dangerous.

I painted on a smile and addressed Rachel, my heart pulsing, my jaw stiff. "Something like that." I pressed my back teeth together like I was having a dental X-Ray. "Actually, Jake and I have split up, so I'm crashing here for a bit."

Rachel's face fell. "You've split up?"

I nodded, feeling Tanya wince beside me, seeing Sophie

look down at the kitchen bench she was standing over, pausing as she loaded a bunch of mugs onto a tray.

"We have," I replied, wishing I was back under my crisp white duvet, still warm, where nothing could harm me.

Rachel walked over, her face set to such a high level of compassion, I thought I might crumble if she came any closer.

I took a step backwards as she approached.

"Are you okay?" She touched my arm.

I stopped breathing and glanced at Tanya for help, but my friend had chosen this moment to slip away to her girlfriend, leaving me with Rachel, just the two of us.

Her touch made my whole body react like an induction hob: instant, glowing heat.

"I'm okay, just a lot of stuff to work out, as you can imagine." I stared into Rachel's crystal blue eyes as I had done so many times before, but this morning, the gesture had fresh meaning.

Because today was the first time I'd done it as a single, available woman.

A single, available woman who was more and more attracted to the single, available woman standing in front of her.

And those were exactly the thoughts I didn't want to be thinking this morning.

It was all too soon, too messy, too much.

Rachel's kind eyes were focused all on me, her head nodding in understanding.

"Of course," she said. "If there's anything I can do, for either of you, just let me know."

For either of us?

Of course, Jake was her business partner, she would say that.

"I will," I said, knowing I had to get out of here as soon as possible, for my own sanity. "You know, second thoughts, I think I need to get going, so I'll take a raincheck on breakfast."

I glanced at my wrist where my watch normally sat, but was absent today. What lie could I make up on the spot to get out of sitting on the balcony with Rachel, the object of my desire staring at me with sympathy in her eyes, making my heart lurch one way, then the other, like it was punch-drunk?

"You do?" Tanya said from the kitchen.

I nodded. "I have to get over to my mum's for Sunday lunch. I said I'd help her out today, because Dad's out this morning and my sister is coming over with her family."

I checked my wrist again: still empty.

"You can't even stay for a quick coffee and pastry?" Tanya walked over and stood behind Rachel.

I shook my head, a rabbit trapped in the headlights. "I just remembered."

Tanya held my gaze, before nodding slowly. "Okay."

"Pour me a coffee and I'll have a swig on my way out, okay?"

I gave Rachel and Tanya a final smile, before fleeing

into my bedroom and collapsing on the bed, my breathing ragged, my thoughts all over the place.

First things first: I should text my parents to see if they were around today. Yes, it had been a lie, but I had nowhere better to be.

Chapter Ten

I knocked on the door of my parents flat and stood back, still overwhelmed by all the changes that had happened in the last 24 hours. A good night's sleep had settled my nerves, but seeing Rachel so soon had emptied the pockets of my life, tipping my thoughts and feelings onto the floor without a moment's notice.

Seconds later, my mum greeted me with a beaming smile. I was no giant, but Mum only just reached over five foot — yet she'd always seemed way taller to me. She was wearing jeans and a blue-and-white stripey top, one of about 20 she owned. As Mum always said, if you found something you liked that suited you, you should buy that item in all of the colours and your wardrobe was set.

She was wearing a racing-green apron over the top of her stripes, and the smeared flour on the front told me she'd been baking this morning, as did the gorgeous scent of sweet, freshly baked pie that hung in the air. I hoped it was apple — Mum made the best apple pie in the world.

"Daughter number two, safely back at the mothership," she said, a soft smile creasing her face. She held out her arms and I sank into her embrace, just like I used to when I was a little girl.

Right now, I was that little girl again, transported back to all the times she'd held me when I was in need.

I was still in need of her reassurance, more than she would ever know.

Even her smell was comforting: lavender and lemon, her favoured essential oil mix.

Mum eventually broke the embrace, rubbing her hands up and down my shoulders.

"Such a long face!" she said, taking my hand and pulling me towards the kitchen. "Come with me, we'll get you a drink and you can tell your mum all about it." She turned then, giving me a grin. "I'm just pleased to have you here, I did a little yelp when I got your text — I always love having you for Sunday dinner, especially one that's a surprise. Although it's a shame Jake couldn't make it, too. Is he working again? That boy needs to have a break. Although I suppose in the business he's in, other people's leisure time is his work time, isn't it?"

I stilled at her words, momentarily surprised she didn't know Jake wouldn't be joining us ever again, but then, why would she? I only left him yesterday and I hadn't exactly been spray-painting my news all over town. Only four other people in the world knew — including Rachel — and just the thought of her threatened to knock me off my stride as I followed Mum down the hall, with her looking over her shoulder, waiting for a reply.

"The thing is…" I winced as I stumbled over my words. "Well, Jake's not coming over because we've split up." I took a deep breath, watching Mum's face as it dropped. "So he won't be coming around again at all."

Her forehead furrowed and she stopped walking, turning to stare at me. She pulled me to her, before taking hold of my shoulders in a vice-like grip. "Oh my, you poor thing. Split up, are you sure? Completely done?"

"Yes, completely done."

She poked her tongue into her cheek. "Is it another woman?" she whispered, like saying it any louder might make it true. She said it with the sure-fire knowledge of a woman who'd seen all this before: man has affair, woman finds out, woman returns to her loved ones and sobs on their shoulder.

I could see Mum was already preparing her shoulder for me, but I shook my head.

To be honest, it would make it way easier to deal with if there was another woman.

But alas, there was not.

Not in the way my mother would imagine, at any rate.

"No, there's no other woman."

Not for Jake, at least.

Mum gave me a concerned stare, then nodded, pulling me into the kitchen where the chicken was sitting in a foil-lined tray, a lemon stuck inside its cavity. The air smelled of the potatoes she'd par-boiled already, now sitting fluffed up all around the pale, uncooked bird.

Mum's roast chicken dinners were the stuff of legend — and just about the only thing Dad let her cook at weekends, when the kitchen was his domain. I'd tried to replicate it at home, but I'd never quite mastered it. On the side was the pie she'd already baked, all golden and crisp, with the tell-tale pastry apple shape nestled on the top.

Mum opened the fridge and poured me a large glass of chilled Chablis: her favourite.

I smiled as she handed me the wine, taking a long glug, instantly feeling better about my day.

Mum poured herself a smaller glass, then took my hand again, dragging me through the parquet-floored living room with its patterned wallpaper and thickly upholstered sofas, and out onto the balcony that ran the full length of their flat. It was scattered with green plants and pots of colourful flowers, along with a white wooden table surrounded by four matching chairs.

This was Mum's favourite part of the flat, what sold it to her. The balcony overlooked an internal courtyard and quite often, my parents' balcony appeared to be the only one in regular use.

I sat down in the cushioned seats, as unexpected panic slid down me: I was going to have to tell Mum the details, and it wasn't the story she was expecting. When I looked up, she was plumping her orange cushion, before sitting down and fixing me with concerned eyes. The same eyes she'd been gazing at me with since the day I was born.

"Where's Dad?" A stalling tactic. I sipped my wine.

"Out on a job." She rolled her eyes.

"I thought he'd retired?"

"He has," she said. "But it's your dad's version of retired, not mine." Mum paused. "Sabrina keeps telling him, but he doesn't listen, you know what he's like. He tells me these are clients he's dealt with for years, but he's been telling me that forever. I just leave him to it now, I can't stop him."

Dad was an architect with his own firm. Sabrina had followed in his footsteps and was now managing the firm, along with two other partners. Dad was meant to have stepped down at the beginning of the year when he turned 65, but he was having trouble letting go.

"So," she said. "What's going on? I thought you and Jake were made for each other, happy as larks." She paused. "If he hasn't cheated on you, what's happened? Men like him don't come along every day." She narrowed her eyes. "I take it you ended it?"

I crinkled my brow. "Why do you think that?"

She smiled. "You're not crying and saying how unfair the world is. If you're not, Jake must be, which means you ended it." She pursed her lips. "Did *you* cheat?"

I sighed, shaking my head. "Nobody cheated and I wish everyone would stop asking me. We loved each other, and now we don't. Well, I don't. That's all, no third parties." Irritation seeped out of my voice, but I wasn't bothered. Ours was a blameless break-up, not a conflicted one.

"So why the sudden change of heart? Are you absolutely sure? Because that boy loves you, that much is clear as day."

My insides flared, but I kept my cool.

"I don't doubt that. But I don't love him anymore and that's quite a key component. I can't just stay together with someone because they want to. I have to want it, too."

Mum ran the tip of her index finger along the top of her wine glass, before flicking her gaze back up to me.

And that gaze was suddenly stifling, taking me back to when I was little and Mum would look at me in the same way. I could never tell lies and I wasn't about to start now.

A hot flush shot through me as I considered the next words that came out of my mouth, and I was blushing before they even hit the air. It's not that I was embarrassed, I was just new to this. And telling my parents was *way* different to telling my friends or my sister.

"I know it seems out of the blue." I paused, my palms clammy, my hands trembling. "But I've kinda fallen for someone else, and it wasn't something I could ignore anymore. Nothing's happened, the other person doesn't even know, but I couldn't be dishonest."

Mum regarded me, before reaching over and taking my hand. "And I'm proud of you for doing that," she said. "I can see this isn't something you've done lightly."

I shook my head. "It was one of the hardest decisions of my life, but also one of the easiest. Once I told him, I knew I'd done the right thing. But it's taken months to work up to it."

"Months?" Mum's voice was etched with surprise. "How many months?"

I nodded. "A lot. Six." Somehow, I wasn't ready to tell her the *whole* truth. "Maybe more."

She took a moment to swallow that information down. "So who's this new fella — is he someone you work with?"

My cheeks burned from the inside out as I cleared my throat. Here goes nothing, the moment Tanya and all my other gay friends had told me about. I was about to come out to my mother and I hadn't even had sex yet. At least, not with a woman.

"No, nobody I work with," I said, the hairs on the back of my neck standing up as I uncrossed and then re-crossed my legs. "And it's not a man, either." I paused, my chest tightening, the words getting caught in my throat.

I bit the inside of my cheek.

Just say the words.

"It's a woman."

A huge gust of something flew up my windpipe, and I forced myself to look at my mother, the woman I'd known my whole life, the first woman I'd ever loved.

She raised both eyebrows and took a giant slug of her Chablis. Then she tried a smile, but it didn't quite stick.

I wasn't sure what I was expecting, but this was new. I'd never faced any judgement when I'd brought up a man I was interested in, but this was obviously different.

It was making me stutter, and making my mum stutter.

I wasn't sure how I felt about that.

"A woman — well, I never saw that one coming." She cocked her head. "This is very out of the blue. Since when do you like women?"

She was still talking to me, so that was good. "It's a pretty recent occurrence." If she thought I had this all worked out, she was sorely mistaken. "And if you're surprised, believe me, I was just as in the dark."

Mum sat forward, staring down at the courtyard before lifting her gaze back to me. "It's not Tanya, is it?"

I laughed. My family clearly thought Tanya was the only lesbian in the whole wide world.

"No, it's not Tanya," I said. "There are other women, other lesbians in London apart from Tanya."

"But you met her through Tanya?"

I nodded. "In a roundabout way, yes. She shares a flat with Tanya's girlfriend, Sophie."

I wished I could see what was going on in her head. Was she surprised? Happy? Disappointed?

Not that her reaction would affect my emotions.

That ship has already sailed.

I recalled Rachel's concerned gaze from this morning, her touch on my arm that had threatened to undo me.

"But you've always had boyfriends in the past. Has there been a girlfriend I've missed, someone you've not told me about?"

I shook my head. "No, it's always been men."

"So you can just change? Just like that?" She took another sip of wine.

"Not exactly just like that." This wasn't a snap decision, something I was trying on for size. "I haven't just decided this on a whim. This has been months of wrestling. It doesn't just happen overnight, that's not how it works."

I hoped she got the enormity of it. After all, I'd never turned up at her door with this sort of news before.

"Of course," she said. "I suppose it happened with Barbara, too."

"Barbara? Which Barbara?" My mind was scanning my mum's friends, but I could only come up with one who fitted the description.

Mum's bottom lip poked out before she replied. "I only know one Barbara." Pause. "Well unless you count Barbara Rudkin, but she was always more of a Babs than a Barbara. If we shorten Barbara's name, she hates it. Even to Barb."

I waved my finger in an anti-clockwise movement. "Let's rewind. Barbara, your friend forever, who was married to William forever, is now a lesbian?" I paused. "With Maggie?"

"Of course with Maggie, who else?"

"I don't know, this is all news to me."

"Well we've both been surprised today, haven't we?"

Touché.

"So how long has Barbara been batting for the other team?" This wasn't how I'd expected the conversation to go.

Mum waggled her head, as if totting up the years. "A while," she said, with a shrug. "She moved Maggie in, told us a few months later, and they've been very happy ever since."

"And you never thought to tell me?" I was outraged that one of her best friends had come out and I didn't know. "Does Sabrina know?"

Mum smiled. "I don't think so, but it's clearly all the rage, I feel like I might be missing out." She laughed at her own joke.

"Please don't leave Dad on my account, I couldn't take the guilt."

She smiled. "I think you're pretty safe — I've put years into that man, I'm not about to walk away now." She shook her head. "Well, this isn't what I expected you to tell me today. But of course, whatever you decide your future is, your dad and I will support you." She paused. "How did Jake take it? I think most men would have their pride dented knowing they'd been usurped for a woman."

I grimaced. "He doesn't know that bit yet, and I don't think he needs to. It's not like anything has happened. Plus, I split up with him because I'm not in love with him anymore. There isn't any other reason."

"And how did he take that?"

"The 'I'm not in love with you' bit?"

Mum nodded.

"Not well. I mean, he coped, but he wasn't jumping for joy. He told me he still loved me."

"And you're sure it's definitely over with him?"

Hadn't she been listening to what I'd been saying? "Yes, Mum, I'm sure."

She held up both hands. "Okay, I'm just checking, because it's a big decision to make unless you're 100 per cent sure. And this woman doesn't know how you feel?"

I shook my head. "I don't think so. I mean, we're friends, but nothing more."

Mum was silent for a few seconds. "Is she gay?"

I nodded.

"What's her name?"

"Rachel." Saying her name felt precious, like she was a diamond I was placing on top of a glass table: handle with care.

"What does she do then, this Rachel?"

"She's a chef. She works at Red On Black, actually."

Mum's face lit up. "Does she really? That's one of our favourites. You've never mentioned it before."

I shrugged. "A bit like telling me that Barbara was a lesbian, I didn't think it was important." I shifted in my seat. "But I was wondering — can I stay here for a bit while I look for somewhere to live and sort my head out?"

Mum nodded, giving me an understanding smile. "Our door is always open, you know that." She paused. "So do you think you're bisexual or a full-on lesbian?"

I smiled as I shook my head: Mum had never shied away from discussing any topic, which as a teenager was a curse.

"I don't know, I only left Jake yesterday, give me time." I gave her a mock scowl.

"But you've been thinking about it for months, you must have some inclination."

"I don't have all the answers," I replied. "I mean, I like Rachel, but does that make me a lesbian? I don't know."

"Barbara says it can swing around all the time," Mum replied. "Although I think her and Maggie are pretty set now." She leaned in with a conspiratorial look on her face. "And she told me it was the best sex she'd ever had in her life," she added with a grin. "So there's that to look forward to."

I held up both palms in the air and grimaced. "Too much information!"

"Too much information about what?" a voice at the balcony door boomed. "What are you blabbing about now, Eve?"

I looked up to see Dad standing there, a wide smile on his face, arms outstretched. He was wearing chinos and a white shirt, and his silver hair had been newly cut since I last saw him. "This is a lovely surprise," he said, his Italian accent pronounced as always. "I was only expecting daughter number one and her brood today."

I got up and gave him a hug, breathing in the familiar smell of his aftershave, Givenchy Gentlemen.

"No Jake, or is he arriving later after he's made the world a fitter place?"

This was going to be a theme for a while, wasn't it?

I shot Mum a look, and she returned it with a serene smile, riding to my rescue.

"There's been a change of plan, Giuseppe." She stood beside him.

"Oh?"

"Alice has news. Do you want me to say or would you rather?"

I shook my head. "Go ahead." I was happy to let Mum do the honours.

"Alice and Jake are no more, and she's thinking of heading down Barbara's road, if you get my meaning." Mum nudged Dad with her elbow as she spoke, but he still looked confused.

"What's Alice got to do with Barbara? Aren't her and Maggie still together?" He was frowning, trying to connect the dots.

I stood up and took his hand in mine. "No, Dad," I said, giving him a squeeze. "What Mum's trying to say is I've left Jake, and I think I might be gay. Or bisexual. Or something. It's up in the air and open to interpretation, but I'm definitely not all that straight anymore."

Dad paused, frozen in mid-stance, his gaze holding me in place.

Mum and I stared at him, waiting for a response.

"Well, say something!" Mum said eventually.

Dad dropped my hand, then leaned in and put his arm around my shoulders. "Gay or bisexual, eh?" he said, shaking his head with a smile. "You know what I think?"

I really didn't.

Dad pulled me close and kissed the top of my head. "I think whoever ends up with my daughter in their life is a lucky person, and I don't much care if it's a man or a woman. So long as you're happy, that's all that counts." He placed another kiss on my cheek, and put the other arm around Mum.

Happiness wrapped itself around me and I felt cocooned, calm. Whatever happened from here on in, my family had my back, and that was a huge weight off my mind.

Now, I just needed to work out what was happening with Rachel, but that could wait. For today at least.

"A lesbian daughter, how exciting!" Dad repeated. "Does this call for more wine?"

"Yes please," Mum and I both chorused back, reaching for our glasses.

Chapter Eleven

I'd left Tanya's the previous day intent on giving myself some time to mull this over. However, the more I thought about it, the more I was sure I needed to act. Now the ball was rolling, I needed to run with it before I lost my nerve.

And so, with trepidation, I booked a table at Red On Black for that night, before telling Mum she had a date so long as she promised to be on her best behaviour. I wasn't sure if I was crazy to take her with me — probably — but the restaurant was just around the corner from their flat, and nobody else I knew would be able to make it at such short notice. Plus, if I invited any of my friends, they'd *know* I'd been here to see Rachel.

It wasn't something I said often, but in this instance, Mum was the easiest option.

Red On Black turned out to be one of those sleek new restaurant spaces with dark wood tables and chairs, low lighting and waiting staff kitted out entirely in black with white bow ties. The glassware sparkled almost as much as the maitre d's teeth as he showed us to our table, my heart in my mouth as I eyed what I assumed to be the kitchen door.

I knew the chances of Rachel springing out of it were remote: she was a chef, not a waiter. However, just the thought of her being behind those doors was enough to make me sweat.

"Okay?" Mum asked, smiling at me as our waiter shook out my napkin and told us about the specials. He had a heavy French accent that added a touch of glamour to his food-reading skills, and a smile that made Mum give him all her attention.

One of the specials was lamb cutlets, and I recalled a conversation with Rachel a month ago where she told me she did over 60 in a single shift. Would her skilled hands touch them tonight?

I nodded at my mum, nervous energy spilling out of me.

"I wonder, could you tell me," she asked the waiter, as if it was the most natural thing in the world. "Is Rachel in the kitchen tonight?"

I clutched my chair. I knew this had been a mistake, Mum could never just leave things be.

Although, I'd brought her here, so maybe I was just the same, too.

The waiter nodded his head. "She is, madam," he said, smiling brightly. "Do you know her?"

Mum motioned to me. "My daughter is good friends with her," she said, avoiding my gaze as my heart slowed to almost a total halt. What the hell was she doing? I gazed at the teal-coloured curtains draping the window, at the woman on the next table whose boobs were enormous and surely fake. I dragged my gaze up to the waiter, who was nodding his head rapidly.

"I'll let her know," he said, pocketing his pen in his shirt pocket. "Who should I say is asking for her?"

My throat was so dry, I was having trouble speaking, but I managed to croak out my name and, satisfied, he turned and walked to the bar to place our order.

When he'd gone, I glared at my mother, outraged, but also semi-impressed with her forthrightness. A waft of something delicious and meaty sailed by as a waiter delivered two plates to the table behind her.

"Since when are we coming in here and doing that right away?" I cleared my throat halfway to add more volume. As I spoke, I had one eye on the swing door the waiter had just disappeared through, in case the next person who appeared through it was Rachel.

Mum waving her hand brought my attention back to the table, as the waiter delivered our glasses of Prosecco, bringing his head close to mine.

"Madam, I have informed Rachel and she says to tell you she'll be out when she gets a second." His breath was minty fresh.

Okay, he'd told her. The ball was still rolling, and it was picking up speed.

When he walked away, I gripped my glass of bubbles and grimaced at my mum. "He's told her."

Dread and excitement put a finger to their lips and tip-toed down my spine.

What was I going to say when she came out? I hadn't thought that far ahead yet.

I concentrated on not rocking in my seat: I wanted to appear calm when Rachel eventually appeared.

Opposite me, Mum grinned, sipping her drink. "It's exciting, and I'm thrilled to be your wing-woman. Isn't that what they call it in the films?"

If she was looking to lighten the moment, she managed it. I gave her a strangled laugh as I buried my head in the menu: did I want the scallops or beef carpaccio to start? The sea bass or lamb for main? And whatever I ordered, was I going to be able to eat it when it arrived?

We'd just placed our order when Rachel walked out of the kitchen doors, her eyes darting around the restaurant before our gazes met across the room. And when they did, it was all I could do to remember to breathe, to remember where I was, to remember my name.

She raised a hand in acknowledgement, an uncertain smile on her face and began walking towards us slowly, as if she was on a tightrope suspended high off the ground.

Was she feeling as trepidatious as me? I had no idea.

As she drew nearer, my stomach dropped. I wasn't ready for this, but then, I didn't think I ever would be.

"You're here," Rachel said as she reached our table, her voice warm, tasting like chocolate brownies. "When

Pierre came into the kitchen and told me there was an Alice outside, I thought it was a joke."

She cast her glance to my mother as I stood up. Our normal greeting was a hug, but today was far from normal, so instead, I just gave her an unsure smile and a pat on the arm.

"It's great to see you."

Seeing Rachel again was making my whole body come alive, and I was glad I'd made the decision to come tonight. I had to see where this went, how it played out. Just being around her was making my heart sing at the top of its lungs.

"This is my mum," I told her; Mum was already standing, her hand outstretched.

"A pleasure to meet you, Rachel." Mum's smile was fixed to full beam. "Alice has told me so much about you, and when she said you were a chef at one of my favourite restaurants, I decided we had to come together and sample your food again." She gave Rachel a wink and I nearly died on the spot. "Any excuse really, I love this place, you've done a fabulous job."

Rachel grinned as she shook my mum's hand. "That's a glowing review, thank you. I'll let the whole team know." She leaned forward conspiratorially. "And I'll make sure you get a little extra something tonight." She stood up straight and glanced my way again. "Only the best for my co-star and her mother."

She was being ridiculously charming and it was working a treat on both my mother and I.

Before, Rachel had just been funny, attractive, a friend. But now I was single and had been stewing on my growing attraction for her, it was as if someone had taken a magnifying glass and trained it on our relationship, escalating my feelings to crazy proportions. Now, instead of my attraction simply being standard size, it was suddenly 20ft tall and running around my head with a megaphone.

Rachel turned her attention back to me, her body language telling me she had to leave. "It really is good to see you, though, but I have to get back — we're in the middle of service." She glanced at the kitchen door, before turning back. "Do you fancy a drink after my shift?"

My heart raised its hands in triumph, fists clenched.

I gave Rachel a confident nod, glancing at my mum, who was waving her hands in the air. "Don't look at me, I'll be tucked up in bed by then. You stay out for a drink if you want."

I turned back to Rachel. Every fibre of my body was leaning towards her as if she were sunlight. "What time do you get off?"

Rachel winced. "I can see if I can get away early. Around 10.45?"

I nodded without even thinking. The time was irrelevant to me. "I'll be here."

"Enjoy your dinner," she said, with a wave.

When she'd gone, I turned back to my mother, smoothing down my napkin, knowing my face was glowing.

"So that's the Rachel who's turned my daughter's head." She gave an approving nod. "She seems lovely."

"Mum." It was like I was 12 all over again.

Her gentle laugh washed over me. "That's not a bad thing, darling," she said. "I've only ever wanted you to be happy, and if that involves Rachel, that makes me happy, too." She sat forward. "And you're going to tell her you like her?"

I took a deep breath. Why else had I come here tonight? I had to know if there was anything else there for Rachel, too. Which meant now was the time to be brave. "I think I am. Seize the day, isn't that what they say?"

Mum raised her bubbles to me. "Here's to you seizing the day. At least you'll do it on a full stomach."

Chapter Twelve

I met her after she finished work, in the restaurant bar. Just like the dining room, it was an understated posh affair: think gold-rimmed padded coasters, along with polished chrome bowls overflowing with flavoured nuts.

Rachel had applied fresh lipstick and as she climbed onto her shiny chrome bar stool, a warmth rolled through my body, saliva flooding my mouth. I couldn't help the smile that slid onto my face when she was sitting beside me, although I tried to tone it down as much as I could. I didn't want to scare her off before I'd even made my declaration.

And then, I had to say something. It was me who'd infiltrated her work space, after all. What should my opener be?

"I keep dreaming about you and I can't stop thinking about you," might not be the best start, so I had to think of something else.

Something to put in front of that thought as a barrier to stop it slipping out.

A stupidity dam.

"So my restaurant is your mum's favourite — what are the chances?"

I nodded. "I know. She and Dad are always going somewhere, I can't keep up."

Her fingers were still just as long, her eyes just as sparkly.

"Is that where you get your love of food?"

I nodded again. "I was always taken to restaurants as a child, and my sister and I were those kids who demanded avocados rather than ice cream. I love seeing kids in restaurants, so long as they're well behaved. Giving me a love of good food was my parents' gift to us, and I'm always grateful." It appeared once I started to speak, stopping was the hard part. "Did you go to restaurants as a kid?"

She shook her head. "Not really — eating out wasn't something we did as my parents didn't have the money. I think my first restaurant experience was when I was a teenager, but I was cooking from a young age — both my parents are great cooks, so I can't complain. Only now, working and eating mostly in restaurants, I crave home-cooked food. It's why I wanted to start the channel, to encourage that kind of simple, tasty home-cooking to continue."

"And you're doing it brilliantly," I replied.

"I am, but I prefer doing it with you."

She would prefer doing it with me. Holy shit. I tried to stop my mind going there, but I knew I was fighting a losing battle.

She had no idea how much I'd prefer to do so many things with her, too. I so wanted this to be more, *us* to be more. Now I'd acknowledged it, it was all I could think of. As my mind threw me an image of Rachel in not very much, I concentrated on being an adult.

I could do this. Although when I looked up and caught the long stretch of skin on show, starting just above the swell of Rachel's breast and sweeping all the way up her neck, I wasn't so sure. I wanted to reach out, touch it, taste it.

"How've you been, anyway? I thought you were staying with Tanya, but then Sophie told me you'd left to go to your parents'."

I blinked, forcing myself to concentrate, swallowing down the real reason on the tip of my tongue.

I tapped my fingertips on the bar as the waiter brought our glasses of Chilean Sauvignon Blanc.

"I was staying with Tanya, but I didn't want to play gooseberry to her and Sophie, even though she promised I wouldn't be. You know how it is."

Rachel gave me a smile, swallowing the lie whole. "I get that." She paused. "They tend to spend most of their time upstairs since I caught them naked on the sofa in our flat when they first started going out."

I let out a screech of laughter. "That's not an image you can scrub out of your mind quickly."

Rachel grinned. "It's not. But back to you. How are you after the break-up?"

Emboldened.

Scared.

Nervous as hell around you.

"I'm coping. It wasn't an easy decision, but it was the right one. I mean, I wasn't in love with Jake anymore, so it wasn't really fair on him to carry on." I paused. "How's he doing?"

Rachel nodded. "He's doing okay, but I can tell he's hurting. He doesn't want to talk to me because he knows we're friends. But I've told him I'm his friend, too. Maybe he will eventually." She eyed me with care. "I never saw it coming, I have to say. I thought you two were solid."

I gulped as her gaze caressed me, undressing me with every beat. "We were for a time."

Until I met you.

My legs were trembling, and crossing them proved an effort, my muscle tone deserting me.

I had to front up before I dissolved and fell off this stool in a heap.

"Actually, I've got something to tell you." *Deep breath, deep breath.*

Rachel smiled, sitting forward. "I've got something to tell you, too, although now might not be the best time, not when relationships are probably the last thing on your mind."

Relationships? What was she talking about? Was it possible she was thinking the same thing about me, too?

"Tell me your news first." If Rachel felt the same, I was about to find out.

I smoothed down my shorts and cleared my throat, my shoulder twitching, a shudder working its way up my body.

"Well," she said, sipping her wine, going a little coy on me. "Did I tell you I've been using Tinder?"

My heart drooped as I shook my head.

Those were not the words I wanted her to say.

"No."

A smile danced onto her face. "Well, I have. I mean, I've been single for ages, and I thought, what the hell? A couple of friends have had success recently, so I gave it a whirl. And meeting my sister's girlfriend spurred me on. And guess what? I got a date." She sat back, smiling, waiting for my response.

She'd met someone else? When I was ready to jump right into that void, to offer myself to her?

Unexpected, hot tears stung the back of my eyeballs, but I swallowed down, squeezing my eyes shut to stop any outbursts. I wasn't going to fall apart in front of her, so instead I stared at the floor and got a grip.

My duty here, as her friend — *her supposedly straight friend* — was to be encouraging. I knew that. I dug deep and painted on my best smile. Even though inside, my heart was quietly snapping in two.

"That's great," I said, sweeping my enthusiasm into my arms and dumping it in her lap. "So who is she?" The perk in my voice was so false, but Rachel was oblivious.

"Her name's Hannah and she works for a bank. Which

is unusual — I normally go for arty types, creatives. Not that dissimilar to you."

Okay, now I wanted to wail.

"When are you going out?"

I sounded so casual: I was anything but.

"We already did this week."

A punch to the guts.

"Are you seeing her again?"

Rachel nodded, a smile creasing her face. A smile that was placed there by another woman, a woman who was not me.

By putting this decision off, I'd been the architect of my own downfall.

How terribly ironic.

"Yes, next Tuesday — it's my next night off. I mean, we haven't slept together yet, we're both holding off on that, but it was nice to be on a date, meeting someone new. My work doesn't really allow it — in the last 18 months, you, Jess, Lucy and Tanya are the four new people I've met — three taken lesbians and one straight woman. So it's nice to meet someone there's a possibility with, you know?"

I nodded. I did know, only my possibility had just fallen down the back of my life and it would need something special to reach down and grab it back. It seemed so unfair I'd taken this long to get to this point, and now, it'd suddenly been taken away.

But I couldn't puncture Rachel's bubble, because she was smiling like she'd just won the lottery. And perhaps she had, because she'd met a proper lesbian, not a perhaps-lesbian like me.

Perhaps this was better all round for Rachel and, in the end, what she deserved. Someone who knew who they were and exactly what they wanted.

"That's really great news," I told her. "I'm pleased for you."

Rachel grinned. "And what was your news?"

My news.

Well, my news had kinda been blown out of the water, hadn't it? I scrabbled to think of something and then: "I was thinking of coming back to the channel in a few weeks, if that works. I need to get back on board, once the dust has settled and I've spoken to Jake."

That was so not my news.

But Rachel looked thrilled. "That's brilliant! What a week this is turning into."

She could say that again.

Chapter Thirteen

The following morning my mum was perched at the breakfast bar on her iPad when I walked in. The kitchen smelled of bleach, so she'd clearly done her morning clean — she was fastidious when it came to hygiene. The black-and-white Victorian tiles under my feet gleamed, and the sides were clear, everything in its place.

"So, how did it go?" I could almost feel the anticipation leaping off her as she spoke.

"It went." I pursed my lips as the coffee gurgled out of the machine, the warming smell hitting my nostrils. I loved the smell of coffee and it was the only thing I had to cling onto this morning. Rachel was about to start dating someone else, and I'd missed the boat.

"What does that mean?" Mum took her reading glasses from her face, leaving them dangling around her neck. "Did you tell her you like her? I think she liked you. I could tell by her eyes. They sparkled when they were on you."

"That was probably heat from working in a kitchen." I paused. "Turns out she doesn't like me at all, and why would she? She thinks I'm heartbroken and if I was in the market for someone else, it would be a man. Which is the logical conclusion to jump to."

"But you could set her straight. So to speak."

"Not when she'd just told me she'd gone on a date with another woman called Hannah."

"Oh." A wince. "That wasn't in our plan."

"Since when has this become *our* plan?"

"Since you're living with us — and I thought last night would push things along."

"It did, sort of. Now she's off the market, so I have to forget about her and move on."

Mum paused, eyeing me. "But you're still a lesbian?"

I gave her a look. Why did she need to categorise at a moment like this? "I'm sad and disappointed more than anything else."

"And Jake's definitely off the table?"

I ground my teeth together, just like my dentist told me not to. "Yes, mother. Just because plan B is off the table, doesn't mean I'm returning to plan A when it clearly wasn't working in the first place."

"Okay, no need to jump down my throat. This is new to me, too, I'm just getting my bearings." She leaned forward, one elbow on the granite breakfast bar. "You know what my motto is?"

"Have some more wine?"

She sucked in a breath, ignoring me. "My motto is never give up. Unless she's got a wedding ring on her finger, she's not off the market yet. And she's had how many dates? One?"

"Second one coming up. And she was quite upbeat about this woman. Who, by the way, has probably known she's a lesbian for a while, so comes with far less baggage than me."

Mum got off her stool and walked over, putting her arms around me, bathing me in a soft smile.

"Everyone comes with baggage of some sort, and this other woman might have all sorts of issues you don't know about. And I'm sure she's had relationships, too — most people have when they reach their 30s. But you know the one thing you have over them all? You *know* Rachel, you get on with her, and I'm sure if you tell her how you feel, she might surprise you. But until she knows all the facts, you can't say she's off the market. There endeth your mother's wisdom lecture for the day."

Chapter Fourteen

I think Mum must have called Sabrina and asked her to come over, because the following week, she turned up on the doorstep at 7.30pm one evening telling me Simon was looking after Flavia and we were going out.

I'd learned very early in life never to argue with Sabrina, because it never really got you anywhere. And so, ushered out the door by our mum, Sabrina took my arm and steered me through the people-strewn pavements, like I'd never been out in London before and needed looking after.

She wasn't far wrong on the second point.

However, when she steered us into the road with Rachel's restaurant, I tensed up. Suddenly, the fact my parents lived a stone's throw from where she worked wasn't all that appealing.

My sister, clearly forewarned, tightened her grip in response, before plunging us into a bar on the next street, all garishly patterned carpets and windows frosted with old English crests. She plonked me down on a padded seat under a large window, before promptly returning with a bottle of chilled Sauvignon Blanc, the perfect accompaniment to a warm summer's evening.

I smiled, trying to fight off the feeling of desperation that had been slumped on my shoulder all day long as I'd stared at the spare-room walls, before trying to eat and failing miserably. I remembered this feeling from failed relationships past: some people fed their misery, but I starved mine.

"I assume Mum called you," I said, as Sabrina poured the wine, condensation running down the chilled glass and wetting her fingers.

"She sent me a text. And to tell you the truth, Flavia had been winding me up all day, so I jumped at the chance of helping my sister. Children are all well and good, but sometimes a little adult company is needed." She raised her glass in punctuation. "Along with a little adult grape juice."

I smiled and took a sip, grateful to have a supportive family around me. Not everyone did. Tanya, for instance, whose family were a bunch of terrible bigots.

"Thank you, anyway. There's only so long I can stare at a wall and ponder the mess I've made of my life. At least if I was at work I'd have something to take my mind off it."

"You're the only teacher I've ever met to moan about the length of their holidays." Sabrina squeezed my leg. "Come on then, bring me up to speed with the full breadth of how much you've fucked up your life. I need to know details. Mum said you've been looking at moving out, viewing some places."

I nodded, my heart sinking. "I did. I went to view two places a bit nearer work — one house-share that was lovely but *sharing*—"

"—was it the term house-share that gave it away?"

I ignored her. "—and one flat the size of our parents' balcony." I shrugged. "It's tough on my salary. I might have to move further out."

"I'm sure something will come up." She paused. "And mum said Rachel had started seeing someone else."

"Nothing's ever very secret in our family, is it?"

"You should know that by now," Sabrina said. "She's taking the whole lesbian thing very well, isn't she?"

"It's all thanks to Barbara," I replied.

Sabrina scrunched her forehead. "Barbara who lives down the road, Barbara?"

I nodded. "Uh-huh. You know Maggie who she lives with? Turns out they share a bed."

"No!" Sabrina's face was a picture, the same one I was sure I'd made when I found out.

"Apparently. So now one of Mum's best friends is a lady lover, she thinks she's an oracle. She probably knows more than me, which is a little disconcerting." I paused for added emphasis. "And apparently, the sex is amazing, according to Barbara."

Sabrina's face contorted. "Barbara has sex?"

"Lots of lesbian sex."

Sabrina held up her hand. "Stop it, I feel queasy. I don't want to think about Barbara naked."

"Don't be ageist."

"I'm not, I'm being Barbara-ist." She let out a low whistle. "You just never know, do you? But back to you — Rachel's now off the market?"

I nodded, my stomach doing a somersault as it did every time I thought about it. "Yes, she met someone online, and their second date is tonight. So as we sit here, she's probably putting on her lipstick and checking her hair, in preparation to get laid."

"She might not put out till the third date," Sabrina said.

"Is that still a thing?"

She shrugged. "No idea. I slept with Simon on the first date, I was never one for protocol. What about you?"

I laughed for the first time that day. "I vary, but never a first date. You must be the slut of the family."

Sabrina gave me grin. "Someone has to be." She licked her lips. "Are you planning on stepping in and trying to win her back?"

I gave her a look. "I can't win back something that wasn't mine in the first place, can I?"

However, when I moved my glance around the pub, my heart leapt up my windpipe and lodged in my throat.

I ducked my head, burying it in my armpit as my blood pressure marched upwards like a determined adventurer.

I had no idea what Sabrina was making of it, but if

I just kept my head down and pretended Rachel *hadn't* just walked into the bar looking drop-dead gorgeous and wafting an air of certainty with her, then perhaps I could convince myself it wasn't happening.

What were the chances of us being in the same bar in the *whole of London*?

I held my breath, fear gristly in my mouth, but when I chanced another look up, Rachel was standing at the bar.

So far, I was incognito.

Now I just had to get my breathing working again, and avoid eye contact at all cost. As far as I could make out, she was alone, but how long would that last?

When I looked at my hands, they were shaking.

"Okay, what's going on? Why have you just started to have some kind of panic attack in front of me?" Sabrina was staring at me wide-eyed.

I nodded my head towards Rachel, standing at the bar, her dark hair shiny under the pub lights, her black top draping her body in an alluring fashion. She had one foot casually propped on the chrome footrest that ran along the underside of the bar, and somehow, even that was beyond sexy. I gulped and glanced at my sister, then back at Rachel.

"She's here," I whispered, as casually as I could manage, which it turned out wasn't very casual at all.

"Who?"

I cleared my throat as Rachel ordered from the bartender, a smile on her face as she did so.

Of course she had a smile on her face, she was waiting for her date. I had to get out of there.

But then I glanced at Sabrina, then at our almost full bottle of wine. She wouldn't let me leave it, Sabrina would see that as a complete waste of money, and she'd be right.

However, she wasn't to know my heart might stop beating at any moment, and was there a price on that? A price on me collapsing and dying in front of her this very second? Mum and Dad wouldn't be pleased at all.

"Rachel," I blurted out, convinced that Rachel would hear.

She didn't.

Sabrina followed my gaze, before turning back to me, her mouth hanging open. "Oh shit, so she is," she whispered.

I glanced up again, then put my head down and moved the wine bucket in front of me, nodding as I crouched in front of it. I knew I looked ridiculous, but I didn't care.

This situation *was* ridiculous, and I wanted to try to stop it escalating.

Sabrina joined me behind the bucket now, clearly thinking she needed to hide, too. "Is she here on her date?"

We used to play hide and seek a lot when we were little, but never had the consequences been so high.

I bit my lip and nodded. "I think so."

She glanced up at Rachel. "Nice black top and silver shoes combo."

I agreed, but now was not the time for fashion analysis.

Just at that moment the door opened and both our heads swivelled to take in a woman in black jeans and a light grey top. She was a good few inches taller than my 5ft 5, and she carried herself with purpose — like she knew what she wanted in life.

As soon as I saw her, I knew she was Rachel's date — call it a sixth sense.

Sure enough, with Sabrina and I still hunched behind our wine bucket like we were studying a particularly interesting groove on the wooden pub table, the assured woman tapped Rachel on the shoulder with a smile on her face. And when Rachel twisted round and returned that smile with added interest, my heart sank to the bottom of my self-made ocean of despair.

Under the table, Sabrina took my hand in hers and squeezed, just like she used to when we were kids and there was a thunderstorm, when we'd huddle in the same bed. My sister had always been there for me, through thick and thin, and this was a particularly threadbare moment.

A moment I never expected in my life.

A storm that had come in unexpected, and turned my life upside down.

Storm Rachel.

But neither of us could avert our eyes from this particular storm: we wanted to track its path with precision, know exactly where it was going.

Were they going to kiss?

The answer was no. Rachel leaned in and gave her

a peck on the cheek, and signalled to the bartender for another drink.

The assured woman put a possessive hand on Rachel's arm and my whole body tensed.

I wanted to spring like catwoman from behind my protective wine bucket and whisk Rachel away, telling her what I was feeling, what she needed to know.

Instead, I sat, clutching my sister's hand, trying to regulate my breathing and put a lid on my bubbling pan of emotions, threatening to reach boiling point and spill out all over the pub.

Rachel and her date collected their drinks and sat at a table on the opposite side of the bar.

Please let Rachel sit facing the wall. Please let Rachel sit facing the wall.

Rachel sat facing the wall.

I let out a breath.

If I tried to stand up and function, I might collapse on the floor in a jumble of shattered pieces.

I wasn't sure questioning my sexuality was doing me much good. Is this what women did? Made you break into a thousand pieces?

Her date had long blonde hair and perfect teeth.

I wanted to push her off her chair.

"Are we going to have to hide behind this bucket for the entire time we're here?" Sabrina asked. "And can we raise our voices above a whisper?"

I held in a laugh, but Sabrina was right: we had to sit up

at some point. Plus, there was a group of people standing in between us now, too, so I didn't feel quite as exposed. So slowly, we did just that. Across the pub, beyond a mass of arms, legs and handbags, Rachel and her date were oblivious.

"I approve of your choice, anyway." Sabrina's tone was still hushed. "And you're prettier than her date, too."

I scoffed. "Have you seen her date's waist?"

"Yours is hardly massive," Sabrina replied. "Plus, who wants a twig in bed? You want something to grab hold of. At least, that's what Simon tells me."

I rolled my eyes at my sister's clumsy attempts to make me feel better.

"Let's talk about something else, take your mind off it." She paused. "How are Man United doing?"

I turned my head. "They lost 4-0 last night."

"Right," she said, nodding. "Shall we talk about Barbara?"

"No," I replied, a little too loudly, forgetting for a moment this was a covert operation. Having raised my voice, I ducked behind the ice bucket again, but this time I managed to headbutt it. The resulting thwack seemed to reverberate around the pub as I clutched my head in pain.

"Ow! Fuck-a-doodle-do!"

When I eventually peeled my fingers from my face, the group that had been shielding us had dispersed, and I was now looking directly into the very concerned eyes of Rachel, the one woman I desperately didn't want to see.

I squinted through the pain as my stomach flipped, knowing we'd been rumbled.

Next to me, I felt Sabrina sit up straight as if she was trying to impress in an interview, and I knew without looking she was fixing her smile and buffing her hair. It's what my sister did.

Rachel was on her feet now, moving across the pub's headache-inducing carpets — good at disguising beer spills and vomit I assumed — until she was standing in front of our table, peering at me over our improvised ice-bucket fort.

I wanted to stop my life and hop off.

"Are you okay? I heard that from over there." Rachel's voice was comforting and reassuring all at the same time.

"Fine, just being clumsy."

I rubbed my head: was there a bump already? "This is my sister, Sabrina — this is Rachel."

"Lovely to meet you." Sabrina stood up, flashing Rachel her widest smile.

"And you." Rachel's gaze never left me. "And how exactly did you headbutt the ice bucket?" She was trying not to laugh.

Beside me, Sabrina snorted. "She has special talents."

"It's been one of those weeks." *She had no idea.* My cheeks flared under her intense scrutiny, my heartbeat sprinting up my body at speed. I ignored the tingling in my ears, and ploughed on. "But listen, don't let us interrupt your date. She looks lovely."

Getting the words out was an effort, making them sound sincere was a whole other level.

"Yeah," Rachel said, not sounding nearly as convinced as me.

Perhaps there was room for manoeuvre.

"I should be getting back," she added, tilting her head. She smiled, but it didn't quite cover her whole face. "I would stay to check you're okay, but I can see you're in capable hands. I'll see you soon?" She gazed at me then, with something in her crystal blue eyes I couldn't quite detect.

"So long as I'm still alive. No guarantees."

She grinned. "Okay. I'll text you." With that, she gave me a final look, before going back to her table.

I watched her go, her date studying me with interest, then switched my attention to Sabrina, who had a look on her face telling me she was enjoying this just a little too much.

"I don't want to know what you're thinking, because I don't care." I was plainly lying, but that's the thing with sisters, isn't it? You can lie, they can totally know you're lying, and yet, you can carry on as if nothing had happened. Sabrina accepted my words without a murmur, and then embraced her role of chief distractor, and I loved her for it.

But while externally we were drinking another glass of wine and chatting about Mum and Dad, about the business, about my niece Flavia and all the cute things she was coming out with, internally I was only a quarter present.

The rest of me had one eye on Rachel, checking how

her date was going, trying to assess whether or not they were going to sleep together later. Because once they slept together, the rules changed.

"You okay if we leave the rest of the wine?"

Sabrina nodded. "I know you've only been part listening to me anyway." She gave me a wink, before picking up her bag. "Come on, let's go and get some food elsewhere. Your choice, whatever you fancy. I might even buy it for you to cheer you up."

"You're the best sister I've got." I stood up and cracked my knee against the table. Seriously, why was I being so fucking clumsy today?

No time to ponder, because I knew I had to say goodbye to Rachel, and in the process possibly be introduced to her date.

I shuffled round our table and walked towards her, tapping her on the shoulder and awkwardly raising my hand.

"Bye then, good to see you."

Rachel turned her head, then stood up.

Sabrina had already walked ahead to the pub door, and in that instance, when Rachel's gaze locked with mine, it was just the two of us, in the pub on our own: no date, no sister, nobody else.

The chatter faded, the lights dimmed, and my mind imagined what might have been if I'd just acted sooner.

The two of us sitting in this pub, on a date.

I so wished it was me sitting opposite her.

However, this was not to be my night, and that point was rammed home seconds later when a man carrying three pints and not looking where he was going bundled into me, pushing me sideways, his locked elbows giving me nowhere to go.

I fell into Rachel, knocking her backwards and she landed on the table with a thud, crashing into her bottle of Heineken and sending it toppling, along with her date's bottle too, the remaining beer rushing across the table's surface in an unstoppable frenzy and ending in her date's lap.

As for me, I landed with a crunching sound on top of Rachel, my thigh jammed between hers, the moment paused, freeze-framed in my head.

Yes, I wanted to get between Rachel's thighs.

But no, this was not how I imagined it might happen.

Somewhere beyond my sightline, I heard the distinct tone of my sister's snigger, alongside someone swearing loudly, then a chair being scraped along the ground. I guessed that was Rachel's date.

If I wanted to make sure I was memorable to Rachel, I was going about it the right way.

I'd meant to leave almost unnoticed, but now here I was, on top of her, on a pub table.

Not exactly discreet.

I put my hands on the table either side of Rachel, ignoring when my right hand connected with something wet. I pushed myself upright, wiping my hand on my jeans before offering it to her.

Rachel groaned as I pulled her up, wincing as her hand reached round to feel what I guessed was her wet back, now covered in beer.

The man who'd caused the ruckus was standing very still beside us, beer dripping from his hands, still clinging to what was left of his three pints, an apology pinned to his face.

"I'm so sorry," he said, before giving us a non-committal shrug and darting across the pub.

Rachel stared downwards, pulling her beer-stained top slowly away from her body.

"I'm sorry, too, but there was nothing I could do — he kinda fell into me."

Rachel shook her head. "I know, I saw it." She glanced at her date. "Are you covered in beer, too?"

Her date nodded, wincing: she was standing up and looked like she'd wet herself.

I tried to focus on that and not on Rachel's top which was clinging to her breasts.

Now was not the time, Alice.

I held up my hands as if surrendering. "Anyway, now I've landed on you, I'm going to go." I gave Rachel a lame smile. "Sorry again," I added, before reaching my hand across the table. "I'm Alice, by the way."

"Hannah," her date replied, frowning.

I gave Rachel a final nod, smoothed myself down, then grabbed my sister's arm on the way out of the pub.

Chapter Fifteen

The following week I was sitting on my parents' balcony, watching the couple below have tea. They were older, probably retired, and they poured their tea with such precision and grace from a white china teapot into patterned china teacups, it made me long for such traditions to be more commonplace. Here I was with my white mug of coffee — how terribly uncouth.

My mum said she never saw anybody else out here, but these two were as regular as me, and that was pretty much every day. I'd started to go to coffee shops just to get out of the house, but none had coffee as good as my parents'. Plus, decamping to the balcony made it feel like I was elsewhere, drinking my coffee alfresco. It was a safe space to think, to contemplate life.

Rachel hadn't been in contact since *that* night, and I was trying not to be too disappointed about that.

Why would she, when she had a girlfriend now — and probably one who didn't headbutt ice buckets?

And then there was Jake. He'd sent a couple of texts this week about two unpaid bills we needed to sort out, and even getting them had made my heart break a little. It was all so final, as it had to be, but it didn't stop me mourning the end of another relationship.

When was I going to meet the one?

Or at least, the one I wanted, who wanted me right back.

I recalled my affirmations which I'd been a bit slack on doing, to say the least. "I am deserving of love and I am open to that being from a woman". I repeated it a few times, my eyes closed, my thoughts focused. After all, I had to believe it to make it come true, didn't I?

"And if that woman could be Rachel, that'd be great," I added, for good measure.

My heart stuttered as I thought about her and her date again. And then about me landing on top of her, feeling her taut body underneath mine.

I *so* wanted that to happen in reality, in a different context. I wanted to sit with her, look into her eyes, tell her everything that had been rolling around my head these past few months. Reveal to her that I liked her, and not just as a friend.

I wanted my life to move forward so much, but now I'd made one move, I'd ended up stuck in another rut. Waiting for my real life to begin.

I chewed on my lower lip as a waft of toast passed my nose. The couple below were having breakfast.

Whereas I hadn't been eating, because I didn't when I wasn't happy. Heartbreak was the best diet I'd tried, hands down.

But that's the thing: I was half-happy, I was glad I'd jumped. But I couldn't be fully happy until I'd fulfilled my plan. Told Rachel how I felt. But when was that going to happen? I had no idea.

"I am deserving of love and I am open to that being from a woman."

I was so very open.

My phone ringing interrupted my thoughts, and when I looked down, I saw it was Rachel.

Blimey — maybe there was something in these affirmations?

As I looked at her name prominent on my screen, all rational thought flew from my head, and my skin tingled.

All over.

Steady.

Be cool, be calm, don't blurt anything out. And definitely don't headbutt anything.

I swiped my finger across the screen.

"Hello?" I was going for confident but casual. Everything I wasn't in that moment.

"Hey, how are you?" She was doing confident and casual, too. "I hope you've recovered from last week and are feeling a bit more steady on your feet?"

I forced a laugh, while the pulse in my neck was trying to breakdance.

"Just about. Sorry again about covering you in beer."

"It wasn't too bad, we didn't let it ruin our night."

I *really* didn't want to hear about her night.

"So I was ringing to let you know a time for the shoot on Saturday, if you're still on for it?"

The shoot, of course. Why would she be ringing about anything else?

I nailed down my disappointment, gave it a stern look, then cleared my throat.

"I'm still on for it."

"Great. I just spoke to Jake, and he says he should be gone by midday. I want to make it as easy as possible for both of you, so I'll shoot his bit, then Tanya says she can shoot our segment. That way, you don't have to see each other if it's still too soon. Jake's fine with that."

Jake. The mention of his name made my palms itch, made me swallow guilt.

"Thank you, that's thoughtful," I replied. "So I'll just see you at Tanya's at midday?"

"I'll look forward to it, I've missed you on set — as have our viewers. All the comments are asking where you are."

"I'm sure they'll survive." I paused. "And you're sure Jake is on board with me coming back? I don't want to make him feel weird when I've already buggered up his life enough of late."

"Absolutely. I asked him that, and he said this is business. Well, words to that effect."

I let the sentence hang — we had to see each other at some point, but the longer we could put it off, the better.

"And also, just to let you know, I booked that new

restaurant — September — remember we were talking about it last month?"

"How can I forget a restaurant called September?"

Rachel laughed, and my insides warmed.

"Exactly. Anyway, I spoke to my friend Amanda who's the chef there and she's reserved us a table — you can't get in otherwise, it's bonkers. Is next week okay? She's reserved us Wednesday, and I can get the evening off if it works for you."

"You still want me to come? I thought you might want to take Hannah." I tried to sound like it meant nothing, even though it meant everything.

"A restaurant like September needs a professional opinion." She paused. "Plus, I like going to restaurants with you."

My stomach tingled at her tone, which had gone an octave lower. "And I like going with you." More than she could possibly imagine.

"That's settled then," she said. "I have to go now, got lunch to cook for 150 people, but I'll see you at the weekend."

She rang off and I stared at my phone.

Shit, I was going to be on camera with Rachel again.

Chapter Sixteen

Tanya met me at a flat near her block, after I'd run screaming from another I'd viewed just up the river. Now I'd realised I couldn't afford anything on my own near where Jake and I had lived, I'd decided to focus on the area around Tanya — being that little bit further out, it was more affordable.

Tanya had come straight from work so she was dressed in power heels, her shiny hair falling around her shoulders, her face looking like she meant business, make-up painted on solid. She gave me a hug, before stepping back to assess me, her finger and thumb clutching her chin as if pondering what I was worth.

"What are you doing? I don't need any smart comments from you today, because I've just seen yet another rubbish flat where the owner said the room was a large double, but those wide-angled filters on phones have got a lot to answer for."

Plus, the flat had been painted bright pink and the stain of it was still on my eyeballs as I stared into the Thames beside me.

"Now you're straying over to the dark side, I'm just checking to see if you're exhibiting any more tell-tale lesbian signs than before."

"And what's the verdict?"

"Everyone thought you were gay anyway, so there's not much to work with."

"You make a girl feel really special, you know that?"

"It's all part of my charm, just ask Sophie."

"And how is your girlfriend?"

"Still with me," Tanya said, an extra spring in her step. After the nonsense Tanya had put up with concerning her family, I was so pleased she'd opened up and let Sophie in. Tanya had a chequered history when it came to dating, but Sophie had managed to cleave open Tanya's heart, which was no mean feat.

"And how is my lovesick friend?" Tanya gave me a gentle smile.

"Fed up of house-hunting. I'd forgotten how soul-destroying it is."

"Today's first flat was a no-go?"

"A bright pink sharing nightmare."

She nodded. "Right. And the next one is a one-bed flat?"

I nodded. "Yes, it's something I can afford on my own, which instantly makes me suspicious."

"Me, too."

We arrived at the block of flats, only a ten-minute walk from Tanya, and went to take the lift, but it was out of service. Not a good start.

We climbed the four flights of stairs, already replete with the aroma of urine even though the flats had only been built a year previous, and met the estate agent just showing out the previous viewing. He gave us a grin, before patting down his overly gelled hair and ushering us in.

"Ladies," he said, which didn't endear him to me at all. "Is it the two of you looking?"

He had on a cheap blue suit and a novelty summer tie, with a beach scene and cocktails stamped all over it.

"Just me," I replied, walking down the narrow hall and into the cramped room with a small kitchenette in one corner, a pull-down table on the wall and a small, battered two-seater sofa in the middle.

This wasn't going to be my future home: it was the sort of place people came to die.

Tanya gave me a panicked stare as if even being here had stained her day.

Once we'd viewed the bedroom — more akin to a coffin — we made our excuses and left.

We took the stairs two at a time, almost not breathing till we arrived at the bottom and sucked in a good lung of fresh air. It was another few seconds before Tanya spoke.

"So you're not moving in there, just so we're clear."

I laughed. "I know, but it doesn't solve my housing issue, does it?"

Tanya moved her hair out of her face. "The way I see it, you don't really have a housing issue."

This was news to me. "How do you work that out?"

I squinted into the sunshine as we retraced our steps back to hers.

"You're living with your parents at the moment, which isn't the end of the world like it would be with mine. I mean, your parents are brilliant and funny, whereas mine would give Donald Trump a run for his money. So it's not an immediate crisis, is it?"

I shook my head. "No," I replied. "But living with your parents in your 30s isn't a very sexy look, you have to admit."

"Living with your cool parents in Marylebone temporarily till you sort yourself out isn't so shabby." Tanya paused, leading me to a bench by the river and sitting us down. Once there, she twisted her body so she could see my face when she was making her point. "Plus, my spare room is still there, it's you who ran away from it."

"You know the reasons why," I replied. "Plus, I don't want to play gooseberry to you and Sophie."

"Sophie and I can cope, we're adults. You're going through a tough time, and I want to do all I can to help you."

Tanya wasn't soppy often, but she was my best friend, one I knew I could count on. "Thank you, that means a lot." And it did. Behind her hardened exterior was a heart of gold.

She put an arm around me. "You mean a lot to me. And that applied when you were with Jake, and it applies now you're thinking of taking a trip to gay town. It applies wherever and whoever you end up with."

I gave her a sad smile. "I know," I whispered.

"No movement on the Rachel front, I take it?"

I shook my head. "Not now she's got a girlfriend."

"I'm not sure she'd call her a girlfriend." Tanya raised an eyebrow. "She's only been out with her twice, and after their second date, Sophie said Rachel had more to say about you than Hannah."

That was the best news I'd heard all day. "Me? What did she say?"

"That it was nice to see you, even if you did pin her to a table."

"Slight exaggeration," I replied, coughing over my embarrassment. "Let's not discuss it too much, I'm still getting over it. Sabrina was with me and she's still texting me about it."

"I can imagine," Tanya said. "My point is, Rachel still thinks you're good friends, so you shouldn't shun our building just because of her. Maybe get control of your impulses to throw yourself at her, but other than that, my place is big enough and it's a good interim option for you."

I stared out to the Thames, thinking it would be lovely to live near the river. I never had before, but coming over to Tanya's flat had always brought a sense of inner calm.

Was she right? Should I take the easier option and move back in with her? It seemed logical and yet, being so close to Rachel also seemed like it might be the death of me.

"And just to reiterate, Sophie says she doesn't think this new woman Rachel's seeing is going anywhere."

Really? A tiny shoot of hope sprang up in me as I sat up straight. It was small, but it was there.

"They looked okay when I saw them."

"Well Sophie says otherwise, and I'd trust her. She and Rachel have been having quite a few chats lately, and they've all involved you."

What did that mean? Whatever, I couldn't help the smile that invaded my face.

Rachel's girlfriend might not be her girlfriend, *and* she was talking about me.

"And while you're sitting there grinning, I have some other news." Tanya paused. "Sophie's moving in with me at the end of the month, so Rachel's spare room is free if you don't want mine."

"That sounds like the perfect solution to my housing issues, why didn't I think of that?" I slapped Tanya on the arm. I knew she was joking, but I didn't need to think about Rachel home alone, in need of some company. I would *love* to give her that company, but not if she was bringing her girlfriend home.

Shit, imagine that: me having to act like her straight friend while she kissed Hannah.

A full shudder went down my body even considering it.

If Hannah ever did go away, I had to tell her.

"I thought you might say that, but *my* offer of my spare room still stands. Remember our pact at university?"

I smiled as I thought back. Tanya and I had met at

university 18 years ago, and we'd always said that wherever we were in our lives, we'd always have a room for each other. Tanya had lived with me very briefly in our 20s, but I'd moved in with her three times so far. She was my port in a storm, and she'd never let me down. I'd even moved in with her and her previous girlfriend Meg for a couple of months.

"I remember," I said. "But in our 30s, the pact is wearing thin, isn't it? Am I still going to be coming to you in my 40s and 50s?"

She laughed. "Whenever we need each other." She looked away, then smoothed her hand over the bench. "You know, this bench played a role in Sophie and I getting together."

"It did?"

"Uh-huh. You know when Gran died and my parents were trying to get rid of Delilah?"

I nodded. Tanya had had a terrible time last year after her gran died, leaving behind her much-loved dog.

"I used to come here to think about what to do — with Delilah and with my mum. Sophie always seemed to be walking a dog past here and we'd sit and chat. It was her who convinced me to take Delilah, and her who helped me do it." She smiled at me, her eyes sparkling with emotion.

"When you find someone who makes you feel something you've never felt before, like we did, you shouldn't just ignore it." She nudged me with her elbow. "And if Rachel does that for you, don't give up just yet."

I didn't reply, just looked out to the river. Where Rachel was concerned, my feelings were churned up good and proper.

"Anyway, I hear from Rachel you're coming over to record a shoot on Saturday — which I think is great. You shouldn't stop doing that just because you split up with Jake."

"Let's see how Saturday goes before we make any big decisions."

Tanya nodded. "Okay, no big decisions before then."

Chapter Seventeen

"And that is a wrap!" Tanya said from behind the camera, giving us a double thumbs-up.

I turned to grin at Rachel, swallowing down the bullets of emotion ricocheting around my body. I'd made it through the shoot and things hadn't been *too* awkward. Tanya had told me to loosen up a couple of times, but I'd managed to trade words with Rachel without blushing too much, and I blew out a long breath, happy we were done.

Jake had been true to his word and disappeared before I arrived, which I was grateful for. We'd been split for three weeks, and I was still dreading the first time we laid eyes on each other. I'd rather we didn't have an audience when it happened, but all things considered, this morning could have played out far worse — and I had Tanya to thank for that. She'd volunteered to go behind the camera to stand in for Jake, and she'd kept things running when I'd stuttered around Rachel at first, before we'd settled into our established rhythm.

"I'm just nipping downstairs to see Sophie, back in a

tick," Tanya said, scooting across her lounge and out the front door before I could process her leaving.

And now I was alone with Rachel.

Deep breaths, I could do this.

"So that went well." Rachel picked up the saucepan she'd been using — this morning she'd made healthy muffins, with a sinful toffee sauce to dip them in. The live chat would go mad for them when we posted the show, which was no surprise — who didn't like muffins and toffee sauce? I'd tasted them, too, and they were beyond delicious.

When I'd licked the spoon, I'd had a fleeting image of licking the toffee sauce from somewhere else, but I'd quickly shut down that part of my brain. Those thoughts were for private time, not on camera.

"It did, I remembered what to do despite being absent for a few weeks." I pushed my hair back off my face, my hands needing something to do.

"You're a natural in front of camera." Rachel glanced my way, before busying herself at the sink washing up the saucepan, her shoulders hunched.

"I wouldn't go that far."

I ground my teeth together, rooted to the spot.

My eyes were glued to Rachel's shapely bum, small but perfectly formed, currently clad in denim shorts. My gaze slid down her pale legs, then up her back — I could make out the delicate curve of her shoulder blades through her royal blue cotton tank top.

It was as if when Tanya left, she took a little of the oxygen from the room, and now I was struggling to breathe.

For want of something to do, I fanned myself.

"It's hot in here," I said, my body burning up.

Rachel put the pan in the drying rack, then turned to me — and the look in her eyes nearly took all my remaining breath away.

She looked... *hungry*.

Her gaze held me in place, and right at that second, I would have done anything she wanted me to do.

Anything.

Then, as Rachel's eyes travelled up and down my body, before landing on my face, I wondered again if she was feeling it, too.

This connection, this longing, this want. This overwhelming emotion that had settled on the room, and was threatening to swallow me, whole.

I had to say something to break the tension. I searched my brain for a topic of conversation.

"How are things going with Hannah?"

Of all the subjects in the world, that was the one I came up with?

Rachel winced, her body language telling me more than any words could. "Not so good."

But before she could tell me anymore, there was a knock on the door, and I'd been so focused on what Rachel was going to say, it almost made me jump out of my skin.

We both looked to the hallway, then back at each other.

"Tanya must have forgotten her key," Rachel said, biting her lip.

"Right." I dragged my gaze away from her and walked to the door.

I opened it, almost not paying attention to who was there — but all that changed when I saw who *was* standing there.

It wasn't Tanya.

It was Jake.

If my body had been alive with want before, seeing Jake was like having a bucket of cold water poured over my emotions. As he stared at me, I felt like I'd just been caught with my pants down, and my first instinct was to slam the door shut in his face and pretend he wasn't there. I wanted to dash back into the warmth of whatever had been going on between Rachel and I.

But I knew that wasn't possible.

I knew, because Jake was staring at me with a pained expression on his face, his foot twisting back and forth as it did when he was nervous and would rather not deal with the situation.

I understood his pain.

"It's you," I said, only now processing the correct emotions you were supposed to have when seeing your recent ex for the first time since you split. Anguish slithered down me, and I recalled that he was the wronged party here, and I the aggressor. "I thought you were done."

He nodded. "I was — but then I realised I'd left my

wallet on the balcony, which I know is not ideal." He pulled himself up straight. "How are you? You look like you've lost weight."

He was putting so much emphasis into being nice and civil when I really didn't deserve it, but that was Jake.

I shrugged. "Eating hasn't been a top priority." I took a deep breath. "How are you?" *After I took your heart and ripped it to shreds?*

Jake shrugged, playing it down as I knew he would. "I've got a few new clients and the channel's really taking off, so I'm keeping busy." He paused. "But I still miss you."

My heart caught in my chest and I didn't know where to look.

Because I didn't miss him, not like that. And knowing he did made me feel terrible.

However, I couldn't help how I felt: my heart was now fully focused on a new target. Unbeknown to him, Jake had just gatecrashed my target practice.

Just as I was thinking that, the lift doors slid open to reveal Tanya, looking flushed and happy, keys hanging from her fingers.

When she looked up and saw us, she froze, not stepping out of the lift.

I went to say something, but nothing came out.

Jake turned and smiled at her, giving her a little wave.

Tanya held up her index finger. "Just remembered I forgot something," she said, lying through her teeth, pressing the lift button again. "Back in a bit."

The doors slid shut, leaving Jake and I in the hallway.

"Have you finished recording?" He looked past me, at the still ajar front door.

Ignoring the fact I hadn't replied to his statement of missing me.

I nodded. "Just now." I put my weight on one foot, then the other, breathing deeply and trying to avoid his stare. He was being too kind and that would be my undoing.

"Can I come and get my wallet?"

Could I cope with Jake and Rachel in the same room? I was about to find out.

I stepped back and held the door open. Jake followed me in, and when Rachel looked up, she tried to cover her surprise.

"Hey, you're back," she said, drying her hands on a tea towel, watching Jake with interest.

He nodded. "Just going to get my wallet, I left it on the balcony." He glanced at me. "You want to come out there with me?"

No of course I didn't, but I couldn't say no, could I?

I nodded, avoiding Rachel's gaze and followed my ex out onto the balcony, the sunshine blinding, in contrast to my mood. I wasn't sure what Jake wanted to say, but I was pretty sure whatever it was, I didn't want to hear it.

I squinted as he picked up his wallet and folded his arms across his chest.

"I'm not going to pretend this is easy, because it's not. I still love you, and that's going to take a while to leave me."

"Jake," I said, but he held up his hand, taking a deep breath.

"Let me finish, this is hard enough."

He'd practised this, hadn't he? I shut up and listened.

"But because you haven't told me you love me, and because by moving out and leaving me you made that pretty clear, I get it. We're done. But we also have to work together, which makes things tricky. Today has been massively awkward, but let's try to be adults about it where the channel is concerned, agreed?"

I nodded, sensing he wasn't quite finished.

"I'm sure it'll be tricky at first, but with time, who knows, we might even become friends. I'd like that, and I think it's only fair to Rachel we're not at each other's throats every time we're filming."

I took a deep breath, nodding. "I agree with everything you said, and I appreciate your honesty."

He shrugged. "I don't have much of a choice, do I? I thought about being an arse, but where would that get us?" He looked at the ground and swore lightly under his breath. "I'd rather steer clear of you because, look at you," he said, waving a hand in my direction. "Being around you and not being with you is *hard*. Really hard." He looked down, clutching one of Tanya's balcony chairs as he took in a deep breath.

If he cried, I might start, too.

"This is a transition for all of us," I replied. "And I want the same thing you do: for us to be friends and to make the channel a success. I'm still on board with that."

He straightened up and ran his hand though his curls, but I could see it was shaking.

"I better go." He'd said what he came to say.

I nodded. "See you at the next shoot."

He gave me a long stare, and I didn't look away.

I wanted to tell him it wasn't his fault, that he'd been a great boyfriend, but it didn't seem fair.

Instead, I watched him go, and only when the front door slammed did I start to shake.

* * *

I took a seat on Tanya's balcony. A year ago, I thought I'd marry Jake and have his children.

Now, as I looked up, I found myself staring into the eyes of the woman who'd unwittingly started the fire that was only growing daily. And she had no idea.

I put my head in my hands as I heard a chair being dragged along the ground, and the reassuring presence of Rachel alongside me.

"It was always going to be hard, you know. Seeing him for the first time."

I sat up, wishing I had my sunglasses, but knowing they were still on the table in my parents' lounge. "I know — and I wasn't prepared."

"Might be the best way, so you didn't fret about it for ages."

She had a point. "I just hate the way he looks at me. Like he loves me and he doesn't understand, which I completely get. But I can't explain it to him because it's all too overwhelming for me to grasp sometimes."

Especially with Rachel sitting beside me.

"Why don't you try to explain it to me, and then maybe you'll get it clearer in your head. Maybe that's what you need to start feeling calmer about everything."

I looked up and saw a smile caressing her lips, encouragement in her eyes.

My insides turned to jelly and a minor tremor slid through me.

She wanted me to tell her, and I *so* wanted to, more than *anything*. But then again, how could I when there was an emergency siren blaring in mind? She was the catalyst, the whole reason my life had gone into a tailspin.

I shook my head, not knowing what to do.

She threw up a hand. "You have to start talking about it — you can't just bottle everything up." She paused. "That's a really bad strategy, it's one I've tried and believe me, it gets you nowhere. Honesty and admitting what you're feeling is the best way forward."

If she knew the truth, I wasn't sure she'd agree, but I wasn't opening my mouth just in case the wrong thing came out of the wrong compartment in my brain.

When I left Jake, I'd sworn to myself I wouldn't look back, I'd only look forward. So I'd smashed my rear-view mirrors, and I'd been true to my word.

But looking forward now meant looking at Rachel and admitting what I was feeling, and there was no way that was happening. Not when Jake had just told me he loved me and I'd said nothing.

I'd seen the way he looked at me, what he'd hoped might happen, and hadn't. And if I told Rachel what I was feeling, I'd be on the receiving end of that same look I'd just given Jake, and I couldn't take that.

However, when I looked up, Rachel reached across with her hand and laid it on my arm, and my whole body flinched, like Rachel was an electric current and 5,000 watts had just shot through me.

Rumbled.

I could hide my words by sealing my mouth shut, but I couldn't hide what my body was doing: with Rachel's hand on my arm, it began to shake.

I sucked in an audible gasp of breath and looked up into Rachel's questioning gaze; with my defences down, the look I gave her was unfiltered, raw, real, and I knew she'd caught something. Something new, that she might not have caught before. But also something she might recognise.

Desire.

I looked down and wished I could be anywhere but here. Why had I agreed to carry on with these shoots?

Being around Jake and Rachel was *impossible.*

"Alice, talk to me," Rachel said, her voice honeyed, oozing through me and making it hard to breathe.

What could I say? Nothing. So instead, I shook my head. "I can't." I'd thought I was ready, but maybe I wasn't.

I shook off her arm, taking a deep breath and standing up, rolling my shoulders in a bid to steady myself. "I have to go." Where had I put my bag? I needed it if I was going to flee.

"But I thought you were sticking around? Tanya said you were having dinner later?"

Damn it, I was having dinner with them.

I turned, and Rachel was standing next to me, her lips shiny and red in the lunchtime sunshine. I dragged my gaze away from them and looked out onto the river below. "I forgot that," I said, shaking my head. "I'm just a bit all over the place after seeing Jake."

Which was partly true. But then again, partly not.

Rachel nodded. "It's understandable, but I still think you should just tell me why you broke up in the first place. Because you seemed great one day, and then not so much the next. I really do think it would help."

I brought my face level with Rachel's and looked into her crazy-gorgeous eyes.

I went to shake my head, but then I stopped.

Did she really want to know? Really?

"I just fell out of love with him, and then I found myself attracted to someone else." I licked my lips, feeling a bead of sweat run down my back.

My stomach was turning cartwheels, and my mind was screaming at me to shut up, but I was paying no attention.

Now, all my focus was on Rachel, and suddenly, my mum's voice was in my ear: "Just tell her."

Rachel's gaze slid down my face and landed around my mouth, as her tongue skated across her bottom lip.

I thought I might die there and then, but I held it together.

"You were attracted to someone else?" she said, as the air around us grew hotter, steamier, thicker. Or was that just my imagination?

I nodded. "I was. I am." *You can do it.* "And that someone is you."

It came out of my mouth as a whisper, but once it left, the words seemed to pop in mid-air, and then explode like the most expensive firework in the pack. It felt like it wasn't just Rachel who'd been privy to that utterance, but also the whole of south London.

I'd just told Rachel I was attracted to her and so far, she hadn't laughed or run away.

Instead, she kept her footing, and gave me a slow, sweet smile. "Me?" she said, matching my whispered tone. "You're attracted to me? But you like men."

"And women, it seems." A zap of desire shot down me, and I concentrated hard on staying upright.

"Since when?" she asked, her eyes aflame, her gaze questioning. But I saw a flicker of something behind her eyes then, something warm, pleased.

I really hoped she was pleased.

"Since I met you."

I'd never been more sincere. Because since meeting her, my world had changed, and I was still assessing the consequences.

Since meeting her, every day was a new discovery about who I was and what I liked, and most importantly, who I might like to be.

Rachel and I made excellent friends. Would we make excellent lovers, too?

If the heat in my cheeks and the thud of my heart were anything to go by, I'd say the odds were high.

She stepped back now, looking at me like she'd never seen me before, like I was a completely different person.

Was I? Perhaps I was. I had, after all, just divulged the one thing that had been lying heavy on my mind.

That ever since I'd met her, during all of our recent restaurant dates together, I just wanted there to be more. And that feeling had only been getting stronger and stronger as time went on.

"I think I need to sit down," Rachel said, doing just that, a puzzled look on her face. "So am I the reason you split up? Because if I am, that's a lot of responsibility on my shoulders."

I sat down opposite her, trying to gauge her mood. I couldn't quite pin it down.

"You're not the reason," I said, shaking my head. "I'm the reason." I stabbed my chest with my index finger. "I'm the one who fell out of love with Jake, I'm the one who started having feelings for you." I paused, wincing.

I wasn't sure how this was going down, but it wasn't how it'd happened in my daydreams.

In those, we'd already be kissing by now.

But as I looked over at Rachel, the over-riding look on her face was shock.

I hoped she wasn't feeling horror, too.

I ran a hand through my hair. "I hadn't planned to tell you like this. Blame Jake for that, shaking me up."

I sucked in my top lip.

Rachel still wasn't saying anything.

"But I don't want this to ruin our friendship. I know you've got a girlfriend, so my timing sucks. And I know this is out of the blue. But I don't want to lose what we've got, because I treasure it too much."

That elicited a response: she was nodding now. "I value it, too, I really do. This is just a bit... left field, that's all." She paused. "You're my straight friend, which means I don't think of you like that." Another pause, then a solid, blinding stare. "Or at least, I try not to."

This time, the tremor that hit my body was a lot larger and I balled my fists together as it rolled through me, not daring to take my wide eyes from Rachel.

I wanted her like nothing I'd ever wanted before in my entire life and now it was on the table, I never wanted it to be knocked off. I knew then, I was going to do everything in my power to make it happen.

I also knew I was going to replay her last sentence over and over.

Or at least, I try not to.

Rachel had been thinking about me, too. And that thought excited me and scared the shit out of me in equal measure.

"You've thought about us, too?" There was too much hope ladled on top of that sentence as it emerged from my mouth: it was frosted on top like the most calorific cake of want, ever.

Rachel was flustered now, bouncing her gaze around the balcony, anywhere but me. "Of course, but that's because you're cute. I mean, look at you," she said, wafting a hand up and down in front of me.

That was the second time that had happened today, and I glanced down at myself. Was I really that alluring?

Apparently, yes.

"But you had a boyfriend, so I shut off any thoughts of that. I can admire someone from afar, and that's what I did with you. But if you're changing the rules…" she trailed off. "Damn it, why didn't you say something before I went on my date?"

Why hadn't I said something earlier? She was seriously asking me that? "I was a bit busy freaking out, what with having left my boyfriend and needing to find somewhere to live."

Rachel put her head in her hands, then appraised me again, this time letting her gaze linger on my body, like she'd been given permission.

"Look," I said, sitting up, trying to take control of the

situation. "We can just carry on as we have been. Nothing has to change. I know this is a big thing I've told you, and I don't expect you to drop everything and change your life for me. And whatever the outcome, I'll deal with it."

She took a deep breath before replying. "But what if I can't deal with it?"

The sun was already hot on the balcony, but the stare Rachel was giving me was making me burn up.

What if she couldn't deal with it? This was the response I'd wanted, but now it was happening, I wasn't really sure what to do with it.

I couldn't deal with my emotions right now, never mind Rachel's. I tried to hold them, but it was like trying to hold onto hot cakes straight from the oven. They were simply too hot to handle.

Our gazes locked and every drop of blood I had rushed downwards to my very core.

I opened my mouth, desperate for fresh air to fill my lungs, because Rachel's eyes were slowing down every bodily movement I had.

Every. Single. One.

Then she was standing up, holding out her hands to me, and I stared at them, gulping.

I wasn't ready. I couldn't do this.

I'd never told a woman I fancied her before, and now my stomach was doing forward rolls again and again, until I felt dizzy, sick.

How did lesbians cope? All the ones I knew just walked

around like life came easy to them, when all the while, this was what they had to endure?

I raised my hands and let Rachel pull me up, her touch, now so different, holding me in a trance.

And then our faces were inches apart, her gaze fully on me, and I'd never felt the heat of someone's stare as much as now.

Was this my moment? Our moment? The moment we kissed for the very first time?

A bang somewhere close made me open my eyes before we got there.

What was that?

Shit, it was the front door.

I pulled back slightly.

The front door meant Tanya was back from downstairs.

We both jumped apart immediately, my whole body shaking as I walked over to one side of the balcony, assessing the river below. Still there. I clutched the thick, clear plastic balcony wall that came up to my waist and closed my eyes. I was breathing like I'd just sprinted 100m, perspiration coating my back.

Damn Tanya and her terrible timing! I was just about to be kissed.

And now I wasn't.

My heart was pounding in my chest, my brain weeping at the injustice.

After what seemed like an eternity, but was probably only a handful of seconds, I turned to stare at Rachel, every part of my body now thumping, every wall of my body dry. The headache that was winding itself up like candyfloss on a machine was going to be epic, I already knew.

But it was all worth it. Yes, we might not have kissed, but things were so much clearer now.

I'd told Rachel I liked her, and she liked me, too.

Today was already one of the most important and historic days of my life.

"Hey you two, I take it Jake's gone?" Tanya called out from the main room.

Her words were thorny, such an unwelcome intrusion.

Would Tanya be able to tell what had just nearly happened? Did lesbians have a sixth sense about this?

I shook myself, trying to clear my mind and body of what just nearly happened; then not looking at Rachel, I cleared my throat. "Yeah, he went a few minutes ago, so we were just digesting it on the balcony."

Sort of. Kind of.

I had to try to appear normal so I didn't come undone. One pull on my emotional thread and it could happen.

"Good plan, especially in this sunshine." Tanya appeared at her balcony doors moments later. "Anybody want another drink?" She was oblivious to the naked heat hovering between us.

"I'd love a coffee," I said, glancing at Rachel, giving her permission to leave, flee the scene. Did she understand my non-verbal communication yet? I was about to find out.

"I've gotta run," she said, glancing at me, then at Tanya.

"I'm working later and I told Jess I'd do a couple of cakes for her before I went." She took a deep breath and looked at me, and a torrent of desire rattled through me.

Damn, I wanted to rush over, take her in my arms and kiss her into next week. And after that? Well, after that, my mind was going *everywhere.*

"I'll see you on Wednesday for dinner?" Rachel said, her lips moist, holding my attention. I wanted to taste those lips so badly, but I'd have to wait till Wednesday.

Could I wait till Wednesday? Four whole days?

I nodded. "Wednesday, right." Was it a date now? Did Rachel still have a girlfriend? I didn't know.

She reached out and squeezed my hand as she passed. "Great job, today," she said, her gaze dropping to my mouth as she passed.

I wobbled anew.

"See you, Tanya, thanks again for letting us use your flat."

"No problem!" Tanya said, as Rachel gave me a heart-stopping look as she left.

I closed my eyes to recover, then gathered myself once more.

Rachel liked me, too.

Focus.

Tanya watched her go, then turned to me, leaning against her doorframe, arms folded across her chest.

"Everything okay here?" Tanya asked, fixing me with her gaze.

"Everything's fine," I replied, as breezy as I could. "Just weird energy, what with seeing Jake and all."

She nodded, moving her mouth one way, then the other.

Then she clicked her fingers together. "Coffee. Coming right up."

Chapter Eighteen

I hadn't seen Rachel since our nearly-kiss, and afterwards, I hadn't stuck around. The thought of sitting through dinner with Tanya and Sophie when my whole world had been turned upside down hadn't been appealing, so I'd made my excuses and left.

Tanya hadn't believed a word that had come out of my mouth: she wasn't stupid, she knew something was up. However, she hadn't asked, and I hadn't told.

Tonight, though, was the night of our monthly dinner out.

Four days had passed since we'd told each other how we felt, and I hadn't been able to think of anything else. At home, I'd been a bag of nerves, getting my easel out and painting for something to do with my hands and mind rather than fret. I wished I smoked, but I didn't. I contemplated daytime drinking, but knew that would get me nowhere. So instead, I painted.

Rachel and I had exchanged a couple of texts planning tonight, but nothing more.

I had no idea where all of this was going, but tonight, I was nervous as hell.

My nerves had meant I'd applied more lipstick than normal, put on my favourite black shirt, and that I'd polished my brown brogues with a brand-new cloth. I hope Rachel appreciated the effort.

She was waiting for me at our table when I arrived at September, but I couldn't read her smile or her body language.

Because this wasn't just dinner with a friend, was it?

As I walked towards her through the crowded restaurant, with waiters bustling by and the smell of Italian summer in the air, I saw none of it: all I saw was Rachel, her features tense, her hands clenched as she got up to greet me. She gave me an awkward hug and we sat down, eyeing each other like we were both hiding an enormous secret.

Only it wasn't true anymore, was it? It was an open secret, and one I wanted to blow the lid off as soon as possible.

"How's your week been?" I asked once we'd ordered wine and food.

I settled back in my wooden seat, not able to get comfortable. Which was probably down to me and not the chair.

"Good," she replied, nervously flicking her hair out of her face. "I've worked every night, so I haven't had a lot of downtime."

"Consider yourself lucky." I really needed to learn how to filter my speech.

Rachel raised an eyebrow. "That doesn't mean what

happened on Saturday hasn't taken up all my brain power this week."

I took a deep breath: it wasn't just me who'd been tormented all week long. "Really?"

"Really." She laid her hands flat on the table and held me with her gaze. "I've got to tell you something else, too. Get it all out in the open."

I winced: brace, brace. Should I bend forward and cover my head with my hands as they tell you to do on an airplane?

"I split up with Hannah." Rachel sat up, squeezing her hands together. "I mean, we weren't really going out formally — we'd only had two dates — plus she wasn't out to her family and out to the world, and as you know, that's a no-go for me." She paused. "But your Mum brought you to my restaurant, so I'm guessing your family know?"

I nodded, and Rachel visibly relaxed.

"Plus, there was also the reason that Hannah was just another woman, and she's not going to win in a shoot-out with you, is she?"

I wasn't sure how to reply, apart from punching the air, but I kept my fists in my lap, where Rachel couldn't see them.

"Well, say something," Rachel said, her neck reddening.

Right, I needed to respond.

I sat forward, reaching over and taking her hand in mine. I wasn't sure where my bravado came from, but I was doing what came naturally. What felt right. "I'm thrilled you broke up with Hannah, if that doesn't sound too callous."

Rachel smiled, shaking her head. "There isn't much point when my heart tells me it wants something else, is there?"

My breath caught in my throat as I stared at her. She stared right back, and the moment lingered like a late-afternoon sunbeam, both of us basking in its glory.

Rachel wanted me, and I wanted her. And that was nothing but glorious.

The waiter brought our bottle of wine and we untangled our hands and our stares, Rachel's cheeks flushed, and I'm sure mine were, too.

The liquid glugged into our glasses as I twisted in my chair, until eventually it was just us two again, and we were back to staring, a triumphant smile tugging the corner of my lips.

"What about you? How's your week been with your parents? It must be kinda nice spending some time with them."

I smiled. "It is, and you've met my mum, she's pretty cool. Plus, I'm spending loads of time painting, which is great. I love to paint, but I don't get nearly enough time to do it when I'm working. Marking, admin and running a department take up all my time."

Rachel sat forward, giving me a low whistle. "That's incredible — I love creativity like that. It's sexy. I'd love to see your paintings some time."

I gulped, swallowing down a flood of emotion. She

found painting *sexy*? "I'd love to show you some." I was pleased I could still carry a conversation with Rachel without tripping over my words. Even when one of the words was 'sexy'. "But in between all that and thinking about you, I'm still living with my parents, which isn't optimal. Still looking for a place to live."

"I need a new flatmate now Sophie's moving up ten floors to be with Tanya," Rachel replied, before holding up her hand. "And that was a joke, by the way. I'm not suggesting you move in with me." She paused, her gaze heating my skin.

"That might be a little soon," I replied. Although part of me was all for it, if it meant seeing Rachel every day. "Imagine what everyone would say." I paused, shifting in my seat as an image of Rachel naked waltzed through my mind. "Imagine what Jake would say."

Yes, there was that added difficulty, too.

Rachel looked down at her cutlery, then back up at me. "It's quite complicated, isn't it?"

"You could say that."

She sat up straight and reached over the table cloth, a sudden surety in her movements as she grasped my hand in hers.

And then she turned her smile on me, and she might as well have taken a blowtorch to some ice. I duly melted.

"I've been looking forward to this meal for ages, but now all I want to do is be away from all these people. Does that make sense?"

I nodded. "It makes perfect sense."

"So here's my plan: let's enjoy the meal, get the bill and then go for a walk, make the most of this summer evening. What do you think?"

A sense of calm washed through me. "I think that sounds perfect."

And I had just the place in mind.

Chapter Nineteen

Rachel had never been up Primrose Hill — a fact I couldn't get my head around.

"My grandparents brought my mum here, my parents used to bring me and my sister here, and now we bring my sister's little girl, too."

"I can see why you love it," Rachel replied, smiling as we walked to the top, the summer air stroking our skin. At just after nine, the light was evaporating all around us, the twilight moving in, yet it felt anything but dark to me.

It felt light and airy, even though my skin was tingling all over. I was the proverbial cat on a hot tin roof.

When we reached the summit minutes later, it was just us. I stared out over London, Regent's Park and the city beyond, which was starting to twinkle in the distance.

"I still love walking down the hill and straight into Soho, after seeing it from up high. It's always made me feel like I know a secret. That the city's not really as big as it seems once you've seen it from up here."

"I guess everything's a matter of perspective, isn't it?" Rachel held my gaze, and a mix of fear and desire slid over my skin, making me unable to turn away — and I didn't want to.

"I guess so." *Deep breaths, keep breathing.*

"How's your perspective on life since Saturday?"

"It's tilted, that's for sure," I replied.

"Are you feeling freaked?" She took my hand as she spoke.

My whole body shook. "Not as much as I think I should be," I said, taking a gulp of warm air. "I know it should be this huge life shift, and I'm sure it will be — but I'm not freaking out as much as I thought. I've been thinking about this for longer than you, and now we're here, it kinda seems like the logical conclusion." Pause. "But if you think I'm calm and in control, I'm not. Not by anyone's standards."

My body was currently an emotion blender, the dial set to high.

She ran a thumb across my knuckle and I shook again.

"It doesn't have to be scary."

Rachel's soft gaze dripped down me. "And if it helps any, I'm scared, too." She squeezed my hand. "Because while I might have got used to the idea this week, this is not just anyone — this is *you.*" Now it was Rachel's turn to take a deep breath. "There's already an us, and taking this further is a gamble."

"I know." And I did. It was something I'd been pondering all week, and I wasn't sure what conclusion I'd come to. Could I risk our friendship for something more?

But when I thought about it, I knew that line had already been crossed — a very long time ago.

The fact was, I couldn't *not* risk it anymore. Like Tanya had told me, life was too short, and I had to keep the ball rolling.

I was ready to play, all my cards on the table.

"But I can't keep *this* in anymore — my feelings for you, I mean. I'm done pretending." I turned to her, taking her other hand, my bravado metallic in my mouth. "I want to move the needle, I want there to be a different kind of us. And I know this is a gamble for you, but I need you to know, this isn't an experiment. I'm not trying you on for size." I gulped again. "I've been trying to put a label on my feelings, and when it came to me a few weeks ago, I knew I had to do something." A full body shiver. "The fact is… I can't stop thinking about you."

She gripped my hands harder as her expression softened.

"You can't?" Her tone was pure sugar syrup.

Something fluttered behind my ribcage. I gulped before replying, the heat of her gaze burning me. "Not for any minute of any day."

Then it was her turn to shudder. "And since you told me, I've finally got permission to not stop thinking about you, either."

And then, there were no more words.

Instead, Rachel snaked an arm around my waist, and it was the perfect move in the perfect moment.

A weird calm descended on me, almost like I was having an out-of-body experience.

She pulled me close, her eyes on my lips, brushing my hair from my face. I felt the tips of her fingers brush across my skin, lingering, pressing her claim to me. If there was anyone else around, I was unaware: it was as if someone had drawn the curtains around us, concealing us from the world. I was only aware of the slight breeze on my face, the beat of my heart, the uneven note of my breathing.

I raised a hand and brushed a finger along Rachel's jawline, and she stilled.

And then, finally, she leaned in and pressed her lips to mine. I melted at her touch. This time, nobody and nothing was going to come between us. And hot damn, *could she kiss.*

The pleasure was disorientating: a low hum in my stomach, a flash of electricity across my hyper-sensitive skin. My fingers roamed from Rachel's face into her glossy hair, spearing her soft locks and trying to pull her closer.

I simply couldn't get enough.

All my hesitation, my what-ifs were drowned out by the rising tide of arousal: every part of my insides were swooning and reeling like never before, and everything I'd ever known about kissing was swept aside, because I'd never been kissed like Rachel was kissing me. Ever.

She was soft, masterful, in control. She was like the best dance partner I'd ever had, and I'd never danced before. But with Rachel, it was like I was suddenly blessed with the gift of dance, and even if I wasn't, it didn't matter, because she was leading me.

I melted under the dizzying strokes of her tongue, swaying against her, and felt her hand slip down my back and settle on the base of my spine, pressing me to her. The pressure of her strong, firm body against mine was magical.

As her lips swept over mine, I knew for sure this was the start of something important.

Something that was making my heart thrum.

The start of something I never even knew I wanted.

If this was what being a lesbian felt like, I was ready to sign on the dotted line, no questions asked.

And still she kissed me, her mouth now even more demanding, exploring and delving until I was a trembling mass of nerve endings.

I could have happily stayed in this moment forever; bought a house here, raised a family, then pirouetted into old age with Rachel's lips on mine, with never a single thought of them leaving. After all, why would you stop something when it felt this good?

Rachel moved her hand from my back to my breast, her thumb stroking over the tip. The delicious friction made me moan into her mouth, but I wasn't embarrassed: far from it, I just wanted more.

Rachel seemed to understand, putting her fingers on the hem of my black shirt, and then I felt the warmth of her hand settling on my bare skin of my stomach, which lit a flame in my heart. It was like being on fire, the excitement travelling over my skin, before settling low in my belly.

And then suddenly, the hand was on top of my shirt and Rachel's lips broke with mine. "Sorry, got a little carried away," she said, her voice so low, it was almost horizontal. "Probably not the best thing to feel you up in public."

Her smile could have lit a dark night.

I cleared my throat. "I can think of worse things." My voice was coarse, like rope, the words seeping through the clouds of desire fogging my brain.

I couldn't take my eyes from her lips, knowing their power, the pleasure they could convey. I pressed my lips back to hers, and just like that, my body lit up once more, as if Rachel was my one and only power source, with an ability to light me up like the national grid.

"I think we just took our relationship to the next level," she said moments later, her eyes dark ovals, flashing at me. "And that was just us kissing." She let out a throaty laugh.

I laughed, my body feeling dangerously out of control. In her arms, I was safe; once out of them, I might collapse like a string puppet, so I was clinging to her.

"I know," I replied, only just managing to get my words out. If that was first base, I couldn't think about scoring a home run: it would send my mind and body into meltdown.

"Are you going back to your parents' house tonight?" she asked eventually, her voice still breathless, her eyes glazed.

Her hand returned to my back, stroking my bare skin,

and it was all I was focused on. The sparks of electricity from her skin on mine. I nodded, my brain still having trouble forming full sentences. Apart from the next one. "Do you want to come?"

Did she? Did I want her to? Was I ready?

My mind began to spin.

Rachel gave me a soft smile, kissing my lips again. "I'd love to, more than anything," she said, stroking my cheek. "But I'm not sure tonight's the time. I don't have my work gear and I have to get up early tomorrow."

My newly emboldened libido stamped its feet, but I knew she was right. I'd waited this long, I could wait a little longer still.

I kissed her lips again, swaying from them once more. "You're right, we should wait till the time's right." I mumbled the words so close to her lips, it was almost as if they were toppling into her mouth. "So long as you promise me we can carry this on very soon. Because that was the best kiss I've ever had."

She gave me a slow grin. A grin that undressed itself in front of me with every centimetre it took. A grin I was powerless to pull my eyes from. "I was right there with you, and I agree. You're a natural."

She really thought that? My first-ever female kiss and I hadn't fudged the exam? "I'm glad you thought so."

And the next look she gave me made my stomach wobble, my legs quiver, and my very core pulse anew. "Let's just say, I can't wait to get you alone and naked, just the two of us, and see where things go. I know it's going to occupy my mind from here on in."

I grinned. "I'm glad." I paused, running my fingers down her smooth skin, feeling the heat of her stare. "So if you're working and I'm living with my parents, when will I see you again?"

To finish what we started, I wanted to add, but I didn't dare. I wasn't that brave just yet, although I had a feeling once we met again, my boundaries might surprise me.

I knew for sure that kiss had surprised the hell out of me.

"At the shoot on Saturday?"

The mention of the shoot was a sobering slap in the face. "With Jake?"

Jake and Rachel in the same sentence now just felt wrong, all ends up.

She chewed on the inside of her cheek. "Yes, for the shoot. But I'm hoping after that, we might have some time. Aren't you dog-sitting for Tanya?"

I raised an eyebrow. "How do you know?"

"I live with Sophie, remember?" And then she blushed. "I might have been taking a keener than usual interest in your movements of late."

Oh might she? I smiled at that. "Are you working on Saturday night?"

A shake of the head. "I got it off yesterday, so if you're free, maybe we could have a second date? I could cook at mine or at Tanya's if you're staying there? Me, you, Delilah?"

I gulped. A second date, in a room with a closed door. If I let my mind wander, it might explode. "A date with you and Delilah sounds perfect."

"I was hoping you'd say that," Rachel said, before her mouth closed over mine and I lost the power of speech once more.

Chapter Twenty

"There's my best friend who's been ignoring all my calls of late." Tanya sat back in her chair as Jess gave me a wave from behind the counter of Porter's, the café she ran that was just around the corner from Tanya's. It was one of those cafés with a mouth-watering menu and the kind of rich, syrupy coffee that made your hair stand on end, and it was always packed.

Jess and her fiancée Lucy had become close friends with Tanya this year, bonded by living in the same area and connected friends, but mainly by their dogs. It turned out that dog ownership opened you up to a whole new set of friends. Walking your dog in the park was a little like waiting for your child at the school gates — if you did it long enough, you were bound to start talking to other people who were doing exactly the same thing.

Plus, when Delilah had been attacked by another dog last year, it'd been Jess who'd driven Sophie and Delilah to the vet and saved the day. That was something that Tanya would never forget.

I returned Jess's wave and sat opposite Tanya.

Could she tell the difference in me?

Now I'd been properly kissed by a woman, my world view had changed. With one flick of Rachel's tongue, it'd turned pink in an instant. Maybe more than one.

"I haven't been ignoring them, I've just been busy."

"Busy doing what? You're still off for another few weeks, aren't you?"

I nodded. "I am, but I've been painting a lot and getting ready for my student showcase."

"Well I'm pleased to hear that, you're always happier when you're painting."

"Am I?"

"Yes, you are." She leaned forward. "Are you painting anything or anyone in particular? I heard on the grapevine you might have gone on a date with a certain woman on Wednesday?"

My clit sprang to life as I thought back to Wednesday, back to that kiss. On Primrose Hill with London watching on.

Now, it was the London of us.

Jess arriving at our table interrupted the conversation.

"Hello, some of my favourite women. How are we today?"

I grinned up at her. "Couldn't be better. And the smell coming from your kitchen is only making me happier." The air in the café was filled with the scent of butter and lemon, telling me this morning had been a mammoth cake-baking session for Jess.

Since coming over to this area more often, I loved coming into Porter's whenever I could: as well as the stellar food, Jess and her team were brilliantly welcoming, and I'd felt at home from the start.

"I've just baked a chocolate Swiss roll with vanilla cream, my new fetish, and a lemon drizzle cake. So if any of that takes your fancy, let me know. In the meantime, the usual coffee?" she asked me.

I nodded. "The larger and blacker, the better, thanks."

Jess turned, then turned back almost immediately. "I almost forgot to say — Lucy and I have set a date for our wedding." She looked so thrilled and flushed with love, it was beguiling.

"That's brilliant news, congrats!" Tanya got up and gave Jess a hug. "When's the big day?"

"This time next year. It's going to be six years since we officially started seeing each other then, so we decided to be sentimental."

"I'm so happy for you." Tanya was beaming, and I wondered how long it would be before she announced her plans, too. "Meg will be pleased — she was worried you'd set the date sooner, and then she might not be able to come. But by that time, the baby should be big enough to be left, right?"

Jess's best friend Kate was married to Meg, Tanya's ex — but they were all still good friends. I loved Meg dearly — truth be told, I was heartbroken when she and Tanya split up, because Meg had been a big part of my life. Plus, she ran a florist called Fabulous Flowers, so their house had always been covered with gorgeous blooms. I was thrilled when she and Tanya got over their differences, and Meg was finally allowed back in our lives. She was currently eight months pregnant with her first child, and I couldn't wait to meet the heir to the Fabulous Flowers fortune.

Jess grinned. "Well she's the size of a gigantic house, so I hope it'll be out by then — she's due in a few weeks, it's getting exciting." She paused. "Although I'm leaving the 'having kids' part to her — Lucy and I have got enough on our plate with Spinach."

I grinned as I recalled Jess's tenacious French Bulldog.

Tanya waited for Jess to leave, before pulling in her chair and fixing me with her smile. "So," she said, splaying her hands like she was opening a book. "Tell me about Wednesday. I want to know all the tiny details, however small."

I shuddered: damn my body. "We just went on one of our usual dinner dates at a cool new restaurant. We do it every month and have been for the past nine months, and you've never been *this* interested before."

"I know you do, but I don't think you've had one since (a), you decided you might like a slice of Rachel; and (b), since you told Rachel this and she dumped her very short-lived girlfriend like a hot brick." Tanya poked her tongue into her cheek. "And don't tell me you just talked about how good the food was, because I won't believe you." She sat forward, her gaze drilling into me. "Do you even remember what the food was?"

I harrumphed like a teenager. "Yes! The chef did amazing things with asparagus."

Tanya erupted in laughter. "Now I really don't believe you." She put a hand under her chin. "And did you taste anything else other than the food?"

What colour were my cheeks now? I didn't want to look in a mirror any time soon.

"We kissed, okay?" I said, a little too loudly, just as Jess was arriving back at our table with coffee.

I looked up, guilt written all over my face. If she'd heard, she said nothing, instead putting the coffees down and hurrying back to serve another customer. I guessed she was used to overhearing things she shouldn't and being discreet. It was all part of running a café.

"And? You're always telling me to open up, so shouldn't you take your own advice?"

I narrowed my eyes at her, but knew she was right. Why was I being so defensive?

My body heated up all over again just thinking about it. "It was incredible. It's like the whole world just made a lot more sense, you know?"

Tanya's face softened. "I do know," she said, sitting back with a smile. "And you're feeling okay about it?"

I nodded. "I'm feeling just wonderful about it." I'd never spoken truer words. When I thought about Rachel's kiss, it still tasted sweeter than any of the aromas coming from Jess's kitchen.

Tanya gave me a grin. "Welcome to the club."

"I'm not a fully paid-up member yet."

"Yet," Tanya replied. "But you do know what it's like to kiss another woman now."

I beamed at her. "I certainly do."

It had been beyond anything I'd imagined, and adrenaline still coursed through my veins when I thought about it. Rachel's kiss made me want to dance, to sing, to pump my fist into the air.

"And how did you leave it?" she asked. "Declarations of love, marriage proposals?"

"Both of those," I said, giving her a playful slap. "We're seeing each other to shoot at yours in precisely," I checked my phone, "two hours. Which is why I thought I'd meet you first, fill you in somewhere that wasn't your flat. Just in case Jake shows up, or Rachel, even worse."

"Even worse?"

"Because I get anxious around her. Because it all means so much."

"You're scared."

"Petrified. But also beyond excited. Does that make sense?" I hoped it did, because the other option was that I was going mad.

"Perfectly — it's normal. You're losing your virginity all over again, things are going to be weird."

A shiver ran through me, from my scalp to my toes. "Losing my virginity and my sanity."

"Why do you think there are so many crazy lesbians out there?"

I gave her a look.

"So today might be the day?"

"Maybe," I said, desire flushing through me. "I don't want to overthink it." *Because I'd been doing that all week.* "But when she kissed me, I wanted to quote poetry afterwards."

"That sounds like it was some kiss."

My mind swam. "You have no idea." I paused. "But what if she wants to take it slow? I don't want to be pushy. I mean, I can't really afford to be pushy, can I? I'm not the proper lesbian."

Tanya let out a howl of laughter. "She won't want to take it slow, trust me. Plus, I think you might be more ready than you think. You can't have been around me this long without picking up some tips, right?"

My mind scrambled thinking about it all again. "Remember that barbecue you had ages ago, when you'd just starting going out with Meg? It was completely full of lesbians, bar me and my then boyfriend?"

"Zach?"

"That's the one."

Tanya shook her head. "But go on, what about it?"

"I remember back then, all this chat going on about women. I remember wondering if I'd ever truly know what you were all going on about."

"And soon you will." Tanya paused. "You think you've been thinking about it all these years and never acknowledged it?"

I screwed up my face: it was a question I'd been asking

myself, and I still didn't have a satisfactory answer. "I don't know," I said. "I mean, it's crossed my mind before, but I think that's normal, isn't it? And then, being a lesbian or bi isn't such a big deal these days. At least, that's what I thought when it wasn't about to happen to me."

"And now the rules have changed?"

My skin tingled at the memory of Rachel's touch. Soon, I'd know what it felt like all over my body. "Totally," I said, my voice gravelly, my insides churning anew. I blew out a slow breath. "Now I'm trying not to think too far into the future, because what it holds is everything I want and everything I'm terrified of."

Tanya reached over and squeezed my hand. "It's not that scary, trust me." She swept some hair out of her eyes. "And just do whatever comes naturally, okay? I'm sure you've got this, though, you don't need me to tell you anything. You've always been better at relationships than me, I doubt anything's changed just because you're with a woman now."

I covered her hand with mine. "You're not so bad these days yourself."

She smiled at that. "I have my moments." A pause. "But if it does go well and tonight you're breaking out the Cuban cigars, does that mean I need to have another queer barbecue to celebrate?"

I shook my head with gusto, waving my hands. "No barbecues, no celebrations. I'm taking this one step at a time, okay?"

Tanya grinned. "I'll wait for your signal to buy the steaks and get Delilah a new rainbow unicorn outfit." She paused. "You're still on for staying over tonight and looking after my little doggie?"

I nodded, patting my overnight bag at my feet. "All ready to smother her with affection while you're dancing to bad wedding music in Wales."

"Good to hear," Tanya said. "And just so you know, I put fresh sheets on your bed, just in case things get a little heated after the shoot. Feel free to make them dirty." She gave me an exaggerated wink.

"Are you trying to make my head explode?"

The grin Tanya gave me this time was the width of London Bridge.

Chapter Twenty-One

Rachel turned up first, and gave me a hesitant hug. "It's good to see you," she said, her eyes sparkling, but I could feel a barrier between us and I understood. Jake was due any minute, and his addition to the mix was anything but normal.

However, there was no time to analyse, as Rachel got busy getting her ingredients ready and running over her script, giving me key points to seize on as normal. It was very much business as usual, unless you were inside my mind, or, I suspected, Rachel's.

Ten minutes later, Jake bustled in, more stubble than normal on his face, and he looked tired and grumpy — not like Jake at all. He set up the camera with minimal chat, and within ten minutes we were shooting, Rachel cooking up a Mexican feast of tacos and home-made guacamole with charred corn, with me tasting all her cooking and declaring it divine.

A bit like her.

Presenting the show was surprisingly normal, given the circumstances. We were professional when it came to the show, although every time our eyes met, my heart threatened to collapse. But giving anything away on camera wasn't optimal — not with Jake behind it and an army of commenters poised on the other side of the screen.

My feelings for Rachel were very much my own, and I wanted to keep them that way for as long as possible.

"And that's a wrap," Jake said, giving us a thumbs-up from behind the camera. "You two were really on form today — there was a real connection, even more than normal." He crossed his arms over his chest, giving us a look. "Who knows why? But just wait till the fans get a look at this — they're going to want even more from you, just a warning!"

I didn't even dare look at Rachel as I knew what her face would be doing: the same as mine, freezing in case we betrayed any hint of what had changed.

Jake's phone buzzed and he picked it up, frowning at the screen as he answered. "Hiya." He paused, heading towards the front door. "Just gotta take this, back in a minute."

The door slammed shut and both of us exhaled, dropping our heads in unison.

"Well, that was the longest half hour of my life." Rachel clutched the edge of Tanya's wide central kitchen island, before giving me a pained smile. "How was it for you?"

"Strangely normal, so long as I didn't focus on my ex behind the camera," I replied, grabbing the empty ingredients bowls and taking them to the sink where Rachel was running water and beginning to clear up.

But when I stood beside her, my heart caught in my throat as she turned, her gaze searing my skin.

"Where did you come from and why can I think of nothing else but you?"

Had someone actually said those words to *me*?

"I'd like to say somewhere exotic, but I'd be lying," I said with a slow smile. "And if it makes you feel any better, I haven't thought of much else but you since Wednesday, either. You or that kiss."

We were back together at the island now, where the filming had taken place, where we'd been standing for the past hour.

But now, without Jake or the cameras rolling, the air had become thicker, more charged.

I went to pick up a pan from the hob, and Rachel did the same. When our fingers touched, I stilled — as did she.

When I looked into her eyes, I knew this was another place that would now be etched onto my memory, just like Primrose Hill.

In an instant her lips were on mine, devouring me hungrily before my brain had a chance to process what was going on.

There was a guttural moan and then Rachel pressed against me, making every part of me swoon.

Fuck me, the woman could kiss.

I clung to her body, my fingers skating across her ribs

and up to her breasts, my whole being screaming "yes, yes, yes!"

If our last kiss had lit up the runway, this one was landing my emotions expertly. With every press of her lips to mine, I knew I was going to be freer, lighter, more myself than I'd ever been before.

And that thought, along with Rachel's moan as I slipped my tongue between her willing lips, made my breath catch, wondering if this had been me all along and if it had, why had I been hiding? And why was I still hiding?

Both our breathing was scattered as we pulled apart, Rachel's eyes scanning mine, her hand around my waist, her other on my breast. As she moved her thumb over my left nipple it stood to attention, as did my clit, but Rachel never took her eyes off me, and I didn't look away either.

I didn't dare.

"I want you so badly," she said, running her tongue along her bottom lip, which made my heart suck in a breath.

"I know." I leaned back in to kiss her, a fire so hot inside me I felt like I needed to be hosed down.

If the YouTube fans could see this, the comments would explode.

Just as my lips connected with Rachel's again, there was a knock at the door and we jumped apart so fast, my arm knocked one of the pans from the hob. The crash it made as it landed on the floor broke the moment spectacularly.

Rachel bent to pick it up, as I steadied myself, before walking down the hallway and opening the door to Jake.

He smiled shyly, racing past me clutching his phone.

"Great work today, ladies," he said, unscrewing the camera from the tripod, before frowning. He stopped, shook his head, pressed something and tutted.

"Everything okay?" A strange lump of fear gurgled in the pit of my stomach.

He looked up, detaching the camera, nodding. "Yeah, fine. Just I forgot to turn off the camera after we stopped, so it looks like it's been filming this whole time. So I hope you weren't badmouthing me when I was out of the room, because if you were, I'm going to hear it later when I do the edit."

The ball of fear in my stomach steamrollered down an imaginary hill and landed at my feet, weighing me down with its ferocity.

Jake had filmed us kissing? Holy fucking hell.

I looked over at Rachel, who was standing as still as a statue, her eyes giving nothing away.

My throat went dry and I couldn't get any words out; I just stared at Jake.

Maybe he wouldn't watch till the kiss.

Maybe he'd get bored of us chatting and washing up in the beginning.

But hang on, what had we been chatting about?

I closed my eyes because I knew.

We'd been chatting about kissing.

And then we'd kissed.

Oh. My. Fucking. God.

"The look on your faces tells me I should stop the editing when the show's done — don't worry ladies, I promise I won't listen to whatever it is you were talking about." He paused, staring at me with a flicker of something in his eyes.

I ran up to him. "Look, I don't mind doing this edit." Could he see the fear in my eyes? He knew me, after all. "I know we've been alternating, but I'm happy to do this one. You've probably got a ton of clients to see."

I couldn't let him take this, it couldn't come out this way.

But Jake had already packed up the camera and was putting the canvas bag on his back. "No problem, it's my turn. Besides, you did all the editing in the beginning, and you trained me for a reason." He put his hand on my arm, fixing me with his kind eyes. "It's time I did one solo. You can trust me. I know you're the video expert, but any issues, I'll give you a call."

I didn't want him to call me after he'd watched it, I knew how that call would go. "No, really, I mean it—"

"—So do I," he replied, stressing every word. "How am I going to learn unless I do it? You told me yourself, the best way to learn was just to practise, and I need the practice. I promise, I'll call you if there are any issues, okay?"

What could I do, apart from rugby-tackle him to the ground and prize the camera out of his bag?

I seriously considered rugby tackling him.

"Anyway, I should get going. You still at your parents?"

I nodded, my eyes glued to his bag, the future bombshell.

A buzzing began in my brain. Maybe I could distract him and then prize it from his buffed shoulder?

Instead, I said: "Yes, but I'm staying here today — Tanya and Sophie are away for the weekend so I'm on Delilah duty."

Dread knitted itself into every muscle in my body, but I was standing stock still, grinding my teeth together.

"Say hi to them for me," he said, giving me a final look. "And you know what? Today wasn't too bad at all. I think all of us still working together is going to pan out just fine. Here's to us being modern and cool." He turned, wearing a huge smile. "You agree?"

I looked at Rachel, she at me, and we both mumbled our agreement.

He laughed, beginning to walk out the room. "Try to work on your enthusiasm!" he said, over his shoulder. "I'll see myself out."

I watched him go, my eyes never leaving the bag as it swung on his shoulder, disappearing into Tanya's hallway.

When I looked up, Rachel was wiping her wet hands on a tea towel, clutching the island again. "What are we going to do?" She slammed the island with her fist. "Fuck, fuck, fuck. He can't see that edit. I'm his business partner and you're his ex-girlfriend." She exhaled. "This is a disaster, Alice!"

"I know," I replied, my voice raised. "I tried to get it off him, but you saw — he wanted to do the edit."

She ran around the island to where I was standing. "But he can't do this one. We can't let him go, can we? Shall I go and see if he's gone yet?" Her eyes were wild as she put a hand to her dark hair, sweeping it off her face. "I'm going to try and stop him. He might still be waiting for the lift."

She ran past me, a blur of nervous energy and I heard the front door open, then an even louder "fuck!" escape her lips. This one with extra defeat ladled on top.

I took that to mean the lift was gone, and with it, Jake and his camera.

I ran down the hall, to where Rachel was standing in the doorway, watching the lift numbers descend, her face scrunched in pain.

"He's gone then?" My stomach churned as I thought through all the terrible consequences of what had just happened. I couldn't believe I'd let him go. What were we going to do?

"You think we should try to run down the stairs and grab him?" Rachel's face twitched as she spoke.

"And say what? Forbid him to do the edit? If we do that, it's going to come out. We'll have to tell him why."

"It's going to come out anyway, whether we get the edit or not." She shook her head. "I'd just rather not blow up our business in the process."

Rachel slumped against the doorframe, before closing

the door and walking back into the living room, head in hands, shaking it from side to side. She flopped down on the sofa, leaning her head back on the white cushions. "How did this happen? How has my life come to this when this morning went so well?" She turned her face to me as I sat down next to her. "What are we going to do?"

I winced, my heart thumping in my chest. "I think we have to warn him before he watches it." I paused. "Or maybe he won't watch it?"

Rachel gave me a look. "He'll watch it, especially after seeing our faces."

She had a point. "You think he already suspects after what he said about us today?" My mind was all over the place, trying to piece together the day so far. So much had happened and it was barely lunchtime. This was turning out to be a monumental Saturday.

"I don't. That's in our heads, not his. I guarantee when he sees us kissing, he'll be surprised."

I covered my face again. "Fuck-a-doodle-do."

"You could say that." Rachel let out a long sigh, before putting a hand on my thigh.

Despite everything, my attention was immediately drawn to it, as my core throbbed.

My body wasn't bothered about Jake, it only had eyes for Rachel. Which is what had got us into this mess in the first place. I sat up, collecting my thoughts, gulping as I looked at her hand.

She followed my gaze, then gave me a gentle smile,

before withdrawing it. We didn't have time to think about anything else right now.

"You think we should Google it? Is there an etiquette on how we should handle this?"

"Help, my ex-boyfriend has a recording of me kissing his female business partner?" Rachel raised both eyebrows, before giving me a gentle laugh. "I doubt it."

I blew out a raspberry as Rachel took my hand and kissed it lightly.

More sensations.

A tell-tale scratching on Tanya's wooden floor signalled Delilah had woken up, and sure enough, she soon appeared, jumping onto the sofa and licking my face with no invitation.

"Hey there, girl," I said, giving her fur a good shake, wiping my mouth. "Look at you all perky. You don't have any worries do you? Not like your Aunty Alice and Aunty Rachel. You haven't kissed anybody recently, have you?"

Rachel was grinning beside me. "Delilah's only kissed you," she said. "Then again, you are pretty irresistible." She leaned in then and kissed me softly on the lips. My breathing stilled.

Damn, this was beyond everything I'd ever dreamed of.

"You're not so bad yourself," I told her, putting a hand on her cheek, just as Delilah popped her head between the pair of us and licked first Rachel, then me.

"Way to kill a moment, Delilah," I said, as she barked in my ear. "You want to go for a w-a-l-k soon?"

Delilah wagged her tail at that, glad to be made a fuss of.

I looked up. "We might have to take her out. You up for that?"

Rachel nodded. "Sure."

"Did you have any plans today?"

"Only making a dinner to impress you later. And now, of course, to worry about when Jake might see us kissing." Rachel winced, shaking her head. "It's like a scene from a really bad farce, isn't it?"

"Only it's real life." I stood up. "You know what, let's look on the bright side."

"There's a bright side to me fucking over my business partner?"

I put Delilah on the sofa next to me, before taking Rachel's hand and pulling her up, planting a brief kiss on her hot lips.

That action brought me back to the here and now, to us, to what really mattered.

Yes, this situation was far from ideal, but we'd deal with it.

Together.

I squeezed her hand and kissed her again. And then I wanted to kiss her all over, but I parked that thought for now.

"This is not on you, it's on *us*. And the bright side is that it'll be out in the open, no more secrets. Jake might not be happy, but at least we can be honest."

Rachel didn't look convinced.

I was choosing to think positive. "I'll call him when we get back from the walk and tell him — and then, if he watches it, he does. I used to do the editing on Sunday, so he probably won't do it today. Didn't he say he was going out later?"

Rachel nodded. "And he had clients this afternoon."

A weird sense of calm descended on me. "There you go, then. We're reprieved for today, and I'll call him later." I sighed. "If he's going to find out, I'll be the one to tell him."

Rachel cocked her head. "Since when did you get so Zen? I'm the one who does yoga and affirmations and I'm freaked out."

"I've been doing affirmations, too, and they clearly worked." I gave her a grin. "You must be rubbing off on me."

Rachel got right into my personal space, stopping when her lips were inches from mine. "Shall we take Delilah for a walk so we can get back and I can rub off on you some more?"

My heart took a large intake of breath. "Fuck, yes."

Chapter Twenty-Two

We took Delilah out for a short walk along the river, walking side by side and brushing arms at every opportunity. Two women walking in the opposite direction had smiled at us in the afternoon sunshine, and it occurred to me I'd been mistaken for being queer a million times before, but this was the first time it had been true. Life was rich with possibility and I was walking on air.

When we got back, Rachel had a couple of errands to do in her flat, but she promised to reappear back at Tanya's in two hours, replete with ingredients to cook for me tonight, and wine to drink.

I sat on my disappointment that she was leaving me, and focused on seeing her later. Then I tried to call Jake, but there was no answer. I left a message and tried to put it out of my mind. Until I spoke to him, there was nothing I could do. I had to hope he didn't watch the edit before then.

Before I knew it, Rachel was knocking on my door.

When I opened it, she looked so beautiful, I had to grip the door frame.

She was wearing denim shorts that folded up to just above her knee, a fresh white shirt printed with bananas and hair that dropped into her stunning eyes, the colour of the ocean.

She looked fierce — and my heart told me so.

"You look incredible," I said, my eyes drinking her in.

She slipped a hand around my back, drew me to her and kissed me fully, confidently.

When she pulled back, I could do nothing but gape, my heart staggering around, gasping for breath.

She took advantage of my stunned silence to walk past me into the flat, like she owned it.

I closed the door, gripping the handle to steady myself as I turned.

Rachel was at the island, placing her bags on the counter, giving me her best sexy grin. "Ready for the best paella of your life?" she asked, waving a bottle of red in my direction, before placing the ingredients in front of her.

It was almost like we were doing a YouTube shoot.

Only, there was no camera, there was just us.

"I am," I replied, walking towards her, resonating a confidence that was all for show.

Inside, I was back to a frazzle of nerves.

As I neared her, I could still taste her on my lips — and it took me right back to Wednesday night when I'd been engulfed by Rachel.

Rachel had me all off balance and from the look in her eye, I think she knew.

"So did you get your jobs done?" I could do this, I could have a conversation, eat dinner and do date things.

I could try not to think post-date thoughts, take control of my imagination that was going on a freewheeling thrill ride.

She nodded. "I did — and I did it all as quickly as humanly possible so I could get back to you."

"I'm glad."

I was standing on the other side of the island, but I was acutely aware of her. Of her body. Of her presence. Of all of her.

"What did you do?" Her gaze was scorching my skin, and my neck muscles locked up. "Did you get hold of Jake?"

I wasn't going to let Jake into this moment. "I left a ton of messages, I'm sure he'll call me back when he gets them." I paused, channelling my best Marilyn Monroe face. I was going for allure. "Other than that, I made a fuss of Delilah, sat on the balcony and wondered when you might get here."

Rachel gave me a slow, smouldering smile, before sweeping a hand through her black hair.

She picked up the paella rice, locked her gaze with mine, then put it down.

A beat, a rise in temperature, a subtle shift of the head.

Then all of a sudden I was walking towards her and she was walking towards me.

Our bodies collided at the top of the island, and I groaned as we connected. In an instant, she was cupping my head and then her mouth was on mine once again, greedy, claiming me for her own.

I fell against her, dizzy, and it was in that moment I knew that no food would be cooked tonight, and no wine drunk.

Her kiss was just the same as before — perhaps better. The intensity seeped down me as we connected; a punch of heat, the drench of desire.

Minutes later, when we pulled away, my lips swollen, my thoughts a mess, I pulled on Rachel's hand, my gaze intense.

She didn't utter a word, just nodded, and then pulled me. So much had never been said with so little.

As Rachel walked down the hallway, I followed the shape of her strong, broad shoulders, the perfect shape of her. A shape I was about to see in all its glory.

When we got to my room, the scene of such desolation only weeks earlier, I didn't notice much apart from Rachel: the soft sheets and the tasteful decor were all in the background, in my peripheral vision.

Looming large in my eyeline was Rachel, and when her lips met mine, her kiss was deep and explicit, requiring an instant response: it was marked urgent.

I responded as directed, kissing her back with all the intent I had, pouring everything into that moment, not caring about the next one, or the one after that. All that mattered was that moment, that second: if I focused on that, the future would take care of itself.

Rachel's arms were around me and on me, pulling me in, getting us as tight as we could possibly manage.

And then she was tugging at my shirt, undoing my buttons, and my insides were shaking.

As she worked, Rachel smiled at me, licking her lips. "You nervous?" Her breathing was laboured, heavy.

I nodded, silent.

"Don't be, you're perfect," she replied, kissing my lips lightly, before discarding my shirt, then my bra, and gazing at me. "Beautiful, too."

I had no words, my body on fire, my pulse about to take off.

She ran her hands over my stomach, and I closed my eyes, my body trembling under her touch. Her hands swept up my back, her mouth leaving a long line of hot, wet kisses up the side of my neck. My senses were overloaded and when she backed me up against a wall and brought her mouth to my breast, I stopped breathing, no longer certain who I was. Every ounce of blood I had plummeted southwards, and every hair on my body stood up as Rachel's tongue slid around my nipple.

I swear, if I'd been breathalysed right then, I'd have failed.

Intoxicated with lust, officer.

Guilty as charged.

My hands were all over her now, too, wanting to feel what I'd been imagining this long. Without thinking, they were on her buttons, popping them with a skill I had no idea I possessed. As the fabric fell open, I gaped at Rachel's beautiful breasts encased in white silk.

I'd wondered how I'd feel when this moment happened. The answer was, spellbound.

Now it was my turn to explore, and all I wanted to do was feel, taste.

My feelings weren't hesitant, but my actions clearly were, because Rachel shrugged off her shirt and took my hands, kissing first left, then right.

And as she did, tiny fireworks lit up my body.

But it was when she slipped off one bra strap, and then the other that the fire inside really took off. As the straps fell, so did my walls, crashing down around my ears. Now was the time to take control, to do the unthinkable I'd been thinking all along.

Now was the time to be who I really wanted to be.

"Give me your hand," Rachel said, with a soft, sure gaze. She flipped her bra down, and then twisted it round so the clasp was at the front. And then she brought my shaking hands to the clasp.

"Undo it." Her eyes were now all steel and slate.

My insides quivered, but I did as instructed, Rachel's gaze never leaving me, the thump of my heart echoing in my very core.

When she took my hand and placed it on her breasts, I knew that was my cue. And so I took it, kissing her lips like they were the only place on earth, before taking her breasts in my mouth.

When I did, it was like an out-of-body experience, like this was someone else doing this altogether.

But then I felt my feet on the floor, my mouth sucking Rachel in, and I knew: this was all me.

And then Rachel took over, bringing my mouth back to her, making me wilt with the scorching heat of her kiss.

A shift of her thigh. A press of her hand. Hot breath in my ear.

And then five words in my ear. "I want you so much."

Rachel's breath hitched, as did mine, and I parted my legs, pulling her close.

I wanted her, too. So much, it terrified me.

"But this is too important to rush," she said. "I want your first time to be absolutely perfect."

I was dazed, confused. All I knew was, if it involved Rachel, it was bound to be perfect.

Her tongue caressed my ear lobe, before she drew back, taking my hand and tugging me off the wall. I would have followed wherever she wanted to go. I couldn't make sense of my emotions, only that they were panting, gasping for breath.

We moved to the bed, laying side by side, our mouths on each other, kissing like there was no tomorrow. Rachel's tongue in my mouth was heavenly, her thigh between my legs divine.

We rolled so she was top, her kisses raining down on me like trained missiles, allowing no room for manoeuvre. Her mouth travelled over my shoulders, her tongue on my

collar bone, over my breasts, swirling my belly button. Long
minutes later she was reaching and undoing my belt, my
button, my zip. Denim slid down my legs, closely followed
by my pants, and then I was naked, with Rachel's hands
cupping my bare butt cheeks, whispering sweet nothings
into my soul.

Her thigh eased my legs apart and I trembled; this was
it, my dreams coming true. Rachel was on top of me, her
hand skating through my clutch of hair, and this time, I
was awake.

This wasn't my dreams, this was for real.

She stared into my eyes, her hand creeping lower, her
gaze questioning. "You doing okay?" she whispered, before
planting a gentle kiss on my lips.

Then her hand was between my legs and I gasped,
locking her gaze, my skull trembling.

"Touch me," a voice said, and it took me a moment to
realise it was mine. It wasn't loud, it couldn't be: all my
energy was focused on my body tensing, waiting for the
explosion.

Rachel never took her eyes from mine as she slipped
her fingers through my wet heat, pressing her lips to mine
in one swift move.

We both groaned at exactly the same moment; I couldn't
do anything else.

Everything about that moment was perfect: with one
flex of her hand, I came undone.

Rachel's fingers sliding inside me was like a light

being switched on; they answered a question I didn't even know I'd asked, stripping away all my doubts and all my defences. With one move, I wanted to open up to her, give her everything, *be* everything she dreamed of.

With Rachel inside me, her lips on mine, I was soaring.

It was at once the most intense experience of my life, but also the most natural; the one that allowed me to finally breathe for the first time. It was familiar, yet exquisitely foreign.

When Rachel pressed herself into me, I cried out, pushing myself up to her, wanting all she could give.

I was dizzy and unbalanced, and as I gripped her shoulder and spread my legs as wide as I could, I never wanted to be anything else.

Our kisses grew more urgent as I began to shake; Rachel's fingers and mouth were everywhere.

She found my clit and I squeezed my eyes tight shut, my breathing ragged; she found my g-spot and I groaned anew.

She adjusted her rhythm to my body's response, and she was everything I expected: a skilled, sensitive lover.

As her fingers rocked me I arched into her, excitement streaking through me like a thunderbolt. And as she brought me to a taut crescendo, to the peak of pleasure, I cried out, a sobbing writhing mass under her as she slid her fingers deep one last time and I came in a series of intense spasms that racked my body, leaving me exhilarated and washed out all in one move.

I sunk my head into my pillow, speechless, shaking. I was a mass of frazzled nerves, on hyper-alert.

Never had I looked into the eyes of my lover unable to speak, my body going through such extreme pleasure it was as if I could fly.

For the first time, I wasn't trying when it came to sex: I just was.

And all the while, Rachel still had her shorts on.

As if reading my thoughts, she gave me a kiss — more sensations raining down on me — and a wink. Then she stood up and slowly, deliberately, undid her top button, lowered her zip, licked her lips — *holy fucking hell* — and slid her jeans down her slim, toned legs, closely followed by her black boy shorts with white waistband.

Tanya had been right. I was already more of a lesbian than I *ever* thought possible.

I could feel myself getting wet all over again.

I cocked a finger in Rachel's direction, beckoning her in. "Come here, you love goddess," I said, trying to arrange my limbs in the most alluring position possible, but when I saw the lust in Rachel's eyes, I knew I didn't need to worry.

It was the same hunger I'd seen when we were filming weeks ago, although now, it was ramped up to the max.

"Are you okay? I know this is new for you." Her face spelt concern.

"Was it okay?" I let out a strangled groan as I eyed Rachel's grin. "It was like nothing I've ever experienced before."

"I'm honoured to be your first." Rachel crawled over me on her hands and knees, lowering herself gently on top of me, naked.

I groaned again, and she laughed, kissing my eyelids, my nose, then my lips.

The storm of emotions currently crashing over my body were too much to handle, and it was all her fault.

"You were… magnificent." I shook my head. "Amazing." I kissed her again. "Incredible. But I knew you would be." Another kiss.

Rachel nuzzled my neck, embarrassed, wriggling out of the spotlight.

"But I do have one complaint."

She lifted her head, raising a worried eyebrow. "You do?"

I pulled her close as an aftershock streaked through me: our skin on skin contact was off the charts.

"Uh-huh," I said, spinning our positions before she could protest. "I haven't touched you yet."

Desire rumbled through me as I raked my gaze down her body. I shook my head. "And you're just as gorgeous as I thought you'd be." I ran a hand over her breasts, down her stomach, briefly going between her legs before bringing it back to her lips.

Rachel shuddered, closing her eyes.

That was all the encouragement I needed.

I wanted to devour her, taste her, make love with her, just as she'd done with me.

I was still nervous, but I was also emboldened.

Because now I'd experienced it, I knew this was something I could get used to, a feeling I was already craving again.

As if sensing my internal dialogue, Rachel took my cheek in her hand and held me with her gaze. "Just do whatever feels right — you can't get it wrong, trust me."

I nodded, grateful for her words.

I licked Rachel's soft neck, her broad shoulders I'd admired earlier, her firm stomach. I shook as I took her nipples in my mouth again, hearing her groan. Before long, my fingers were skating through her trimmed, coarse hair, and there was a hitch in Rachel's breathing as I stopped, flicking my gaze up to her.

She seemed to understand, as she drew me down for a searing kiss. Then she took my hand and placed it on her heat, closing her eyes and letting out a low moan as she guided my fingers to just where she wanted them.

And as soon as I was there, I took over, as if I'd known how to do this all my life.

Making Rachel squirm this way was a whole new level of incredible, as if today hadn't already gone far enough. But with every kiss I left on her skin, with every twist of my hand, with every stroke to her body, I was reaching a peak I thought I'd already hit, the delicious climb taking me higher and higher, until I could hardly breathe, think, or feel.

And moments later, when I kissed Rachel's breasts

and slid my fingers around her pulsing clit, she came all over my fingers. Her groan was my new favourite sound, her smell my new favourite aroma.

She came again, then again, before she stopped me, holding my arm in place, pulling me to her, kissing my lips.

I didn't want to stop, not now I'd found something *so me*, something I was instantly good at.

Something and someone I was instantly lost in.

I'd expected to feel different when *I* came, but making *Rachel* come? It was a whole new level of sublime.

Moments later, a slow grin spread across her face and she regarded me with hooded eyes. She was just as punch drunk as me.

"Was that... okay?" I had no gauge on this, I'd just gone with my instincts.

Rachel let out a throaty laugh before she replied. "It was pretty much perfect." She paused, her eyes holding mine. "How was it for you?"

"I don't have the words," I replied, kissing her lips. I crawled up her, and we both groaned as our bodies locked together once again.

I'd told Sabrina I wanted something that took my breath away.

I was pretty sure I'd found it.

Chapter Twenty-Three

The following morning, after waking me up with her head between my legs and having me for breakfast — another new experience and one I wondered if we could repeat daily — Rachel insisted on getting up and cooking the paella from the night before.

"We've got all the ingredients, and I know you're hungry. At least, I know I am, and you worked just as hard as me." She placed a kiss on my mouth and gave me a grin as she spoke. I could smell myself on her lips, and I found it a turn-on; with Jake, I'd always cringed a little. What had changed? The person kissing me. Another revelation in my ever-growing bundle marked 'new'.

I pouted, content to stay in bed with Rachel naked, rather than eat food. However, as if on cue my stomach rumbled, and I could no longer deny I was hungry. After all, I hadn't eaten for nearly 24 hours, seeing as it was now 10am.

I ran my hand down Rachel's strong arm, still impressed with her toned physique, honed by hours of work in the kitchen. "What time did Sophie say they'd be back? I feel like there's still plenty of you I haven't run my fingers over."

Rachel kissed my lips again, her breath hot. "I think you gave it a good go last night."

"I can't help it," I said, purring as I spoke. "I can't get enough of you."

"I'm not going anywhere, and we have to eat." She swung her legs out of the bed, before standing naked before me, arms in the air, yawning. Her breasts were perfect handfuls, her hair artfully messy. "If you get up, I promise you can feel me up while I'm cooking, okay? It'll be the opposite of when we film. You can let your hands roam wherever they want."

Lately, every time we'd filmed, I'd wanted to press her up against the stove and do all manner of inappropriate things, so I was completely down with that. I nodded, grinning her way. "You've sold me."

I paused, remembering what we still had to do, my ardour suddenly cooled. "Talking of filming — you get chopping, I'll try to get in touch with Jake, okay?" I frowned as I finished, putting two fingers to my temple.

Rachel nodded, slipping her denim shorts from last night back on, along with her bra, before bringing her head inches from mine, capturing my attention completely. "Good luck, stay calm. And remember: you've done nothing wrong."

It didn't feel that way, though. And I had to sort it out before Jake watched the recording. "I know."

Rachel trailed her tongue along her lip. "Don't be too long, though. I need your lips close to me today." She paused, her stare making my breath hitch. "Both pairs."

My insides tightened at her words and I nodded, letting go a breath as she left the room, watching her denim-clad arse all the way.

The woman was so sexy, I was weak.

Dealing with Jake right now was the last thing I wanted, but it needed to be done. I grabbed my phone, my body still wobbling.

It went straight to voicemail. Dammit, where the hell was he? I left another message for him to call me, sent him another text, then dropped my phone on the bed covers, sighing.

I wanted to get this done and move on, as I was doing in all other areas of my life. Until I'd spoken to him, I felt like I was lying, and I needed closure. Plus, it wasn't just about me: it would do Jake good, too. Knowing the truth might finally free him as well.

When I got out to the kitchen a few minutes later, having got dressed, brushed my teeth and made myself presentable, Rachel was in full flow, onions and garlic already sizzling in the pan. I was sad I'd missed her professional chopping — I was always transfixed.

When she heard my footsteps, she looked up, clocking my face. "Still no luck?"

I shook my head, walking over to her and wrapping my arms around her waist.

Rachel leaned back into me, still stirring the onions with her right hand.

I kissed the side of her neck before replying, surprising myself at how effortless this was. I was slipping into the morning-after just as easily as the night before.

"No. Where the hell is he? Or maybe he's watched it and he doesn't want to speak to me." I winced. "I wouldn't blame him."

Rachel stroked my hand with her own. "I guess we'll find out soon enough."

"I guess we will," I replied, kissing her neck again. "Damn, you smell so good. That's another thing I have to get used to with women, isn't it? I'm used to smelling better."

Rachel grinned at me. "If that's the only downside, I hope it's one you can manage."

I smiled. I couldn't think of many downsides to being with Rachel this morning. Before this had happened, all I'd felt was guilt: for leaving Jake, ruining his life, and for not being honest with myself or any of my friends. But this morning, when I didn't think about Jake seeing us kissing, that was replaced by a feeling that I'd been right to pursue this. To pursue Rachel, more to the point. I was still no closer to a label, but this morning, the only label that mattered was that I was happy.

Rachel had brought about a kind of happiness that filled me with such brightness, it was scary.

I let her go, and she picked up a chorizo from beside her, stripping its skin and chopping it finely.

"You think Tanya and Sophie are going to be okay about us?" I hadn't really considered there would be any issues, and I hoped there weren't.

"Course, why wouldn't they be?" Rachel leaned over and kissed my lips before concentrating again.

"Don't cut your fingers, Chef. They're already quite precious to me."

She gave me a grin and a bubble of happiness fizzed up my body.

"But what about you: how does it feel for you? Last night was a big night in your life."

I exhaled. "It was. But you made it ridiculously easy." I was drawn back to her lips: this morning, my whole world was Rachel-flavoured. "And weirdly, it's like we've been doing it forever."

Which was crazy, I knew, but Rachel already felt so familiar. I was beginning to see that sleeping with someone you knew so well added another dimension to the scenario.

Especially when that someone was capable of supplying a never-ending stream of gold-standard orgasms.

That part was *definitely* new.

"I know what you mean." Rachel grinned my way. "Can you open the rice for me?" She indicated with her head and I followed her gaze to the risotto rice on the counter.

As she did so, she brushed her little finger over the top of my knuckle, and even that tiny action sent shockwaves tumbling down my spine, through every sinew of my body, landing between my legs. I held it together, but it was no mean feat.

I had so much more to give her, and she to me.

I also knew it had *never* been like this with a man. Not even with Jake. And Jake had been nothing but the perfect boyfriend: loving, gentle, kind. However, even at the height of our love-making, even when he was being the most considerate lover, he didn't hold the power Rachel held in her little finger.

I'd be lying if I said that didn't scare me. Last night was just the beginning; we'd barely scratched the surface. Yet one touch from her was enough to send me into orbit. It was a lot to take in, and I wanted to keep it to myself for a while.

I picked up the rice and studied my new lover: her long fingers, her strong arms, her strong cheekbones.

She was breathtaking. Everything I'd wanted, in fact.

"Rach," I said, hoping my voice didn't betray my nerves.

"Yeah?"

"Can I ask a favour?"

She looked at me. "Anything."

I was in love with her voice already, and her mouth.

"Can we hold off telling the world for a while?" I tore open the top of the rice. "Just for a little bit? I kinda like our little cocoon." Letting the world in on this seemed a little rude when it was still so new, so untouched.

She turned to me with such kind eyes, I stilled again.

"Course. We can talk about marriage on our next date, no rush."

I furrowed my brow.

"Kidding!" Rachel reached out and squeezed my arm. "Jeez, you're kinda easy to wind up."

"So my sister tells me. My childhood was one long drama of me sobbing, my sister smirking and my mum trying to placate me."

"And what will she think about you sleeping with a woman?" She threw the chorizo into the pan and it sizzled, filling the flat with delicious Mediterranean flavours.

Beside me, Delilah appeared from her basket, barking: she clearly had Spanish roots.

"Hello you," I said, leaning down and making a fuss of her. I walked over to the balcony to throw open the French doors on what was already a gorgeous day. "Hold that thought," I told Rachel with a smile, waiting for Delilah to pee on her designated pee pad. She was well trained, and I assumed that was Sophie's doing, seeing as she was a dog walker.

I left her on the balcony barking at passing birds, and walked back into the flat, sniffing Spanish aromas, before getting Delilah's breakfast. When she heard it hit her metal bowl, she was beside me in an instant. I left her chewing and washed my hands, before coming back to Rachel who was now adding rice, spices and stock. Once the sizzle had died down, she looked at me.

"You were saying about keeping this between us?"

I nodded. "It's a big change and I want a little while to get used to it; to know what to say, how to react. Let all the feelings in me settle." I wasn't sure if she knew what she'd done to me, but it was monumental, life-changing.

"Sure. So long as I'm not a dirty little secret — my days of lying and sneaking around are done."

I shook my head; she was anything but. "Of course not. My family already know this is on the cards."

"I'm not just a notch on your bedpost?"

I shook my head before leaning over and kissing her lips. "If you are, you might be the most important one." My voice shook as I spoke. "Do you remember your first time?"

An emotion I couldn't pin down swept over Rachel's face as she nodded. "I do. I met a woman in a club, got roaring drunk, snogged her up against a wall all night long and then we went back to hers and that was it. I remember coming home on the bus the following morning, back to my university halls, thinking everyone could see the difference in me, that it was so obvious. They couldn't, but that's what it's like when you're 19."

"I wish I'd known you then." And I did. I wanted to know everything about Rachel; every, tiny, intimate detail.

"I don't, I was a mess. But that night changed my life, even if it wasn't the best sex I'd ever had. Far from it." She shivered as she held my gaze. "I hope your first time was better than mine?"

She looked so vulnerable when she spoke, my heart

lurched. As far as I was concerned, Rachel walked on water and could do no wrong.

"It was everything," I replied, kissing her hand, drowning in her uncertain stare. "I'm a lucky girl because I was in the best hands possible."

Rachel blew out a relieved sigh. "I'm the lucky one." She put down her wooden spoon, before turning to flick on Tanya's coffee machine, grabbing two black mugs from her cupboard above the kettle.

She stopped, staring at me. "I was worried how you might react."

"You were?"

She nodded, holding my stare. "Worried this was just something you needed to get out of your system."

She shook as she spoke. Behind her, the coffee machine lit up to say it was ready. "But when I was with you, I didn't think that at all. Because last night was very real for me. Frighteningly real."

I walked over to her and took her face in my hands. I'd been so wrapped up in how huge this was for me, I hadn't stopped to think about Rachel and how she was feeling.

How she might worry.

She had no need; no need at all.

"Don't ever doubt me — and if I'm feeling something, I promise to talk to you, okay? I'm not saying this is going to be plain sailing, but I hope I did enough to convince you that last night wasn't something I did lightly."

I kissed her lips and it shook me to the core.

Even more so when Rachel put her arms around me and squeezed me tight.

"You did plenty," she said. "And I can see what it meant to you. You're radiant." She kissed me again, running her index finger along my lips and fixing me with her stare.

I sucked her fingers into my mouth and we both groaned in unison, closing our eyes.

It wasn't just about sex, but then again, *this* was amazing. What was *this*? This feeling, this want, this overwhelming, earth-shattering need? I'd never experienced it before, and I wondered if Rachel had either. Was this every woman she'd been with, or just us? I'd love to know, but morning one was a little early for those kind of questions.

She opened her eyes as she removed her fingers, blinked, then stepped back, blowing out a breath and going back to the coffee. "No regrets?"

I shook my head. "Not about being with you."

Rachel gave me my coffee, stirred the paella, then took my hand, leading me onto the balcony. Delilah followed us, wagging her tail. The heat was already palpable at 10.30, the smell of the Thames rising up: oil, brine and salt. I arched my face into the sun, glad of its rays this morning. The sunshine matched my mood perfectly.

"But if we're being open and honest, one thing that does worry me is you've got quite a few years head-start." I took a deep breath. "I'm kinda out of my depth, aren't I?" Because as much as I was brimming with everything that had happened in the past 24 hours, I still had my fair share of insecurities.

Rachel smiled. "I don't think it works like that, does it? I mean, I've slept with a number of women, some of them were great, some of them stole my heart and didn't give it back, and some of them were just plain terrible."

She held my gaze as she spoke, and I was hanging on her every word. Because after all, when it came to being a lesbian, I was merely the apprentice, and Rachel was the wise, all-knowing mentor.

The sexy-as-hell, wise, all-knowing mentor.

"I've always thought that when it comes to relationships and sex, whenever you start a new one, it's like wiping the slate clean and starting fresh. And you might not have slept with any other women, but in the end, we're coming at this on an equal footing — just two people putting their trust in one another, seeing where things go."

"I like that logic a lot," I replied. "It makes me feel less of a novice."

"You didn't act like a novice last night."

I stared at her when she said that, wondering how I'd managed to get through all those months of being together, filming and chatting, without touching her and kissing her? It seemed almost rude all the time we'd wasted.

But back then, I'd had a boyfriend, so it hadn't been that easy. And said ex currently had a recording of the two of us kissing, and I *really* needed to get hold of him.

My face obviously showed my change in mood, as Rachel sat forward. "What's wrong?"

"Just thinking about calling Jake. But honestly, it's the last thing I want to do. I don't want to burst this bubble we're in, it's too glorious, too perfect."

"You want me to do it?"

"No, it should be me," I replied. "Thank you, though. You just need to be there for me to freak out on after I do it."

"I'm not going anywhere," Rachel said, and the look in her eyes told me she meant it.

"Neither am I," I replied, remembering Rachel inside me last night and feeling my cheeks colour.

"Does the fact I had a boyfriend before bother you?"

She shook her head straight away. "Everybody's got a past."

"But the fact he's a man?"

She chuckled. "I'm not going to penalise you for not being a gold-star lesbian, if that's what you're asking."

"A what?"

"A gold star — it means you're a lesbian who's only ever slept with women."

"There's a term for that?" My mind was officially boggled.

Rachel smiled as she nodded. "There's a term for most things these days."

"Are you a gold-star lesbian?" I wasn't sure what I hoped the answer would be.

She nodded again. "I am — but I prefer to just say

lesbian or queer. Sexuality is fluid, isn't it? I have a friend who was with women for 15 years, and is now happily settled with a man. I also have friends who did it the other way around."

"But you don't think you're ever going to sleep with a man?"

She laughed again, shaking her head. "I think if it was going to happen, it'd have happened by now, don't you?"

"I guess it would." I drank my coffee, picking up Rachel's hand and kissing it. "I wish I had a private space like this, just for us." I gazed at her. "I'm glad we're giving this a while to get used to."

Rachel smiled at me. "Whatever you need." She paused. "Just so long as there's no hiding. I know you said your family would be okay, but what about friends? If this develops between us, they're going to have to know. Because whatever you want to happen, it's never just the two of us — we don't live in that world. There's always someone else, be it friends, family or fans of the channel."

I nodded. "I know that. But right now, I love it's just you, me, and this thing between us that's so powerful."

Rachel's smile was slow and sure. "It's something alright," she said, drawing me to her. I got up and my lips were inches from hers when there was a banging on the front door.

I jumped back, startled. "What the fuck?"

Rachel hopped up. "You wanna get that? If it's Tanya back early, they can have some paella."

I frowned, calculating the time. "Too early for them, surely?"

I crossed the flat and opened the door with a grin on my face.

When I saw who it was, I froze.

Chapter Twenty-Four

"Good morning, lover girl." There was an edge to Jake's voice I'd never heard before. His eyes were bloodshot, narrowed, and he looked... wild. Like I'd never seen him look before in our entire time together.

He almost spat the words into my face.

I surmised he'd seen the video.

"Jake," I began, but he just gave me a look and walked into the flat, sweeping me aside.

Every muscle in my body tightened, as if being twisted by a professional.

He walked into the living space, with me rushing in behind him.

"Cooking already?"

I could see Rachel wasn't sure what to do either, as she stopped mid-stir. "Hi, Jake."

He sneered at Rachel, then me. "Very nice," he said, gesturing with his hands. "Very Sunday morning after laughing it up about me all night no doubt. In between shagging. I hope you had a good laugh at my expense."

I tried to shuffle my thoughts, get them in order, but it was a hopeless task.

"It's not what it seems." My heart was pounding in my chest, but this time, fear, not desire, was its driving force. "I've been trying to get hold of you — I left a bazillion messages."

"I know, I heard them. Each one a little more desperate, a little more guilty than the last." He looked from me to Rachel, not quite sure where to plant his gaze. "But I just need to know — how long has this been going on?"

He was talking to me, now. "Because I thought our relationship — even if it is just business now, but we were a couple not so long ago — would have meant I'd get the courtesy of a heads-up on this, but apparently not."

He shook his head, sucking in a breath. "I mean, how could you?" His face was red as he looked at the ground, then back up at us, his eyes sparkling with tears.

I hated that I'd hurt him. Absolutely hated myself.

"When exactly were you going to tell me?" His voice had gone up a notch, and I stepped forward, going into damage control mode.

I reached out, remembering too late I couldn't do that anymore. I'd forfeited the right a few weeks ago.

"Jake, it's not what you think."

He shrugged off my arm. "Isn't it?" He was shouting now, his eyes wild. "Or is it exactly what I think? Because if you're *not* having an affair, if you're *not* sleeping together, just correct me, go ahead."

He stared at me, then Rachel, and we both dropped our gazes to the floor. I couldn't say anything because I didn't want to deny the truth. And over the past 24 hours, the truth had cemented itself into my soul. Into every part of my being. And it was so very scary.

I wasn't anywhere near straight, I knew that now.

He let out a breath. "I didn't think so. So thanks a fucking bunch for letting me find out by editing our video. Editing *our own video*, Alice. On the channel we work on. Together. As a unit." He shook his head. "What a dumb, trusting idiot I am."

I stepped forward, shaking my head. "You're not, Jake, you're anything but that. And I'm so very sorry you had to find out like this."

He scoffed. "I know we've split up, but spare me by claiming this happened *after* we broke up. None of it made any sense to me, Alice, *none of it*. We were good together, great even. And then one day you run off telling me it's you. What does that even mean? But it wasn't just you, was it? It was her, too!"

The look he gave Rachel, all daggers and glint, killed me. This wasn't her fault, none of it was.

"Just listen, Jake," Rachel said.

"I don't want to listen to you, to either of you!"

His volume stopped me in my tracks, and for a moment, the flat was silent, just the sharpness of his tone slicing through the air, and Delilah's barking as she came in from the balcony to see what all the fuss was about.

I bent down to pet her, looking up at Jake. "You're scaring the dog," I said. "And you're scaring me."

"Poor fucking you." I'd never seen him like this, ever.

"Hey!" Rachel said, scooping up Delilah and going back to the kitchen. "Nothing happened while you two were together, Jake."

"She's right," I added, walking towards him.

He took a step back.

I stopped walking, keeping his attention. I took a deep breath, just saying what was in my heart.

"That's why I split up with you, because I didn't want to cheat on you. And before you go blaming Rachel, she had no idea until I told her how I was feeling two weeks ago." My heartbeat was calming down, but it was still thudding in my ears. "Nobody was laughing at you, and I've been trying to get hold of you ever since you left."

"And I'm meant to believe that?" He flipped his palms to the ceiling, his eyes wide.

"It's true!" But even though it was, I still sounded like I was lying. Guilty by omission.

"But we were together, Alice. We talked. I thought you would have at least had the courtesy to tell me why you were leaving. It would have made more sense to me."

I shook my head. This was so hard to explain. "I thought so, too, but it was too overwhelming even for me, Jake. I couldn't talk to you, I couldn't talk to anyone because I didn't know what I was feeling, what was going on."

"But we had good sex, we were in love." His voice cracked at the end.

Oh god, this was horrible.

"We did, and we were." Now wasn't the time to tell the whole truth. "And you were a great boyfriend. But things changed and it was out of my control. I couldn't help how I was feeling and you don't know the times I wanted to feel different, I wanted to want you like I did in the beginning."

I glanced at Rachel, sensing her shoulders tense. She gave me a look of understanding, shaking her head, Delilah in her arms.

"But you just couldn't help yourself? You were out of control? I can't imagine it, Alice, you were always so in control with me." His eyes were searching mine, and I didn't know what they were looking for. I didn't know what he wanted me to say, I just knew I didn't have the answers he wanted.

I never had.

"And it's about trust, Alice. I trusted you with my heart, and you trampled it. I gave you everything I had, and you threw it in my face. If this was really you, you should have told me!"

"And you'd have listened? Taken it in your stride?" I threw my hands in the air, my temperature rising. "What, Jake, tell me?"

He glared at me, his body shaking.

"I thought we were going to be adults about this, not

scream at each other." I got the irony of screaming that line.

His face reddened and he did a little hop on the spot.

And just at that moment, as Jake extended his arm and pointed his index finger at me, I heard a key in the front door and we all turned as one to see Tanya and Sophie walk into the living space. Into this scene.

"That was before you fucked my co-star behind my back!" Jake screamed, ignoring them. "That was before you trashed everything we had — our friendship, our trust, our time together, like it meant nothing. Nothing at all!"

Delilah began to bark, racing over to greet her owners.

Tanya scooped her up, looking from Jake to me, wincing. "What's going on?"

I turned to Rachel, who shook her head, ushering Tanya and Sophie into the kitchen area with her.

Leaving Jake and I, centre stage, to carry on where we left off.

Jake wasted no time. "You don't respect me, you never even loved me. Were you looking at every woman while we were out? Were you thinking about other women while I fucked you?"

"Enough, Jake! That's enough! And of course I wasn't." I put my palms on my thighs, drawing in a breath before looking up. "This isn't about you. It's not even about me or Rachel — and like I said, please don't blame her, I went to her with this, this is on me."

"She had a part to play, or am I wrong?"

"Yes, but only when I told her how I felt. And I was free to do that, by the way, because we've been split up for over a month now. I can do what I like, and yes I agree with you, we should have told you, and for that I'm so very sorry."

I was sinking, drowning, but I had to get this out, let him know.

"These past few months have been so scary, so lonely, and I desperately wanted us to work. But I couldn't do it anymore when I realised I liked Rachel. That I *really* liked Rachel." I glanced over at her, and she was biting her lip, hands on the counter, not taking her eyes off me. She nodded her head barely perceptibly, and I swallowed down, hard.

"And I knew then, I couldn't carry on with you — or with anyone — without giving this a shot." I dropped my head, chest heaving. "And do you think any of this has been easy? Do you think walking away from a future that's expected and assured, from you who everyone loved, was easy? None of it was! But I couldn't ignore it, this intangible feeling, this thing that was bigger than me, you, Rachel, *everyone*. I had to know. And to do that, I had to break your heart, and that was horrible. And I couldn't even tell you why."

I drew in a huge breath, sinking to the floor, no longer able to hold my own body weight, and Jake did the same. "I wanted to love you, Jake, and a part of me always will, but it was never going to work. It was kinder to let you go."

He shook his head, breathing heavily, then put his head in his hands. "Did I misread everything? Were you always gay?"

I shook as I spoke, my whole body humming with friction. "I don't know. Maybe." I raised my head again. "Just know, I never wanted to hurt you. I loved you, and I'm sorry about everything. The video, us, everything."

He looked up, tears running down his face, sniffing and wiping his hand across his face.

Despite all his words, his hurt was still my fault, even if I'd had no real control over it.

"I'm sorry, too. I'll stop shouting now. It's just, seeing that video, it pushed my buttons."

"I understand." Wetness on my face alerted me to the fact I was crying now, too. Before I knew it, Rachel's bare legs were in front of me, and a tissue was being waggled under my nose. I took it gratefully, looking up, aware I must have been a sight.

But Rachel just smiled, then gave Jake a tissue.

This wasn't what I'd had in mind when I woke up this morning. But at least it was all out in the open now. There was that, at least.

"Jake," Rachel said, clearing her throat.

He looked up at her, defeated.

"I just want to say sorry, too. We should have told you, but nothing happened until this weekend."

Jake winced, and so did I.

"But we shouldn't have let you walk off with the

recording when we knew what was on there. And then we should have warned you." She paused. "I hope we can work this out as friends, and keep the channel going."

He sighed, pushing himself up, standing up finally. His jeans were new, I didn't recognise them. As time went on, I guessed that would happen more often. Our lives weren't together anymore.

"Let's see what happens," he replied, running a hand through his hair. "But I don't want to throw away everything we've worked for either. Not when we've just got going."

Rachel breathed out. "Great." They stood looking at each other, like a living game of chess. Nobody was quite sure whose move it was, and we were all too wrung out to care.

In the kitchen, Tanya cleared her throat. "Erm, everyone." I turned my head. She sounded weird. "I think you should look at this. I'm guessing you're fighting about the video?"

I nodded, my heart sinking, but then looked up. How did Tanya know?

She held up her phone. "I'm not sure how or why this has happened, but your latest video is going bananas. I've got you on subscription and the upload came up when we were driving home, and the comments are going ballistic." She paused. "You might want to take a look at what happens at around 41m 28 seconds, it says." She winced. "Apparently it involves you two sucking each other's faces off."

I stared at Tanya, trying to compute what she was saying. *Wait, what was she saying?*

Rachel's voice was next. "Jake? Did you come round here, chew us out, and all the while you'd uploaded the damn video to YouTube? What the fuck are you playing at?"

There was a standoff in my head as I weighed up what was happening. Jake wouldn't do that, would he? Then again, he probably thought the same when he saw the video. But upload it on purpose? Hurting me, threatening the business? Out of spite?

Jake's mouth was dropping open now, and he was running over to Tanya, grabbing her phone. He watched, stared, and then began to jiggle on the spot, his curls bouncing. He had that wild look again.

"I didn't! I wouldn't do that! I edited it, cut the kissing out and uploaded the real one." He paused, snagging his fingers in his hair. "Although I was obviously a bit distracted."

"Distracted?" Rachel said, her voice blowing smoke. "There's distracted and there's *distracted*!" She twisted to Tanya. "Have you got your laptop handy?"

Tanya nodded and skidded into her room, coming out with it held high. She switched it on, put it on the oval wooden dining table by the window and we all gathered around.

Rachel hit play on the latest episode, gave me a look I couldn't quite decipher, and then scrolled to the end of the episode.

And there we were, talking, washing up, laughing, and then we got closer, then closer still... and I had to look away.

Because we were kissing on screen.

Full-on bloody kissing.

There was a ringing in my ears, or was it coming from outside? I couldn't be sure.

Rachel looked away too, glancing at me as she did.

Our gazes caught and the horror of it, the enormity sunk in. The whole world being privy to such a private moment — our moment — was far worse than I could have ever imagined. I'd wanted to keep this quiet, get used to it, but now it was trashed, ruined.

Perhaps just like our channel. Just like my relationship with Jake. And what about my relationship with Rachel? My relationships with everyone in my life? They'd all think I was a liar and a cheat who'd been hiding this from them.

Was everything ruined before it had even begun?

Jake stopped the recording and closed his eyes. "I can't fucking believe it — I didn't do this on purpose, you have to believe me."

"It's kinda hard to," Rachel replied, shaking her head.

"I know, but I didn't." He put both his hands in his hair and took a deep breath. Then he walked to the sofas, swearing, then back to us.

Rachel was leaning down again, hand back on the touchpad. "Oh fuck, the comments are blowing up—"

"—surprise," I said. "If you were after a ratings boost, well done Jake, you achieved it. At the expense of your two co-stars, but really, well done." My voice was dripping with sarcasm. My turn to stare at my ex with murderous intent.

I was pretty sure most people's coming-out stories did not follow this trajectory.

"I didn't do it on purpose!" His face was so red it was almost purple.

"You know what, I'm fed up of you screaming at us today," Rachel said, her face now rock-hard, set in stone. "If you want to do something useful, go home and take this shit down right now!" She shook her head. "It's already our most downloaded episode. And there was me thinking people came for the food."

Jake's phone buzzed. He took it out of his pocket and put a hand to his head. "Fuck!"

"What now?" I said.

He shook his head. "Nothing. Just my sister." He cast his gaze down. "I hadn't told her we'd split up yet."

"We've been split up for weeks!"

He shook his head. "I know."

I'd had enough of him today — I'd had enough of it all.

Having woken up this morning so happy, now I just wanted to go back to bed and pretend it was all a bad dream. A very bad dream.

"Just go, Jake, sort this out."

He nodded. "I will. And I'm sorry." He paused. "I wouldn't do this to the channel or to either of you. I'll fix it." He gave me a final look, then slipped out, slamming the door shut behind him.

But even I knew he couldn't fix this.

Chapter Twenty-Five

Tanya cleared her throat, then scratched her head, before glancing at Sophie. "We're going to take a coffee onto the balcony and shut the door, give you some space," she said, walking over and punching some buttons on the machine. "I know this is a lot to take in, but I don't think Jake did it on purpose — he was just upset and not paying attention. And it might do your channel some good, get you some attention."

"There's no such thing as bad publicity," Sophie chimed in, putting the second mug under the machine.

"I'm not sure you'd be saying that if the video of the first woman you'd ever kissed was getting shared and commented on from all over the world."

Sophie tensed her cheeks, then shook her head. "Perhaps not."

"No, I didn't think so. Not if you had to face your employer and explain it. If the governors see it, I might lose my job."

Sophie winced. "I didn't think about that."

Tanya took her hand and they shut the door as they walked out, taking Delilah with them.

Then there was just Rachel and I, our breath jagged, a mass of bones and expressions that didn't quite fit our skin anymore.

The room smelt of paella, which just made things more surreal, and the sunlight was beaming in like a spaceship had just landed. My stomach rumbled, but I'd lost my appetite.

I sank down on Tanya's white sofa, shaking my head. Then I got out my phone from my back pocket, and saw I had a missed call from Sabrina, along with another from my boss, and about ten text messages from various friends. I didn't need to click on them to know what they were about. Everybody wanted to talk about the fact I was now a lesbian.

When I just wanted to curl up into a ball and be spirited away.

How could something so right and so personal suddenly become so wrong and so public?

I put my phone back into my bag and glanced up at Rachel, leaning against the kitchen island, her face blank. She was shellshocked, still taking it all in. My heart went out to her.

I wanted to say so much, but I was still shaking.

I stood up, stuffing my hands into the pockets of my blue shorts, staring at Sophie and Tanya outside.

There were too many people in this flat, and there

were too many people in the world currently watching me kiss Rachel. That fact scratched at my skin, never letting me forget it.

I didn't know if I was strong enough for this after all. Yes, Rachel and I were off the scale sexually. But was that enough? Was it enough for all the stares, all the pointing, all the living your life out and proud?

This had floored me. I was ready to do this step by step, but bursting out into the world with almost a sex tape?

The room was suddenly too small, and I spun around, looking for my stuff. I had to get out of here, I needed some air.

Everyone knew everything about me and this was too much.

Rachel intercepted me, snagging my arm gently as I walked past.

I gulped, then brought my eyes level with hers.

"Talk to me, Alice. This doesn't change anything. This is still me and you, everything you felt earlier is still valid."

I shook my head. It's not how it felt. "It changes everything! You know I wanted to take this slowly, and now, everyone knows it all. I feel exposed."

Rachel held my chin with her hand.

Her touch almost made my knees buckle under me.

"I don't get it." Her voice was soft. "Yes, this is a shit thing to happen, but we'll deal with it together and we'll get over it."

"What if it's ruined the channel?"

Rachel's gaze drilled into me. "The channel's not the most important thing here."

I wobbled again. "But everyone knows about us and about me." I took a step back, shaking my head. "They know I kissed a girl — and I'm still getting used to it. You've had 30 years to get used to this, I've had 24 hours."

Rachel took her arm away and folded them across her chest, hugging herself tight.

"It doesn't normally go like this, you know." She blew out a breath, a raspberry sound escaping her lips. "I mean, I've gone out with a number of women before, and never once have any of our kisses been broadcast on YouTube. I'm not normally a commodity. But we weren't accounting for fame, however small ours is, were we?"

I shook my head. No, we really hadn't.

And now, some of the most personal parts of my life — and one of the very newest and most precious — was online for everyone to see.

Including my family, my colleagues, my friends and my students. Everyone I'd ever met in the past and everyone in my future. And yes, we could take it down, but these things lived on — I wasn't naive enough to think that would be the end of it.

Maybe I'd bitten off more than I could chew.

"I need some space to think about this, work out how to handle it." Perhaps if I went home, I'd get some clarity.

"I thought we'd handle it together?" Rachel was sounding perplexed, along with a little confused and hurt.

I didn't blame her, but I just wanted to sprint as far away as I could from this.

"I can't think right now, I just need to get some air. I'm going to go home, call Jake, make sure it's taken down and then I'll call you later, okay?"

She looked at me, trying to work me out.

Only, she couldn't, not yet.

"Don't run away from this, Alice. Remember what we said this morning? We're good together, and this isn't something you did lightly. Yes, this is a setback, but we'll get over it, and we could even use this to our advantage in time."

"Don't you start talking about us lezzing it up being good for the channel." I put 'lezzing it up' in finger quotes.

"I don't know what will happen with the channel, but I have to think positively. But whatever happens with that, it's not just us anymore. Everybody knows. You have to be comfortable with that."

"I am comfortable with it." Lies, all lies.

"From where I'm standing, it really doesn't look that way." She paused. "You said this morning you were, that it wasn't just a phase, but that's not the way you're acting. You're not strong enough for this? What does that even mean?"

I got up and walked to the window, hugging my body. I wanted to pretend today had never happened. Only, that wasn't completely true because that would erase this morning with Rachel, and I never wanted to erase us.

However, today's rude unveiling on YouTube had exposed me and us in ways I never thought possible.

Now, my discomfort was on show for everyone to see, especially Rachel.

I turned, still clutching myself, not feeling confident enough to let go.

"I need to go home." I bit my lip. "I'll text you, okay?"

Rachel's features slumped, just like her body.

"Your call." She shrugged, like it didn't matter at all, before tensing up again. "I know this is big, but it will calm down. And then you're just left with your own life, and you need to decide what you want to do with it: live it the way you want, or retreat into your shell like before. We've only just begun, don't forget that."

My thoughts spun in my head like a roulette wheel, round and round. I clenched my fists in my shorts' pockets, my knuckles hard against the fabric. I had so much to say to her, but I couldn't form a single sentence.

Instead, I gave her a final stare, before shaking my head and walking to get my stuff from the bedroom.

Chapter Twenty-Six

"Afternoon darling, I didn't expect you back!" Mum was chirpy today, her hands covered in soil. Since they'd moved back into the metropolis, she'd turned into a keen gardener, proclaiming the balcony garden the perfect size for retirement.

"You and me both." I knew I looked a mess.

Mum narrowed her eyes. "Everything go okay last night? You don't look like someone who was meeting the woman of their dreams for dinner."

I dumped my bag on the stone kitchen floor and sat at the breakfast bar, knitting my hands together on the counter. "Well, the first part was pretty magical." I blushed. "But since then, there's been a fly in the ointment."

That was the understatement of the century.

Mum gave me a look, before washing her hands in the sink, turning her head over her shoulder as she did. "I'm listening."

And so, while she dried her hands on a bright pink tea towel, I told her the full story.

As the words tumbled out of my mouth, Mum's

shoulders tensed; when she turned to face me, wringing her hands together, her face was pale.

"So it's on the internet now? You and her kissing?" Her voice was brittle, as if it might snap at any minute.

I nodded, the wind knocked out of me. I'd been trying to talk myself round on the way home, but seeing Mum's reaction only cemented my initial feelings: this wasn't something I could just laugh off.

"Oh my," Mum said, before walking over to the kettle and filling it up. The sound of the water filled the air, and I didn't know what to say next. Was her reaction because I was kissing a woman, or just because the video had been uploaded?

I closed my eyes as I heard the kettle switch being flicked. This show going online was testing every area of my life and I wasn't sure of any of the outcomes: Rachel, my family, my friends, my job. It had all seemed so easy when I was in her arms, but now, not so much.

When I looked over at her, Mum was still frowning. "Can you get it taken down?"

I clenched, then unclenched my fists. "Jake was going to do that when he left us."

Mum's face contorted. "Has he seen it? Oh god, what must he think?"

"That I was having an affair behind his back the whole time with his co-star and business partner?"

Mum winced. "Yes, that's exactly how he'd see it."

I nodded. "But hopefully, he can sort it out."

"I'm sure he'll do everything he can. He's a good boy, that one."

Something went off in my head. "Can you stop saying how wonderful Jake is all the time? I know he's lovely, but I'm not with him anymore and I don't love him. I love Rachel, and I don't know how that's going to pan out after all this." I let out a small sob, but no tears came: I was all cried out for now.

And I'd just told my mum I loved Rachel? I hadn't even told myself that before now.

I was in love with Rachel and I'd just walked away from her because I was scared. My timing was impeccable.

"I don't need to hear any more about Jake, Mum. It's his fault this is on the internet in the first place."

I sniffed, wiping the bottom of my nose with my bare hand. Attractive.

I took a deep breath, clutching my hand in front of my chest. "I need you to support *me*, and that means supporting me and Rachel as a couple." I paused, gathering my strength again. "That is, if we still are a couple."

And then the tears returned and I collapsed in a heap of sobs, my body convulsing. The next thing I knew were my mum's arms around me, holding me tight, along with a shushing sound in my ear.

"I'll always support you, you know that," she said, her voice not as shrill as it had been.

"I hope so," I replied, sniffing.

She squeezed me tighter. "Of course I will." She paused.

"It's just… this is all so new, so different. One day you announce you like a woman, the next you're kissing her online. It's all happening at such a fast pace."

I let out a strangled noise. "You're telling me." I untangled myself from her and grabbed a tissue from the box on the counter. "I slept with her last night and it was…" I shook my head. "It was just incredible." I let out a long sigh. "But now this, and Jake is so mad, and Rachel and I had a fight, and I don't know what I'm doing or how I'm feeling." I shook my head again. "It's such a huge mess."

Mum stepped back, and then went to the fridge, pulling out a bottle of Chablis. She got two glasses from the cupboard above the microwave and poured me one.

"Drink?" She held it out to me.

"It can't hurt."

Unlike Rachel and Jake, who'd undoubtedly been hurt by me.

And then I thought about Rachel, telling me not to walk away from this just because I'd stepped on a grenade. But when that happened, surely you needed some time to convalesce, to work out what to do next?

Mum climbed onto one of the breakfast bar stools and I followed suit.

"I know what's happened today is horrid, but you'll survive and grow from it." Mum was puffing out her chest, getting over herself to try to help me in my time of need. I appreciated it.

"Or it might blow my life apart." I took a gulp of wine as a full stop to my sentence.

"You're being dramatic."

"Aren't I allowed to be?"

She let that one go with a curt nod. "For now, but not forever. I'm sure Rachel will be fine, and the show will be okay, too. You just need to give it a little time."

"You haven't seen the video."

She shook her head, a cloud passing over her again. "And I don't intend to," she said. "But you have to work the show thing out with Jake and Rachel, and then work the rest out with Rachel. They're tied up, but they are independent, too."

"But what if I'm not strong enough to cope? If I'd been caught kissing a bloke on camera, nobody would have blinked, would they?"

"They would if it wasn't your boyfriend."

"But not as much. Which makes me wonder — am I ready for this? Ready to be gay and open myself up to such public scrutiny? It's a big change."

Mum frowned then. "You just told me you're in love with Rachel. Is that true?"

I sighed, thinking about her. About how incredible last night had been. What an amazing person she was. How her touch, her voice, her mere presence in a room lit me up. If that wasn't love, I didn't know what was.

I choked up again, nodding.

"Darling, look at me."

I turned my head as she put a hand on mine. "You can't help who you fall in love with, because love doesn't always make sense. If you've fallen in love with Rachel, then don't walk away. Love is worth pursuing, worth fighting for."

"But what if I'm not gay? What if I'm throwing away everything and it all blows up in my face?"

"That horse has already bolted I think," Mum said. "I can't predict the future, and neither can you. What I can tell you is that you and Jake wouldn't have lasted because you didn't love him. But if you love Rachel, you've got every chance of making it work."

"You're okay with me being in love with a woman?"

"It doesn't matter what I think, it matters what you think." She paused, staring at me. "Are you okay being in love with a woman?"

"I'm okay being in love with Rachel." And I was. In all the commotion, I'd forgotten that.

I was still overwhelmed, but maybe in time, I wouldn't be. Maybe, in time, I could get used to this.

"That's all you need to know. You've fallen in love, embrace that. It's a special thing." Mum hugged me. "Give yourself a little time, but tell Rachel what's happening, because she's going to be upset, too."

* * *

Rachel texted me that night, asking how I was. When I got the text, I wanted to crawl through the phone and settle in her arms, but I knew I couldn't. That wouldn't be fair.

I texted back telling her I needed space, that I'd be in touch with her soon. I also asked her not to give up on me.

In her shoes, I'm not sure what I would have thought, but it wouldn't have been positive. However, I owed it to myself and her to sort my head out before I spoke to her again. If I tried to do it tonight, it would just end in bemusement and tears.

I'd had enough tears for one day, so I wanted to avoid that at all costs.

I'd tried to watch TV, but my mind just kept drifting. I'd been ignoring my phone and the internet at all costs, although I had texted Jake to check the show had been replaced, and he'd assured me it had.

I lay back down on my king-sized bed and covered my face with my hand. I hoped the channel would survive, that this wouldn't cause it too much harm. And like Jake had said, it might even give it the boost it needed. Wouldn't that be ironic?

I was still in two minds about carrying on with the show, as it would forever involve Jake. It was like we'd got divorced, but the show was our child, forever tethering us both together. Did I care enough not to give him full custody and wipe my hands of it? If it was down to me, I'd be tempted to walk away. But it wasn't just down to me; this involved Rachel, too.

And where Rachel was concerned, I was treading carefully. I still had no idea how we — if there still was a *we* — would fare in the end.

Chapter Twenty-Seven

To stop me wallowing, the following week I hunkered down in my parents' spare room and painted, throwing myself into creativity. It'd always been there as a way out of my issues before, and I enjoyed the methodical nature of it — coming up with an image, laying the foundations, then layering over and over. It was helping me work out my feelings, too, which was my initial goal.

My mum had given up trying to talk to me, and was now tip-toeing around me, waiting for me to come to her. I knew it was taking a supreme effort on her part, and I appreciated it. I was still avoiding the internet and my phone, still trying to grapple with how I felt.

Only on Wednesday did I feel I was getting it kinda straight in my head. So to speak.

I was 95 per cent sure I wanted it all: Rachel, the channel, Jake's friendship, all of it.

I'd only been without it all for a few days, but already the ache of its absence was a part of me.

Getting a call from my boss to tell me not to worry also helped. He'd made light of the show, telling me the kids would be nothing but impressed, also letting me know that he didn't care a jot. "Last time I checked, it wasn't a crime to kiss a woman."

I'd smiled at that. He had a point.

The only crime I'd committed was a crime of the heart.

On Thursday, I walked to Trafalgar Square, watching the tourists feed the pigeons. I spent the afternoon in the National Gallery and the Portrait Gallery, breathing in the art, hoping it could refresh my spirit.

Did these artists suffer personal setbacks, but still paint on, literally and metaphorically? I was sure they had. The question was, could I? I hoped so, and I felt I was getting stronger by the day.

After the galleries, I had lunch at the top floor of John Lewis, eating scones with jam and cream while staring out over the rooftops of London, a patchwork of black, grey and glass under clear blue skies. Then I fought my way through the shoppers on Oxford Street, past the stands selling sweet-smelling biscuits, via Marylebone High Street with its boutiques and posh restaurants, ending up at Regent's Park. Once there, I walked to the lake, then stared up at Primrose Hill in the distance, wobbling side to side in the afternoon heat.

Standing on top of that hill with Rachel, kissing her lips, and experiencing our electricity for the very first time seemed like such a long time ago, another life. But it had happened.

I could still feel the imprint of her lips on mine as I

touched my fingers to my lips. My spine tingled as I had total recall of kissing her, of staring down at where I was standing, thinking this was now the London of us.

Every fibre of my being hoped there was still an us. Otherwise, there couldn't be a London of us, could there? Something tugged in my stomach as my thoughts rolled through me. If there was to be a London of us, it was up to me to make it happen.

I strolled past the kidney-shaped boating lake, full of screaming kids and loose oars; dodged a barrage of Canadian geese roaming the paths like baseball-bat wielding thugs; and was just nearing the stone-pillared entrance nearest to Baker Street tube when I heard my name being called out.

I turned — and that's when I saw Meg waving at me.

I couldn't help but smile. Meg was Tanya's ex, and hands-down the ex I'd loved the most. Throughout their relationship, I'd always loved hanging out with her, and I was beyond glad she and Tanya were friends again, which meant I could stop and say hello at times like this.

She was sitting alone, sandwich in hand, her giant belly prominent in front of her. She was also patting the bench beside her.

I couldn't say no to a pregnant woman, could I?

"What are you doing here?" My black bag banged on the bench as I sat down.

Meg gave me an awkward, I'm-a-bit-too-pregnant-for-this-but-I'm-still-going-to-do-it hug. "Don't you start, like pregnant women can't move around," she said, rolling her eyes. "I'm meeting Jamie in a bit to see some houses he's interested in. Mum's barred me from the shop and I'm going bonkers at home, so I convinced Jamie to take pity on me and take me out."

Jamie was Meg's brother and also a property developer.

"And what does Kate think about you running around the city when you're due in a week?"

Kate was Meg's wife and I already knew the answer.

She shook her head, her blonde hair super-styled, her skin glowing. And even though she was so pregnant, it didn't stop Meg having that easy-going demeanour that had so drawn me to her when we'd first met. I wondered now if I hadn't had a slight crush on her back then. Thinking about it, I probably had.

"You know, people are beginning to treat me like I have some rare disease rather than being in the latter stages of pregnancy," she said. "I know my own mind, and if I go into labour, I'll get to a hospital." She paused. "Anyway, let's not talk about me or the baby, because it's all anyone talks about. Let's talk about you and what's going on in your life. How's Jake?"

My face dropped. "You are out of touch with my life, aren't you?"

Meg sat up at that. "Am I?" She gave me a quizzical look. "That sounds ominous, so fill me in."

I did just that. And with every passing sentence, Meg's expression grew a little more boggled, until I brought her up to the weekend that had just gone, and how I'd slept with Rachel, and now I was a YouTube kissing star.

When she heard that, she leaned across and squeezed my knee. "Alice, you dark horse. There was me thinking Tanya's jokes about you being gay were ridiculous, and it was true all along!"

I smiled. "I've already told Tanya this is her fault."

"Let me guess, she's happy to take the blame?"

"She was, until I bolted, so now she's caught in the middle. Rachel is Sophie's best friend, you see."

"Ah," Meg said.

"Yes, ah. So Tanya wants to help me but she also doesn't want me to hurt Rachel, and it's not what I want to do, either. But even today, I was wondering who was watching me or taking photos of me." I glanced around the park. "I mean, somebody could be taking pictures of us and posting them in the YouTube comments right now."

Meg smiled. "Imagine that — one day you're captured kissing Rachel, the next, you're with some other woman who's knocked up."

I grimaced. "The comments would be off the chart."

"I dread to think," Meg replied. "But this is a big thing — you dumping Jake for a woman. I imagine you're all over the place, especially with everything that's happened since."

I nodded. "You're not wrong."

She rubbed her stomach, frowning.

"You're not about to go into labour, are you?" I could cope, but I'd rather not.

She shook her head. "No, but the baby keeps kicking and he or she is so big now, it's getting a bit uncomfortable." She grimaced. "Anyway, back to you." She stared at me. "So why did you run away?"

I sighed. "It's just, this is not easy. One minute I'm straight, the next I've got all these feelings swarming around me, then when I act on them, it's suddenly all over the internet and *very* public. That's what's got me. It's so huge anyway, I don't need an audience. It seems a little unfair."

Meg regarded me for a few moments. "But your relationship with Jake was part of the channel, and you were okay having an audience for that."

"But that was different because we'd been together for a while, we were established. And I wasn't likely to get caught on camera snogging Jake because, well... We were far beyond the stage of snogging like that." I paused. "Come to think of it, I don't think we *ever* snogged like that."

Meg raised an eyebrow. "And maybe that's the point." She sipped her coffee. "Are you running from this because of its power, or because everyone's seen you? Are you scared of the power of this love — or whatever it is — or what people are going to think of you kissing a woman?" She wriggled again, trying to get comfortable.

Was I scared? Hell, yes. I was terrified. "I'm not ashamed, if that's what you're asking. I just wanted this to be us for a while — at least 24 hours. Not much to ask. But now it's out there — and I mean *really* out there —

and I don't want to do this in public. I need some time to get used to it, to me, to the two of us."

Emotion bubbled up inside me and I knew my eyes were brimming with tears. I gulped, swallowing down my feelings, closing my eyes.

When I opened them, Meg was struggling to her feet, putting her arms around me, her bump hitting me in the nose. The absurdity of the situation released some of my tension and I laughed, Meg's baby crushing my face.

"Oh Alice, you're going to be fine. If nothing else, you've got a massive lesbian network to fall back on. We've all been through this, only perhaps not in exactly the same way." She squeezed my cheek with her thumb and index finger, before sitting down again with a small groan.

"But things will die down. People are excited to see the start of something that looks so good — and you both do look *so good* on screen — amazing chemistry and now I know why."

I felt my cheeks colour. Amazing chemistry on-screen and off.

"Doesn't the fact we're online and two women mean it's less likely to die down, though?" I sniffed, fishing a tissue out of my bag to blow my nose.

She smiled at that. "It ups the ante, but soon you'll just be another couple, blending into the background. So don't worry about the unwanted attention, that will go away. The real point is, how does she make you feel?

I mean, the whole hoopla has kinda overshadowed the fact you met someone and you've fallen for them. Hard."

I nodded. It really had. "I have fallen for her. And sleeping with her was incredible. I don't have the words to describe how amazing it was."

Meg reached over and squeezed my hand. "If you could just see your face when you said that — it was like the sun had come out. You need to focus on that." She paused. "I remember my first time and how I felt afterwards. Changed." She paused. "I'm guessing it was the same for you?"

A wave of bliss ran through me when I thought about Rachel and I in bed. "It was life-changing and I told her that. I've never had sex like it before, ever." And then I felt ridiculous, telling another lesbian that. Because, they all knew, didn't they? It was like they'd been hiding this huge secret the whole time, and the only way you were going to know about it was to try it yourself.

"Yeah, I get that," Meg said. "Try having it when you're pregnant."

I raised an eyebrow at that. "One step at a time."

She laughed. "I wasn't talking about you," she said. "Pregnancy is making me so horny lately, and Kate's being the perfect wife. The only thing is, lately, every time I come, I kinda think the baby's going to pop out, too."

I let out a yelp of laughter; I hadn't done that in a few days. It felt good. "Now there's an image."

Meg grinned, taking my hand. "It's so good to see you, you know that?"

I smiled at her. "You, too. We should do it more often, now we're allowed."

"We should!" Meg said. "Tell me, is Rachel as lovely as she seems on-screen?"

"She's all that and more."

"So don't run away because you think you can't cope or you think this isn't for you. I can already see from your face that you're smitten, so you owe it to yourself and Rachel to give it a chance at least. Then if she's not the person for you, at least you tried."

"But what if I'm not a good enough lesbian? What if I'm not even a lesbian at all? Will you still talk to me?"

Meg furrowed her brow. "Now you're just being silly — there's no such thing as a 'good enough' lesbian. We were friends when you were straight, weren't we?"

I nodded.

"Even when you were going out with that terrible bloke — what was his name?"

"Ian."

Meg shuddered. "Yes, Ian the mansplainer."

I laughed. "Going out is stretching it. We had a few dates."

"It was long enough, believe me. The point is — we love you for you, Alice, not who you're sleeping with. You have good taste generally — Jake was lovely, Zach was lovely, and I'm sure Rachel is, too. Stop worrying about what other people think and do this for you. And most of all, stop trying to find excuses. It's your life, and you're the only one who's living it. Do you want to see Rachel again?"

Warmth flooded my body, and I nodded. "Of course I do, but it doesn't stop what's happened, or me coming to it with so much baggage. She might not want to take on all my uncertainty, and I wouldn't blame her."

Meg reached over and put a hand on my knee, her eyes full of kindness. "Frankly, fuck the baggage — you're a strong woman, you can deal with it and I'm sure Rachel can, too." She held my gaze.

"But also, if you find the right woman — more to the point, the right *person* — the whole package is amazing. I've got it with Kate — she's gorgeous, kind, cooks a mean spag bol and she's a great lover. Plus, she puts up with my pregnancy mood swings like a champ. You don't know that with Rachel yet, but she could be your one. Yes, you're in the public eye, but you don't have to live-stream everything you do. You can have time just the two of you, and that's what matters."

I looked at her. "You think I'm strong enough to cope? Even though I'm a bag of nerves and scared shitless?"

"You're plenty strong enough," Meg replied. "And if you're feeling scared and unprepared, that's good. That's what happens with all the best things in life: having kids, buying a house, starting a new relationship." She patted her belly. "I've got a new person coming into my life very soon — and he or she is never going to leave. You think I'm not scared?"

I hadn't thought about that. "Are you?"

"Scared out of my tree. But I'm also *so* excited to finally meet this little person. Aren't you excited you might have met someone who could be so important in your life?"

I nodded. "I really am. I've never felt like this before, ever."

Meg shook her head, smiling. "I'd say that's all you need to know."

Chapter Twenty-Eight

I hadn't been back to Woolwich since the video had emerged a week earlier, but it seemed so much longer than a week — it seemed like an eternity.

This morning, the bankside had the familiar Thames smell that clung to your nose, and its tendrils embraced me as I approached Tanya and Rachel's block of flats, my heart thumping that little bit harder in my chest. Just being this close to Rachel sent jitters pulsing through me like electrolytes.

The weather was turning slowly from summer to autumn, with the wind possessing milk teeth — enough that I'd worn a scarf. I rubbed my eye as some dirt swirled up from the pavement and lodged itself there: it was always windier by the river, that was just the law.

Tanya had called me last night, telling me she'd spoken to Meg, and she wanted to see me before the shoot.

So here I was, at 10am sharp.

"The wanderer returns."

I turned to see Tanya walking up behind me, dressed in jeans and a green sweatshirt, Delilah scuttling at her feet.

Delilah jumped at my leg and gave me a bark, and I petted her. Her brown and black coat shone in the morning demi-sunshine.

I was here for the shoot today, coming to meet Rachel and Jake again finally, after last weekend. I knew Rachel had seen Jake, smoothed things out, but I had all that to come. To say I was nervous was an understatement.

"So how are you? Still feeling at least 50 per cent lesbian? Because I've heard it fades if you don't use it, so that's just a warning."

A smile invaded my cheeks. "Don't start."

"Somebody has to. But it's good to see you're out of hiding and ready to face the world. I know Jake and particularly Rachel will be thrilled to see you." She paused. "According to Sophie, Rachel has been 100 per cent miserable all week, even while sleeping."

I kicked a stone and watched as it crashed into the river wall, before giving her a sad smile. "That makes two of us."

"If you hadn't shown up today, Sophie and I had plans to drag Rachel round to yours and bang your heads together."

"Thoughtful." I plunged my hands into my jeans' pockets. I knew now I should have stayed last week, should have talked it over with Rachel. Instead, I'd run like Cinderella hearing the chimes of midnight.

"I wanted to see you before you saw Rachel, to fill you in."

My heart stuttered. Fill me in? "Go on."

"I spoke to Meg yesterday and she told me what you'd told her. That you're feeling more sorted, that you want to move on, that you're ready to do this."

I held her gaze, nodding again.

"Were you planning on letting Rachel know anytime soon?"

Rachel. Even her name made me nervous. "Rachel?"

"Dark hair, piercing blue eyes. You slept with her recently."

I gave her a look.

"It's just... I'm going out with her flatmate, and from what I hear she's not doing too well."

A punch to my heart. "Is she okay? What's wrong?"

"*You're* what's wrong, Alice. Rachel thinks you've changed your mind, that you tried it, but it wasn't for you." She paused. "I told Sophie to tell her that's not it at all, that you were just gathering yourself, but *you* need to let her know, too."

"She thinks I'm not interested?" Was she crazy? Nothing could be further from the truth.

"Can you blame her? You left on Sunday and she's barely had a text from you since. It's been *six days*. Six days is a long time to sit and stew, even if you work the crazy shifts she does. It's a lot of overcooked lamb cutlets, from what Sophie tells me."

I took a huge gulp of air to steady myself as panic slid through me. I hoped Rachel would hear me out when we spoke today.

"Of course I'm interested, I just thought it was only fair to sort myself out first. What use am I to her if I'm still a blubbering mess? But I assumed she'd know I was coming back, eventually."

A sigh. "Have you told her that?"

Well, no. "I haven't spoken to her."

Tanya pulled on Delilah's lead as she was straining on it, barking at another dog walking by. "Well today's your lucky day, because today you can. Promise me you will? Get this show on the road again, full steam ahead? No pussy-footing around? I hate being a go-between, so think of me, if nobody else?"

I nodded my head at double-speed. I wanted to sprint to Rachel now, to tell her everything. "No pussy-footing, I promise."

"Because the sooner you mend things with her, the sooner we can have your coming-out barbecue."

I cocked my head at Tanya. "My what now?"

"Your coming-out barbecue, remember? When you first told me about Rachel, we agreed we would."

"That was before my coming out was the topic of such public discussion."

"You say po-tay-to, I say po-tar-to. I still think we should have it and invite all the gays. We'll have rainbow burgers and unicorn cocktails, it'll be great."

I made a face. "Can you let me talk to Rachel first? Let me see if she still wants me?"

She shrugged. "Okay, I'll let you do that." She glanced

over her shoulder. "In fact, I'll let you do it right now, it turns out."

I swivelled to see Rachel walking towards me, her arm linked with Sophie's.

My breath caught in my throat. We'd been set up, ambushed.

But I didn't really mind, even though I still wasn't quite prepared. Then again, I don't think you're ever prepared to take the first step in the next phase of your life, are you? Sometimes, you just have to take a leap of faith. Feel the fear and do it anyway, as Meg told me.

Tanya leaned into my ear, whispering: "Now play nicely and get this love story back on the road. I demand it, and your YouTube fans most definitely demand it."

She gave my arm a squeeze as Rachel got within ten feet of me.

I didn't even have time to give her a suitable rebuke, as all my powers were focused on Rachel, on how she looked, on how she was making me feel. All my thoughts and feelings, everything I wanted to say to her suddenly raced to the front of my brain, and I was overwhelmed.

Now she was right here, I wanted to tell her *everything*.

I love the way your right eyebrow arches one way.

I love the way your cheek twitches when you're nervous, like now.

I'm sorry.

I'm scared I'm not good enough for you.

I want you.

You're the most beautiful woman I've ever seen.

To make things better, I had to start *somewhere*.

I took a deep breath. "It's so good to see you." And it was. Even standing here awkwardly with Rachel was better than being anywhere away from her.

"You, too," she said, putting out an arm — whether to steady herself or me, I wasn't sure. "You look incredible."

My eyes took in her strength, her beauty, *her*. "So do you."

She was wearing black jeans and a white T-shirt, but she could have been wearing a bin liner for all I cared. So long as she was inside the wrapping, that was all that mattered. Her body, her mind, her everything.

I glanced behind me, and saw Tanya and Sophie walking off arm in arm, giving us both a wave as they left.

When I turned back, Rachel gave me a half-smile. "Did you know we were being set up?"

"I had a feeling."

"I'm kinda glad, though."

"Me, too." A wave of warmth washed through me as I stared at her.

She indicated the bench on the edge of the path. Tanya's bench. "You want to sit?"

We walked over, my nerves jangling like wire coat hangers.

"So how have you been?"

She laughed. "Terrible. I've been channelling my energy into working and then doing a lot of yoga. Sophie keeps moaning about the mat always being out, but what's the point in putting it away? I need to focus on something."

"Did you tell her it was my fault?"

She nodded. "I did."

We paused. There was so much to say, and this seemed almost too public an environment to say it.

And as well as words, I was desperate to touch her, to feel her. To make sure that everything I'd been thinking all week was true.

That her touch was the one I craved most in the whole, wide world. I put out a hand, running my fingers over her knuckle. She stilled on contact, as did I, a rocket of emotion shooting up my body.

Yes, it was still there.

She licked her lips, and my eyes followed.

"You're staying for the shoot?"

I nodded. "Tanya persuaded me, and I figured I had to face my fears. You, Jake, the camera, do it all in one go. Tear off the plaster, quick and dirty."

Once that was done, maybe I could move forward.

"Am I such a fear?" she asked, furrowing her brow.

When I inhaled, I shook. "Yes, because you mean so much." I exhaled. "This, us, all of it."

She put her hand on my arm. "I know." A pause. "I've spoken to Jake, and he wants you to come, too, in case you were worried," she added. "We've been chatting, and we're on board with the channel, whatever else happens."

Those last three words reached in and wrapped their fingers around my heart.

Whatever else happens.

I knew exactly what else I wanted to happen, and she was staring me in the face.

"And by the way, the advertisers have doubled their commitment to us, and I've had a number of enquiries this week," Rachel added. "I just haven't got back to them all as I haven't been in the place to process them. Plus, I've been flat out at work, too."

Guilt lathered itself into my skin. She hadn't felt up to it because of me. I had a lot of work to do to make it up to Rachel.

I quirked an eyebrow. "Let me get this straight — advertisers saw us kiss and are now tripping over themselves to throw money at us?"

"I like to think it's because the channel is truly taking off and because of the quality content we're putting on the internet," Rachel replied, not missing a beat.

"Perhaps it wasn't the worst thing in the world, huh?"

"Not for the channel, no."

She stared at me then, and the world stopped briefly.

I dropped my eyes to her lips, then back up to her.

"I'm sorry." I knew those words weren't enough, but it was a start. A line in the sand from which to jump forward and sort our lives out. "For all of it."

She cocked her head. "For kissing me?"

I smiled. "Not that bit, even if it was caught on camera. That bit is the one part I'll never regret."

"You're talking like it's not going to happen again." She sucked in a breath, her face pale.

I shook my head and took her hand. "On the contrary, that's all I've been hoping will happen again. I mean, not all, but it's a start, right?"

She nodded, but I could still see the uncertainty in her half-smile, in the trepidation of her stare.

I wanted Rachel to beam at me again, full blast, no brakes on, but I knew that might take a little while.

"I missed you so much this week. Throughout it all, even when I was waist-high in doubt and indecision, you were the constant ache. A delicious, constant ache. A Rachel-shaped hole in my life."

She drew in a breath. "Tell me about the doubt."

I shivered, the hairs on my arms standing up. I pulled my cardigan around me and gathered my thoughts. "It was never about you, or us." My muscles tightened even more. "It was more about me. About shaking up my future, my life."

"Like you told Jake."

I nodded, screwing up my face. "And I know that might have sounded like I was doubting you and us, but I wasn't. This is just big, for me."

"For me, too."

"I know that now." I took her hand, squeezing it tight. A montage of the kissing video played in my head, along with me running away, not facing up to it. "And I hope you'll give me a chance to truly explain."

She stared at me.

"I just want you to know, this isn't a phase. You're not a phase. I want this, and I want us. And I'm sorry it took me so long to realise."

Her whole body shivered and I could see her eyes glistening. She shook her head, checking her phone. "We can't do this now — we've got a shoot in half an hour and make-up to apply."

"I know," I replied. "Plus, we can't have panda eyes for the camera."

She laughed, wiping the bottom of one eye. "Agreed."

I was glad I'd said something at least, but there was much more to come.

"But as soon as we're both free?"

She nodded. "It's going to be Monday. I'm working today and tomorrow."

My turn to wince. Now I'd seen her again, that seemed a lifetime. However, I'd waited a lifetime for her, so I'd survive two more days. "Monday it is."

I stared at her lips, then shook myself. I couldn't get into this now. I sat up straight, moved my head left, then right, and put on my game face.

"How do you think we should play this? Seeing as it's our first shoot together since the last, infamous one."

She exhaled, then sat back, considering my question. "Casual." A firm nod. "Like it was nothing. Which it would have been, were we not two women, that's the annoying part."

"The internet is a feral place. But you know what? This time around, it really wasn't so bad. There were a few comments you'd expect, but most people were happy for us."

"Even Jake seems to have got over it pretty quickly," she said, shaking her head. "Maybe he got laid, too."

I grinned. "That might explain it." I paused. "Or maybe our showdown the other week gave him closure, who knows?" I rolled my shoulders. "How about I make a small mention of last week at the end, but other than that, let's just do a normal cooking show. It's really no big deal, and let's just play on that, okay?"

"Did you see we got a mention on the Huffington Post?"

I nodded. "I did — crazy."

"And some PR got in touch to pitch the show to Ellen. Are you up for going on and telling your story to millions of people around the globe?"

I wasn't at all, but if it meant smoothing the path for getting back together with Rachel, I guessed I was going to have to be. Like she said, we were public property now. I shivered before I spoke. "Sounds like I'm having the biggest coming out party in the entire world."

"At least Ellen will be able to sympathise."

I raised both eyebrows. "I guess she will."

I followed Rachel's slim fingers as she scratched the top of her nose: I so wanted to take them in mine, to kiss them one by one, to feel them on my skin, inside me.

A part of Rachel was inside me now, and I couldn't avoid it anymore.

She stared at me, and a million emotions tumbled through me.

Away from her, I could think rationally. But once the proximity was narrowed, rationality vanished. My heart was pulling me in the direction of her, and I was powerless to stop it.

"I missed you so much this week," she said, moving into my space, her lips inches from mine.

"I missed you, too. More than I ever thought possible to miss anyone."

Did her moving this close mean she was willing to give us another try? I hoped so, because I couldn't let her go again.

Not now, when I knew that everything I truly wanted was within my reach.

I stared at her, my heart clattering in my chest. And then I did what was the only thing to do. The thing I definitely couldn't wait till Monday for.

I moved forward and pressed my lips to hers, and as soon as I did, the world righted itself. The touch of her soft, sure lips was all I needed for now. We'd get to everything else in time, but this was step one. This wasn't a kiss of passion, more of reconnection, of saying everything was going to be alright.

And I desperately hoped that was true.

When we pulled apart seconds later, I let out a whimper.

I opened my eyes, and her face was still close, her eyes smiling at me, her pupils dark.

"We should go," she whispered.

I nodded, kissing her lips one more time.

There was so much more to say, but hopefully, we had time to do it.

Chapter Twenty-Nine

We went for a coffee after the shoot and talked things out between the three of us, agreeing that the channel came first, whatever was happening in our personal lives. I apologised to Jake, he apologised to both of us, and we agreed to put it all behind us. It was at times like these I remembered why I'd fallen for him, and knew I was lucky to have him in my life because he was being so good about everything. Probably better than I would have been had the tables been reversed.

Rachel had to leave for work after the coffee, so we rode the tube together back up to Marylebone, talking mundane stuff, arms pressed together. Whenever our eyes met, we both looked away, embarrassed. I wished I could spend the rest of the day together, but it wasn't to be.

When I got home, Mum was waiting at the door.

"Well?" Her eyebrows were knotted together on her forehead.

My shoulders slumped. "It went okay. I mean, we haven't talked yet, but it went fine. We did the show, Jake was really lovely to me and even gave me a hug when we left and told me he wanted me to be happy."

"That boy is an angel, do you know that? He's going to make someone a lovely husband."

"You might have mentioned that once or twice."

"Well, it's true."

She made me a cup of tea in my favourite red mug and we walked through to the balcony. Below, the gardener was trimming some hedges, but the sun was shielded from hitting this particular patch of London, the September clouds covering its brightness.

"And what about Rachel?"

It was a question I'd been asking myself since she'd left.

"Well, we did the show, we made a joke about watching right to the end because you never knew what might happen once the camera stopped rolling."

Mum burst out laughing. "Very droll."

I raised an eyebrow. "You've watched it, haven't you?"

Her cheeks turned fire-engine red. "It just popped up on my iPad, I didn't mean to."

Great. So my mum had watched Rachel and I snogging.

"So now you understand my angst?"

She smiled. "I do, but it's ever so exciting, too. You didn't quite come out, more like you exploded out." She leaned forward and patted my leg. "Barbara gave me that one, I thought it was very good."

I rolled my eyes. A week after it had all happened, and

I could at least do that. If she'd said that to me last week, I'd have jumped down her throat.

"Anyway, we did the show, but then she had to run — she's working tonight."

"Does that mean we should see if we can book a table and run over there?"

"It does not." I shook my head. "This has already involved far too many people as it is, and from here on in, I'd like it to be just me and Rachel."

"Your father and I might already have a booking."

"Do you?" I sat up.

Her eyes sparkled. "No," she said, giving me a wink. She blew on her tea. "So what's the plan of action?"

"We've already agreed we're going to meet up on Monday — she's got the day off, and luckily, I don't start back to school till Wednesday."

Mum sat back, putting down her mug. "And you can wait that long? Sit through today and tomorrow, knowing she's just over there?"

She had a point. "Not really, but what choice do I have?"

"You could meet her after work, bring her back here and she could spend the night? This is your place as much as ours, and I want you to feel that way while you're living here."

"Including bringing back a possible girlfriend?"

"I'd be honoured," Mum said. And the look on her face told me she wasn't joking.

Could I bring Rachel back here? Would she even want to come back with me?

"You might have a point in going to meet her. I'll consider bringing her back here."

She perked up at that. "I promise to be on my best behaviour, and to cook you an outrageously delicious breakfast in the morning."

I grinned. "You make a convincing argument, you know that?"

Chapter Thirty

I decided to listen to my mum. So around midnight I strolled over to Red On Black and hung around its staff entrance, looking for all the world like one of the dodgiest people in the area: hanging around back alleys at midnight had that affect.

The ground beside me was covered in fag butts where the staff had been smoking, and a faint odour of stale urine curled into my airwaves. It wasn't somewhere you wanted to stay very long, but if it was the alley Rachel was going to be stepping out into very soon, I was going nowhere.

The sky in central London was charcoal grey mixed with the orange hue of streetlights, the air interrupted by the occasional car horn and gear change as the Saturday night traffic got people home or to their next destination.

I waited 15 minutes before Rachel appeared, the sole of my Converse flat against the dirty brick wall behind me, the midnight air tickling my skin.

Eventually, the thick white fire door cranked open, making a shrill scraping sound as it was pushed. And there she was, laughing in the doorway with a young man in his 20s who she clearly had a great rapport with because they were very tactile. When she looked up and saw me, she stopped laughing mid-breath and stilled.

If there hadn't been a wall behind me, I might have taken a step backwards. Instead, I clenched my fist, the hairs on my neck standing on end.

Show time.

"Alice," she said, grabbing the young man's attention as she spoke. In the murky light her teeth took on an ultra-violet hue when she gave me a wonky smile, her eyes dark.

"Hi." My shoulders tensed as I offered a tiny wave of my right hand, like that could convey everything I wanted to say to her. It couldn't, but it was all I had in that moment. All the bravado I'd had walking down here evaporated into thin air, leaving just me, exposed all over again. But this time, it was an exposure I was going to lean into, rather than run away from.

I owed that to myself and to Rachel.

The young man left and then it was just the two of us.

A black cab trundled by on the road beside us, its bright orange light glaring in the darkness. As its tail lights receded, I pushed myself off the wall, giving Rachel a tight smile.

"So, I couldn't wait till Monday."

She gave me a slow smile in return that made my stomach do somersaults. "I can see." A pause. "And I'm glad." She stepped forward, stopping a few inches short of me. "So what were your plans? You want to go for a drink? I smell like a very intense steak meal, I should warn you, but if you're happy to go out with me smelling like this, I'm more than happy to come with you."

I sniffed the air around her, dared to go closer, then closer still. My heart was pounding in my chest, and my cheeks flared with what might be.

I sniffed her cheek and closed my eyes: she wasn't joking, she really did smell like seared meat, but she also smelled of possibility — which was the word weaving its magic dust through my heart, telling me it had game. I wanted to believe it.

"I was thinking," I began.

But then Rachel was backing me up against the wall, and whatever I might have been thinking flung itself from my mind as I concentrated on the here and now; on the physical pleasure of Rachel pressing into me, her eyes rich with want.

"That's where you keep going wrong, with all the thinking," she said, pressing a thigh in between mine, before she crushed her lips against mine.

I was instantly transported back to that thrilling Saturday, back to Rachel's firm, knowing hands, back to us. Only this time, I didn't have to use my imagination, because Rachel was right here.

Her tongue slid into my mouth with an assured insistence, and I closed my eyes, losing myself in the moment. The hardness of the wall behind me was in stark contrast to my fuzzy emotions.

And just like before, it all felt so... *me*.

So right.

Rachel's lips on mine answered every question I'd ever had about desire, about lust, about something feeling perfect. She was taking my breath away, *again*.

The past week I'd been worrying about trying on this new identity, worrying how it would fit. Would it bunch around my middle? Would it be uncomfortable? It turned out, Rachel's hot lips sliding over mine was the ideal look for me.

Moments later, Rachel pulled back, her gaze on my face, like she never wanted to leave. "So go on, tell me what you were thinking."

I searched my mind for the answer. "That we go back to mine." I was keen to stress *mine* and not bring my parents into it for fear of losing the sale. "I only live five minutes away, and we can have a drink, a chat." I stopped, pressing my mouth onto hers again and sinking into her delicious kiss. "Or we could just bypass that and go straight to bed." We were seconds off mounting each other here.

Rachel pulled back slightly now, the edges of her eyes crinkling as she smiled.

With every second I spent with her, she grew that little bit more beautiful.

"I like option three a lot."

With that, she took my hand and pulled me off the

wall, giving me a sexy smile, before heading towards home.

* * *

When we walked into my parents' flat, Rachel let out a gasp as she took in the high-ceiled hallway and the polished wooden floorboards. "This is like something out of a design magazine," she whispered, as I hung her jacket on the rack. "I can see where you get your artistic streak from."

"I'm not nearly so stylish. My parents outdo me at every turn."

Desire was still beating a drum in my ear.

"You want a drink?" *Or just some hot sex in the hallway?*

She eyed me again, and a pulse of lust swept through me. "Sure."

I pulled her into the kitchen and closed the door firmly, sealing us in and my parents out. I stalked over to the fridge as Rachel leaned on the counter, and I could feel her gaze following my every move.

Prickles of heat broke out all over my body, and I concentrated on keeping my breathing even, steady.

When I turned, Rachel was staring at the block of photos on the wall beside her — my family through the ages, stretching back as far as my great-grandparents on my dad's side.

"Is this your mum and dad?" Rachel was pointing at a photo on the wall.

"Yes, the year before they were married," I replied.

Our eyes met as I placed a bottle of Pinot Grigio on the counter, and I took a deep breath.

"She's gorgeous," Rachel said, licking her lips. "You look a lot like her."

"You think? People normally say I look like my dad." I didn't really care, these were just words filling the space. I didn't care who I looked like or what my heritage was. I only cared about reconnecting with Rachel. Now we'd kissed once, I was only hungry for more.

I drew up beside her and our eyes locked again.

Rachel's shoulders tensed, and then the air in front of me was filled with her and the need for wine left my mind.

We were kissing again before I knew it, she devouring me, and I, her. But this time, it was behind closed doors, with no passers-by and no cameras. This was just Rachel and I, a meeting of mouths, of bodies; a splurge of want, of need.

Her fingers raced under my top, kneading my nipple through my bra, and I strained against her.

I grabbed her arse, cupping it firmly, and she groaned into my mouth.

My tongue slipped inside her and a fire started in my belly, roaring to life at my very core.

When I pulled away, I gazed at her, this woman who'd changed my life completely. Seeing her standing against the hob and oven was such a natural pose for her, her chest rising and falling in quick succession. Knowing I was the cause of that made me smile.

"You know," I began, weaving my hand into the waistband of her trousers, kissing her lips again. She tasted deliciously sweet. "Seeing you up against the stove makes me think of all the fantasies I've had while we've been filming."

Rachel raised one eyebrow. "Tell me more." She pulled me close and kissed me again, and my thoughts swam. Holding onto anything with her nearby — thoughts, feelings, convictions to take things more slowly this time — was getting harder and harder.

"The usual," I said, a smile piercing my cheeks. "I think about sliding my fingers inside you while you're cooking, about taking you from behind over the hob, about lifting you up onto the counter-top, ripping open your top and sucking your pert nipples into my mouth." My insides stirred at my words, and Rachel's eyes grew visibly darker as I spoke.

"And there was me thinking you were a good Catholic girl, with pure thoughts all the time."

I slid my tongue into her mouth and swirled it all around, wanting to taste every part of her, before pulling back, my body shaking.

"Catholic girls are the very worst, you should know that."

I pushed a thigh between her legs, the first time I'd done this to her, taking control.

There was a hitch in her breathing, but her gaze didn't falter. "Do you want to live out your fantasies?" Her voice was scratchy, broken.

"God, yes." Not wasting any time, I slid down Rachel's zip, before cupping her between her legs.

This time she gasped and shifted, her cheeks redder than before.

But I was done talking. I popped three buttons on Rachel's shirt, before reaching inside and roughly moving aside the fabric of her bra, before taking her nipple into my mouth, snagging it with my teeth.

The metal of her rings hitting the counter chimed as she grabbed it, and as my mouth sucked her in, my hand found its way back to her. I shifted aside the material of her pants in one swift move, before my fingers curled into her without ceremony, three at once.

She was so wet, I could have used a whole fist.

Why had nobody ever told me this could feel so good?

Rachel panted in my ear as I began to move in her, slowly at first, her groans low and insistent, timed with my movement. I moved my mouth from her nipple to her mouth, claiming her totally.

In response, Rachel pulled me close and put an arm around my shoulder, willing me into her. Her breath was hot against my ear.

"Oh yes," she said, as my fingers plunged into her, sending shockwaves of desire tumbling down my body, freefalling for all to see. "Fuck me, Alice. Fuck me like you've always wanted to."

At that, I grabbed her arse, pulled her close and shrugged off any limits I'd ever put on myself. Today, I was being me, living the way that I wanted to. And all of that involved giving Rachel what she wanted, being there for her, pleasing her, loving her.

With that thought ringing in my ear, I eased out of her, then back in, out, then back in. I picked up speed, I hit her sweet spot, I rocked, I rolled.

As I did, Rachel's head fell back, and I saw redness pooling on her neck and chest as her inside walls began to tighten around my fingers, pulsing hot to my touch.

She'd never looked so incredibly beautiful, so elegant, so perfect, so *mine*.

And that thought swept me up again as I rained kisses down on her neck and ears, until she eventually twisted, turned and shook in my arms, burying her head in my neck and gasping into my ear as she came pressed up against the hob, my fingers deep inside her, just the way I'd imagined.

* * *

I'd got carried away, but I wasn't sorry — and Rachel didn't look too worried either, her gaze soft as I led her to my room.

She smiled when she entered, before stripping off and doing the same to me, before we both toppled onto the king-sized bed, its mass of six plump pillows leaning against a white padded headboard

We both took a moment to catch our breaths, my fingers trailing down Rachel's strong, toned arms and over her pale skin, the softness still so new.

"What's the matter?" She opened an eye when I moved.

"Nothing, I'm just marvelling at your body, so be quiet."

A light chuckle. "Yes, ma'am," she replied. "Does it pass inspection?"

I lay back down next to her, both of us still on top of my white duvet, staring into her crystal blue depths.

"You'd pass any inspection you went for, you're a work of art," I told her, kissing the tips of her fingers. My body ached for her in such a huge way, and yet, I was in no rush.

In the kitchen, we'd been laser-focused, getting to the heart of the matter in seconds. I wondered how long it would take before we stopped ripping each other's clothes off the very first chance we got — not that I was complaining.

But now, after that frenetic pace, I wanted to slow things down, just like we had last week. Because as much as I loved the jive, I also enjoyed to slow dance, too.

Rachel smiled at me, tracing a finger along my lips, pulling my body to hers before her lips claimed me again.

I surrendered to her touch.

"I'm so glad you showed up tonight," she said, between kisses. "I'd have been miserable waiting till Monday."

A heady charge of electricity tumbled through me as Rachel's fingers roamed my butt, sweeping themselves up and between my legs, making my heart tick faster still.

"And if you were in any doubt, your playing hard-to-get totally worked," she added. "You're all I've been able to think about all week."

I wrinkled my brow at that, and Rachel immediately smoothed it out with her fingers.

"Want me to show you how much I missed you?"

Her tone and her stare penetrated me, and all my thoughts of taking this slower vanished, replaced by a surge between my legs. Whatever she wanted to give me, I was ready to take.

She took my face in her hands and trailed her tongue along my bottom lip, then along my top. "That's what I want to do to your pussy right now."

My neck tensed, and a shiver of want arrowed down my body.

I wanted her to do that, too.

So. Very. Much.

Rachel plunged her tongue into me again, then used it to tease my nipples, still miles from where I wanted her most. When she'd kissed her way from my eyelids to my navel, then all the way back up, she stared down at me, then rolled onto her back, patting her chest.

"I want you to sit here," she said, patting it some more.

I furrowed my brow. "On your chest?"

"Uh-huh." She gazed at me. "Trust me."

And I did, implicitly.

I swung a leg up and over her, and then foundered.

Rachel grinned, guiding my knees to either side of her neck, before grinning up at me, as reality dawned on me.

I was kneeling, legs spread, in front of my lover, her mouth right in front of my pussy.

Rachel wasted no time pressing home her point, and when her tongue slid through my folds, I let out a guttural moan.

I wasn't an amateur at sex, or so I'd thought. I might not swing from chandeliers, but I was no prude. However, sleeping with a woman was making me rethink everything I'd ever thought about the rules of the game — and far beyond.

As Rachel eased my thighs apart and swirled her tongue around me and into me, one thing was for sure: it wasn't just sex, either.

Rachel's tongue inside me didn't just show she knew what would turn me on and make me shake with lust; her skill also showed such an understanding of who I was and what I wanted. She didn't need guidance, because she just *knew*.

And that was something I hadn't even considered before: sleeping with a woman was stripping away my layers, it was so raw.

I was losing my inhibitions fast, grinding to Rachel's groove, every sensation overwhelming. It was as if my brain just processed one, then another, until it felt like it might short-circuit. But if I was about to blow up, I couldn't think of a sweeter way to go.

I threw my head forward, not sure which way to move my pelvis as I felt the slick stroke of her tongue against sensitive skin.

I didn't believe in magic, but for a moment, I saw stars.

And then my orgasm sprang from my very core and rumbled up my body, pouncing on every sense I had, shaking me awake.

Was I ready to be the new me, to do this for real now?

As Rachel's tongue tore down my walls and shredded every nerve ending I ever had, the answer was a resounding yes.

Yes to her. Yes to me. Yes to this new life, wherever it may take me. Yes!

And that's just what I screamed out as I finally came in a great wave of emotion, flashes lighting up my core as Rachel didn't let up one bit, squeezing my arse as her tongue spun me out of control and I fell forward, sending more shockwaves through me again and again and again.

It was relentless, she was relentless, and in that moment, she was all I'd ever wanted.

Chapter Thirty-One

I woke in the morning to the sound of my dad whistling Simon & Garfunkel down the hallway. Even though I knew he wasn't about to burst in, I pulled the covers over both of us.

Rachel cracked open an eye and narrowed it, before burrowing her head into my chest.

"Is your dad Paul Simon?" she said, after the whistling had subsided — he'd clearly disappeared into the kitchen.

"If Paul Simon's an old-school Italian who got lost on the way back to Italy, then yes."

She grinned at that. "Maybe he's been keeping it under wraps all these years." Pause. "He's not called Al, is he?"

I let out a bark of laughter. "He is not."

She kissed my lips as I laughed, then my right breast, then my left, before sitting up, letting her eyes roam the room as if for the first time. Which, seeing as we'd pitched up in the early hours and hadn't taken much notice of our surroundings, it probably was.

I followed her gaze around the room: the dark charcoal

walls, the bright white skirting, the bare wooden floors, the massive windows stylishly draped in black velvet.

"What did you say your parents did again?"

I smiled. "Architect and designer."

"You can tell — this room is beautiful."

I smiled some more. "I know. It's not most people's parents' spare room, is it?"

She shook her head. "Er, no. I feel like I should have noticed last night."

"You might have been a little preoccupied, what with me having just fucked you in the kitchen." I grinned at the memory, still fresh in my mind.

Rachel glanced down at me, bringing her head down for a kiss before laying next to me. "You've got a point."

I reached out to tuck a stray hair behind Rachel's ear.

"But anyway, enough about decoration — let's talk about us. How are you feeling after kidnapping me and having your wicked way with me last night?" Rachel's eyes were teasing, a smile playing on her mouth.

I grinned right back. "I'm feeling… fantastic. And *very* gay, which is mainly down to you." I cocked my head, before kissing her lips. She tasted of sex and sleep.

"You're not feeling overwhelmed again, like it's all too much?" She pulled herself up on her pillow, her gaze penetrating mine.

I shook my head. "Perhaps that was just last week. Stage fright." A gentle smile. "And while I can't promise there won't be other wobbles, I'm hoping none as bad as last week. My mind's clearer, at the very least."

I kissed her nose, holding her gaze.

"I'm so sorry about last week." I couldn't put it any plainer, and I hoped she could feel my sincerity.

A sadness washed over her face. "Me, too."

"I just," I said, then stopped.

I'd just freaked out was the bare bones of it, a meltdown that had seen my defences stripped, and the only way I knew how to react was to build the wall back up. But I hadn't known then what I knew now — which was that maybe the walls needed to come down, and it was time for my whole life to be rebuilt, from the ground up.

Perhaps this time, the defences would be more sophisticated, smarter, more up to date with the new me. Or perhaps I could be more vulnerable, and perhaps not need them at all.

"I thought I could handle it all, I thought telling people I was seeing you would be a breeze, what with all the lesbians in my life. And you know, weirdly, the whole 'being queer' bit *has* been a breeze. It helps that I'm madly attracted to you, and when we're together, it just feels... right." I let out a long sigh. "If it could just be the two of us all the time, none of this would have happened."

Rachel smiled. "That's not how it works. You can't just be gay behind closed doors. It's not about sex, it's about being yourself, being true to who you really are."

I nodded. "I know that now. And being with you, I

feel the very best version of me I've ever been." I locked her gaze with mine, my heart thumping in my chest. "It's like you've unlocked this part of me that I never knew was there. And it comes out not just when we're having sex, but when I look at you, when I think about you."

Rachel leaned in and kissed me, her eyes watery. "I love that you feel that."

My heart swelled as I stared at her. "In so many ways, you've made this so easy. And in so many ways, this has been the hardest week of my life, too."

"Mine, too," she replied.

My heart lurched at that; I hated that I'd caused her so much pain. I traced my fingers down her cheek, before kissing her lips, then drawing back.

"I can't say sorry enough, but when it all blew up and then *everyone* knew I was suddenly gay — and I mean everyone, in one huge explosion of gay — it was overwhelming." Understatement of the year. "And yes, I know I wasn't very fair on you reacting the way I did, but I hope you can forgive me." I paused, taking Rachel's fingers in mine and intertwining them.

"I can, even though our first week wasn't stellar, with you freaking and running out."

I deserved that, but it still cut deep. "I know, and I promise, I'll try to do better."

Rachel pulled herself up, leaning her head on her bent elbow, regarding me. "I guess that's all I can ask."

Her shoulders relaxed, and so did mine.

"So the whole 'being a lesbian' thing isn't as scary as you thought? You've woken up feeling gay?"

"The first thing I thought about was Ellen, so that's a good start, right?"

Rachel's eyebrows knitted together. "That's a joke, right?"

I grinned. "A little lesbian humour — like I say, when I've been friends with Tanya for two decades, I got skin in the game."

She laughed at that. "Lesbian humour from the newly reformed straight Catholic girl. I've done well, haven't I?"

"I've done even better." I held her gaze as I bent to kiss her, smiling as I rolled onto my back. "So are we good? It feels like we have a lot more stuff to talk about."

She nodded. "So far, you've told me you're sorry, that you're not running off, and you keep kissing me, so it's a positive start." She moved her mouth one way, then the other, and I knew she was preparing to say something big.

"There's a *but* coming, isn't there?" I swallowed preparing myself. Was she going to ask for something I couldn't give? I hoped not.

"But I also need to know that you're all in — not just with me, but with the wider world — however you want to label yourself. I'm out and proud, and I can't be anything else. I've been out far too long. I know the YouTube thing was weird, but are you ready to front-up at college and to your friends?"

Relief swept through me — this, I could give her. "I think after the video, they might already know."

"You know what I mean. You were scared you might lose your job, you were scared to talk to your colleagues, your students. It's all a part of it. It is harder, and it is more out there, but I hope the fact we're together means it's also worth it."

"It does, and I'm going to be stronger."

"Just remember you're not doing this alone, okay? No running off again — if you've got issues, talk to me. Or even Tanya, or Sophie — just don't go running scared."

I knew she was right. "I will, I promise."

Rachel ran a hand through her hair before continuing. "I don't want you to live a small life. I want your life to be rich, to be everything you deserve. Hiding and pretending you're someone you're not doesn't allow you to do that."

There was a low ache in my gut. Everything she was saying was true, and I was ready. In fact, she might not know, but I was already at the helm of my ship, spinning the wheel at a rapid pace. And I was turning this ship around because I was listening to my heart, and not worrying about what I should or shouldn't do, and about what other people thought.

I'd decided that the only people whose thoughts mattered were Rachel and I, and right now, it seemed like we were of one mind, and ready to give this a go.

"I want that, too — so much. And I've already started making changes that you don't even know about. I've spoken to my boss, and you know what? My students all think it's cool I'm on YouTube, and my boss and his wife invited us for dinner."

Rachel let out a howl of laughter. "So you're not losing your job because you kissed me?"

I shook my head. "If anything, my boss was more scared of me leaving to do the channel full-time."

"Wow, I like their big thinking."

I laughed. "Theo has nothing but faith in me, it seems. Unlike me or you."

She put out a hand and turned my face to her. "Not true. I do have faith in you, but you have to have faith in yourself, and I wasn't sure you did. When this happens, some people run and hide their whole life. I was just hoping you weren't one of them. It would have made me very sad."

"It would?"

Her gaze scorched my face as she nodded. "It would." She let out a long sigh. "I know we've only been together a week, but we've known each other longer, haven't we? You're not someone I just met and took to bed — you're someone who's already worked their way into my heart as a good friend, and now as a lover, too. When I thought you might turn away, I was so nervous. I didn't know what I was going to do without you — as a lover or a friend."

"Me either," I replied. "And that's another thing that made me want to hit pause and restart. *You.* You're the one who's been in my heart and my head for months. It feels like we've been leading up to this since we met a year ago. All those restaurant meals were our trainee dates, weren't they?"

Rachel laughed at that, flopping onto her back before turning back to me. "I guess they were. And I loved every minute of those dates, I looked forward to them so much."

"I did, too."

"Can we still go on them?"

"Course," I said. "Only now, they really are dates, with sex at the end."

"I much prefer them now," Rachel said, a sexy grin on her lips.

"I thought you might." I kissed her lips, leaving my face inches from her, losing myself in her rich blue gaze. "The thing is, you're inside my heart now, too, and I can't carry on without you. So I have to be okay with everything that's gone on — the video, us, coming out so publicly. I wasn't sure I was strong enough, but I'm not alone — I've got you and everyone else by my side. And what's the alternative? Life without you. And that, Rachel Cramer, is pretty much unthinkable."

A slow, sure smile spread across her face as she brought her hand to my right cheek, and her lips to mine, electricity sparking all over again. When she pulled back, all sorts of emotions sailed through me, but I couldn't pin one down. Rachel had thrown me into a maelstrom again.

"Unthinkable, huh?"

I nodded. "Completely."

"And life without you is totally unthinkable, too, Alice Di Santo."

Chapter Thirty-Two

Rachel insisted she wasn't nervous, but I didn't buy it.

For one, she was wearing smart trousers and a new pink top. For another, she was unusually quiet.

Rachel took my elbow as I pushed open the giant wooden front door and we walked down the Victorian foyer, our footsteps muffled by the dark red carpet. We'd been together officially for two weeks now, and it was still like all my birthdays had come at once.

"Have you ever thought it might be you who's nervous, and not me? After all, I've met families before, and I'm pretty sure I can charm them. Plus, I know your parents love my cooking, so I have an advantage.

"But you," she said, stopping me as we waited for the antiquated lift to shudder its way down the shaft. "This is a first for you. You've never brought a woman home to meet the family for dinner before, and that's a big thing. Besides, I've met your mum, dad and sister already, so I'm not even that new."

She kissed me again and my blood swayed from side

to side. "Just remember, your family love you and they want what's best for you."

I nodded. "I know."

"When you're worrying, remember they're on your side. I'm a veteran of this shit, okay?" She nudged me with her elbow.

I laughed when she said that. "I sometimes forget, and think it's just me going through this."

"Queer people go through this every day."

We arrived at my parents' front door, and I was just about to insert the key in the lock when the door sprang open. My mum was on the other side, her face full of Chablis splotch.

"Hello you two!" She gave me a hug like she hadn't seen me for years.

Maybe she was nervous, too.

"So great to see you again, Rachel," she added. "You're very welcome." Never one to stand on ceremony, Mum pulled Rachel into a hug, which she accepted with good grace. She'd tried it on Tanya when she'd first met her and she hadn't made that mistake twice. Tanya was better with hugs these days, but when we were at university, they were a foreign language to her.

Mum took our jackets and we followed her through to the lounge where Barbara and Maggie were sitting — I might have known Mum would invite the lesbians en masse — along with my sister Sabrina, Simon and Flavia.

My niece was being entertained by an iPad, and paid us

no attention when we walked in. Unlike the adults who all got up to greet us, giving Rachel a once-over and insisting she take a seat. Simon went to get us wine, and then all eyes were on Rachel, but I knew she could handle it.

"So fabulous to meet such a famous YouTube star!" Barbara was giddier than I'd ever seen her before. Giddy and Barbara were not words I generally put together, being that she was a former business exec and still a stunning woman, even in her 60s. "Maggie and I watch you both in bed every Saturday morning, don't we, Mags?"

Beside me, I heard Sabrina choke on her wine.

Maggie nodded. "And we absolutely loved your pappardelle recipe with the wild boar — it was to die for."

"And the gnocchi," Barbara added. "In fact, we think you're a culinary genius, but don't tell Giuseppe, he might get upset."

Barbara and Maggie were staring at Rachel a little too much, so I turned the conversation around to Sabrina. "How's the build going?"

"Don't ask," she said. "Let's just say, I've asked Mum if we could move in here, but she says not while you're here." She paused. "So any more news on how long you're here? If we have to live in our dust-filled upstairs much longer, there might be a murder."

I gave Sabrina a pained smile. "If you're desperate, I can always move into Tanya's place — but let's talk about it later."

She put a hand on my knee, her eyes wild. "If we could,

you would literally be saving all our lives. Your sister, your brother-in-law and your niece. And you want us all alive, don't you?"

"Flavia, definitely," I replied, as she smacked me in the arm.

Simon returned with glasses of white wine for us in tall-stemmed glasses, sitting down on the sofa next to Barbara and Maggie.

"Giuseppe is having a mini-breakdown in there — I think it's the stress of cooking for Rachel," he said, stroking his goatee. Simon didn't have much hair on his head, but he had an exceptional amount all over his body, including a well-trimmed goatee on his face.

Rachel shook her head, getting up. "He doesn't need to." She turned to me. "Can I offer to help?"

I stood up. "I don't see why not — let me take you through."

I took her hand and led her back out to the hallway, pulling her in for a quick kiss before taking her to the kitchen.

"Everything okay?" My heart was thumping as we neared the black kitchen door.

Rachel smiled and kissed me again. "Just relax, Alice," she said. "The kitchen is my domain. Let me lead the way."

I raised an eyebrow. "You remember the last time you were in there?"

Rachel blushed as I spoke. "I'm trying to block that out of my mind and get into professional mode."

I kissed her again. "Right. I'll let you get on then."

Rachel walked in first, and when I waltzed in after her, I could see my dad was red in the face, with a myriad of pots and baking trays to be tended to. When he looked up and saw us, panic crossed his face.

"Hello Rachel, good to see you again." He wiped his hands on his apron, before sweeping his hair off his face with his forearm. "You've caught me at quite a critical moment."

"I can see," Rachel said, putting her wine glass down. "What can I do to help?"

Dad hesitated for a second, before realising this was an offer he couldn't refuse. "There's a garlic-rosemary sauce that needs whipping up if you really mean it — and a spare apron over there."

Rachel placed the apron over her head and picked up some shallots, and my dad visibly relaxed. "I like this girl already," Dad told me with a smile. "Are you helping, too?"

I shook my head. Helping my dad in the kitchen was way too risky, the whole family knew that. He was very territorial although, apparently not when it came to professional help.

"In that case, get out and let me have a little time, chef to chef."

I threw Rachel a glance, and she just nodded.

"I promise I won't grill her too much," Dad added.

I laughed. "Don't grill him too much either, okay?" I told Rachel.

* * *

Needless to say, my parents fell in love with Rachel — and I didn't blame them. What was not to love? She was a smart, sexy, sassy chef. And tonight I was going home with her, my clothes for tomorrow in my bag.

"You were amazing today." And she had been — she'd dazzled both my parents, as well as improving the sauce my dad served with his lamb, which hadn't changed in years. When I saw the way my dad looked at her when he tasted it, I knew I wasn't the only Di Santo who'd fallen for Rachel's charms.

"They made it pretty easy. Your family were fab, as were Barbara and Maggie. My family are usually the noisy lot, but I think yours could give them a run for their money."

"And that's a good thing?"

Rachel laughed and squeezed my hand. "Definitely a good thing."

We walked along the back street running parallel with the Euston Road, the roar of the traffic muffled by the intervening houses. The yellow glow of the statuesque concrete street lamps lit the way, and across the road, the local chip shop was doing a roaring Sunday night trade.

"Do you think you will move into Tanya's after what your sister said?"

I nodded. "I think so — Tanya's offered and if they need somewhere so they don't kill each other, I can't really say no. Plus, it makes sense as it's closer to you, especially now I'm back at school. I want to see you as much as I can, which is difficult with your crazy hours."

Rachel was quiet for a beat as we stopped at a traffic lights, waiting for the green man. It announced itself with the accompanying beeping sound a few seconds later, and we crossed in silence.

"You know," Rachel began, before stopping outside an off-licence, its display advertising champagne I'd never heard of. "I know this might be a bit soon, but I live alone now. I need a flatmate, but I'd prefer to have you." She chewed on her lip. "What I'm saying is, if you wanted to move in with me, you could." She frowned as she spoke. "If this is too soon, just say no. I don't want to make you feel weird."

I stared at her delicate nose, her soft, sure eyes, her strong cheekbones; the face that had become so precious to me in such a short space of time. And I considered her words, wondering how I should reply.

It was something I'd thought about, of course it was. Sophie had moved out to Tanya's flat a couple of weeks ago, and now Rachel had a spare room. But was it too soon?

Last time something big had come up in our relationship, I'd panicked — it was all too new. But now, I couldn't imagine my life without Rachel, and when I looked to the future, I saw us living together. So why not bring the timeline forward a little?

I leaned in and kissed Rachel's lips, and she smiled in response.

"Do you think it's too soon?"

She shrugged. "I know we've only been together for a short while, but it's not like we just met, is it?"

It certainly wasn't. "Keep talking," I said, staring into her sapphire eyes, currently asking me a question.

"I could promise at least two home-cooked meals a week," Rachel said, kissing me again.

"Cooked in the buff?"

She laughed. "As the allotted health and safety monitor, I'd have to decline."

"You see, that would have sold me." Were we ready? "You think we should do this?"

A customer leaving the off-licence startled me as they opened the door, the shop's bell ringing. I'd forgotten we were standing on a street in central London — I'd been too caught up in our conversation.

She took both my hands in hers and ran her thumbs over my palms. "Damned if I know," she said. "But what I do know is the thought of waking up with you every morning makes me smile."

I stared at her, a smile creeping over my face. "You know, you tell the world you're a cool, laidback chef, but really, you're just a slushy romantic at heart."

Rachel blushed bright red, before casting her gaze to the ground, finally landing on me. "Can we just keep it between us?"

"Your reputation as a Lothario and straight-girl defiler is well documented on YouTube, so I wouldn't worry."

Her face creased up at that. "Straight girl defiler? That does not sound sexy."

I cocked my head. "The act was most definitely better than the words." I wrinkled my brow. "So we're doing this? We're going to move in together?"

Rachel nodded. "Looks like it."

I glanced at the champagne in the display, and a bubble of happiness went pop in my head. This journey started the day I met Rachel over a year ago, and now it was ramping up, just getting started.

We were moving in together. I was going to be living with a woman who was my girlfriend.

Holy fuck.

"You realise Tanya and Sophie are not going to shut up about it, right?" I said.

"Oh, I know, but I can handle them."

"Does this make your block of flats the most lesbian in London?" I asked, kissing her lips.

"I doubt it, but it does make it the block with the best-looking lesbians for sure."

I laughed at that. "Just to be clear, we're above Tanya and Sophie, right?"

Rachel looked at me like I'd gone mad. "Natch," she replied. "And you know the other plus point?"

"Tell me."

"My sister broke up with her girlfriend recently — for reasons I predicted correctly — which means I'm not the single lesbian sister in the family. For the first time ever."

I laughed as we started walking again, threading my arm through Rachel's as we did. "So are we toasting your sister's misfortune, Mystic Rachel?"

"I prefer to see it as celebrating my own. That, and the fact I get to lord it over her for once in my life."

I shook my head. "Glad to be of service," I replied.

Chapter Thirty-Three

"You're so lucky this weather has held, you know that?" I was concentrating on not cutting my fingers while I chopped up this courgette — cut fingers were a major turn-off in lesbian circles, as I was quickly learning.

Tanya shook her head, her new, shorter hair not moving. Ever since I'd known her, Tanya had worn long hair, but not anymore. She'd recently had it cut, and just like everything Tanya tried, it looked incredible on her.

"It's not luck, it's the weather gods smiling on us. The weather god is clearly a woman, and possibly even a lesbian. She knows how important it is for the weather to hold for today and this particular barbecue, because there's so much to celebrate." Tanya counted on her fingers. "My best friend coming out for one," she said, winking at me. "Plus Sophie moving in, you moving in with Rachel, Meg and Kate having their baby. I mean, my cup runneth over with celebration."

"And it's all because of you. I wouldn't have met Rachel without you, and Meg would never have got together with

Kate had you not been such a vile ex-girlfriend, so give yourself a pat on the back."

"Hey!" Sophie said, walking through from the balcony, a barbecue tong in her hand. "Enough slating my gorgeous girlfriend, thank you." She slapped Tanya on the arse before kissing her lips. "Is she giving you grief? Do I need to have a word with our guest?"

Tanya smiled. "It wouldn't help, she's been dissing me for years."

I nodded. "It's true." I finished chopping the courgette into long strips and put them into the bowl Tanya had given me. "What's next? The peppers?"

She nodded. "Yes please, and big chunks."

"I know," I said. "You're such a control freak, you know that?"

Sophie grinned. "And that's why her life runs with military precision, isn't it, sweetheart?"

Tanya brandished the knife she was chopping the onions with, wiping tears from her eyes. "You may mock."

"And we do," Sophie replied, grinning. "Are you impressed with all the baking Tanya's done for today, too?"

I nodded. "Amazed — I never knew she was a baker. Rachel and Jess have some competition."

"I wouldn't go that far," Tanya said.

"I would," Sophie replied. "One thing I know, too — your gran would be so proud of you for carrying on her recipes. Wait till you taste that lemon cake, it's amazing."

I gave Tanya a grin. "Hidden talents."

She rolled her eyes. "I keep seeing my kitchen on YouTube, so I figured I better start using it."

A knock on her front door interrupted us, and Sophie was first to react, looking over her shoulder as she walked to the hallway. "I'd say that's our first guest. Are we ready, kitchen crew?"

Tanya wiped her eyes again as she nodded. "Once I clear these tears, I'm ready," she replied.

* * *

Two hours later and the afternoon was in full swing, the smell of roasted steak mingling with barbecued prawns and roasted peppers. Tanya had made her famous potato salad, and Sophie had rustled up a couple of Nigella salads for good measure. Rachel wasn't here yet — she'd had to go to her parents' to see her aunt who was visiting from the USA — but she was arriving soon, bringing her younger sister Becca with her to meet everyone.

I was sitting on one of Tanya's balcony chairs, with Meg and Kate's two-month-old son Finn on my lap. Even though Meg was her usual perky self, her make-up couldn't hide the bags that had taken up residence under her eyes. It turned out Finn was a night owl, which didn't sit well with his mum, a florist who was used to early mornings. Meg's mum had come out of retirement to run the shop for three months with some part-time help, but Meg was hoping to go back full-time in the not-too-distant future.

"And how was the birth?"

"Don't ask," Kate said, sitting down beside Meg and gazing at her son.

Meg smiled. "I ended up having a caesarean as there were complications, so I'm only just up and about again." She grasped Kate's knee as she spoke. "You're having the next one, aren't you, babe?"

Kate laughed. "Only if Finn starts to sleep soon, otherwise I might be put off."

I stared down at this new life in my hands, currently dribbling and smiling up at me. "Don't listen to them, Finn," I said, kissing his cheek, his new baby smell swamping my senses. "He clearly just has a massive fear of missing out, so he doesn't want to sleep. I don't blame him."

"He gets that from you," Meg said, kissing Kate's hand, before turning back to me. "Anyway, enough about us, this party is to celebrate your coming out I hear — and can I just say, I hope I played a part."

I gave her a grin. "You certainly helped."

"So how are you finding being on Team Queer?"

"Let's just say we've been living together for two weeks and I'm not getting much sleep either, but for different reasons." I felt my cheeks heat up as I recalled the sex Rachel and I had the night before, with my girlfriend showing me just how flexible she was through regular yoga practice. It was impressive, I had to admit.

"I remember those days," Meg said, glancing at Kate. "Do you remember?"

Kate cocked her head, her cropped peroxide blonde

hair not moving. "I don't remember anything before Finn anymore," she said, laughing. But even as she said it, I could see the loving look she was giving her wife.

"So it's going well?" Meg said.

I nodded. "It's going really well. Rachel's awesome and I'm a gibbering wreck. We've been living together for two weeks, so far, so good."

Meg looked over my shoulder and smiled. "Talk of the devil, here's the woman currently putting that smile on your face."

I turned my head and Rachel was standing over me, giving me her special smile, reserved just for me.

"Is this a glimpse of my future?" she asked, kissing the top of my head before making a fuss of Finn.

"You didn't tell me you had a baby as well as getting a new girlfriend," Rachel's sister Becca said, as she bent to kiss me.

"We didn't want to shock you," I replied. "Girlfriend, moving in, baby, in that order."

Becca gave me the same sweet grin I knew from Rachel's face as she laughed. "You're a traditionalist, I like that."

Rachel swept her hand around the balcony, raising her voice as she spoke. "Everyone, this is my sister Becca, who's newly single and looking for a woman, so form an orderly queue."

Becca slapped Rachel on the arm as she laughed. "You are the archetypal embarrassing sister, you know that?" She scowled at Rachel as only sisters could.

"It's a skill I've perfected over the years," Rachel said.

Finn began to cry in my arms, so Kate lifted him up, putting him over her shoulder and patting his back. He quietened down in an instant, while Meg gave me a wide smile.

"She's so brilliant with him," she said, glancing at her wife. "Honestly, I was the one who wanted to have kids, but it's Kate who's the most maternal, which I wasn't expecting."

I was thrilled for Meg — she'd found her one, got married and had a child — she was all-in.

I glanced at Rachel, now chatting with Becca and Sophie over by the barbecue, and a wave of warmth flushed through me. Had I found my one?

"Hey Alice — they bought prawns just for you," Rachel shouted.

I got up and walked over to her. Even though it was October, it was still 20 degrees today, like we were on a balcony in Spain and not south London.

"Have you had one yet?"

I shook my head. "Not yet." I stroked Becca's arm before addressing her. "How are you?"

Becca gave me a grin so reminiscent of her sister, it was uncanny. Rachel's three older sisters all took after her mum, whereas Rachel and Becca had inherited their dad's dark hair colouring and his paper-thin Irish skin. Becca also had crystal blue eyes, just like her sister. Even though she was newly single, I had no doubt some woman would fall for her very soon.

"I'm good, although Rachel sold me this party saying there would be lesbians to meet. She forgot to say they'd all be old and coupled up with children." Becca rolled her eyes, and I had to laugh. She was only 23, after all.

"It's free food, so what are you moaning about?" Rachel said, poking her sister in the ribs. "Plus, you're here to meet Jess and Lucy who are in the kitchen, chatting to Tanya. Becca's going to organise their wedding as a pilot project for her event-planning business — they're her willing guinea pigs. Jess almost kissed me when I suggested it this week."

"I rest my case," Becca said, taking a sip of her beer. "Lesbians getting married and having babies everywhere I look."

"It'll come to you eventually, little sister," Rachel said, putting an arm around me.

Becca shrugged. "Not for a good few years, and anyway, I don't care. I'm off women after my last relationship." She paused. "Or maybe I'll do casual from now on — a hook-up, no emotions and no questions asked."

Rachel snorted. "Good luck with that."

The sound of steel on glass put a stop to our conversation and I turned to see Tanya standing by the balcony doors, tapping a teaspoon on an empty wine bottle. Jess and Lucy squeezed past her and came to stand next to us, Jess giving me a kiss on the cheek.

"Happy coming-out party!" she whispered in my ear, giving me a wink.

"Thanks," I replied.

Tanya tapped the wine bottle again, and the party all swivelled their heads towards her and waited expectantly.

I winced, wondering what she was going to say.

"Before we all get too drunk and eat far too much delicious food — all prepared without Rachel, I might add!"

That got a cheer, to which Rachel rolled her eyes.

"I just wanted to thank you all for coming, and also get you to raise a glass to the main reason I threw this barbecue — my best friend, Alice."

Oh god, here we go. I ducked my head, as Rachel dropped her arm from my shoulder, wanting me to enjoy the moment on my own.

"Alice and I have been friends for years, and in all that time, everyone always thought Alice was the lesbian and I was straight."

Much laughter from the party.

"But not anymore. And no, before you ask, this is not a party to tell you I'm straight—"

"—I hope not!" Sophie shouted.

"—rather, it's a party to celebrate Alice's coming out as not straight. She's not settled on a label yet — am I right?"

I shook my head. "No label."

"But what she's definite about is that whether or not she's a lesbian, bi, pansexual or whatever — she's into chicks now. Or one chick in particular."

More laughs.

"So everyone please raise your glasses to my friend Alice finally getting the orgasms she deserves."

That got the loudest laugh of all, before everyone raised their glasses. "To Alice!"

And then Rachel's arm did come back around me and I was glad. I needed her by my side, now more than ever.

"I'd also like to add something," I said, my voice coming out loud and clear even though my insides were quivering. "Thanks to Tanya and Sophie for being true to their word and throwing this barbecue — and congrats to them on moving in together, too! And congrats to Meg and Kate and their new addition, Finn. He might not sleep much, but he's the cutest thing here, and that's going some to outdo my new girlfriend." I leaned in to kiss Rachel and the whole party hollered.

When I drew back, I gave Rachel a wink. "And for those of you who might say that was the first time you've seen us kiss, you're all liars. I know you've all watched the video, so don't try to tell me otherwise."

Huge laughter for that one, including from me. Because now, even a few weeks on, it seemed like it happened to some other people in another life.

Yes, Rachel and I had been caught on camera kissing and the whole world had seen, but life went on — and what I was quickly learning was nobody really cared. It was me who'd cared the most. And once I stopped worrying about other people, life had become much easier.

I looked around the party now, to all these wonderful

women and their intertwined lives. They'd always been my friends, always welcomed in my boyfriends, and now they welcomed in my girlfriend just the same. In the end, it turned out there was no difference, apart from the one inside of me. That certain something that I couldn't quite put my finger on.

Tanya would tell me it was a lesbian thing, so did that make me a lesbian? Maybe, but I wasn't going to worry about that today. In fact, today I had no worries, because I was surrounded by friends and love, with my beautiful girlfriend by my side.

I glanced at Becca, who was laughing now.

Would I go back to being 23? Not for anyone.

Would I have liked to have known women might be on my horizon then? Maybe.

But I didn't regret my past, not a single minute.

What's more, I was looking forward to my future, which looked the rosiest it'd ever been.

Chapter Thirty-Four

I'd had the dream again.

I woke in a flurry of hot sheets and damp skin, trying to ground myself back in reality. Only this time, when I woke up, there was no crushing sense of doom — because the dream *was* now my perfect reality.

I rolled over and smiled at her pillow, still warm, the radiator doing its usual early-morning creaking and moaning.

It was February half-term and we had a podcast interview today with the Food Network, which was a pretty big deal. Me, Rachel and Jake, together on-screen, all friends and working together beautifully. Even I was still amazed, but after the shock of our outing, Jake had taken our getting together in his stride, proving again what a supremely lovely man he was.

It also helped that he had a new girlfriend by his side, one he met through our new channel sponsors, oil company FrySmart. He certainly had more of a smile on his face of late.

I heard the shower shut off and rearranged myself in

the bed, smoothing down my hair, making sure I looked the best I possibly could for Rachel's return. When she walked into the room, an orange towel wrapped around her, she grinned at me when she saw I was awake, breaking her stride to walk round to my side of the bed and place a kiss on my lips.

"Morning my snoring beast," she said, raising a single eyebrow as she turned away.

"I don't snore!"

"I'm going to record you one of these days so I can categorically refute that claim."

"Defamation of character, your honour."

Rachel dropped her towel and crawled onto the bed, water droplets still clinging to her skin as she climbed on top of me, straddling me naked. Unwittingly, she was recreating my dream, but you'd get no complaints here. Her breasts swung tantalisingly in front of me, and I leaned forward and kissed them both. She smelled of coconut shower cream and her — and she was already my most favourite smell in the whole wide world.

"I can defame your character again if you like," she said, pinning my arms above my head, her mouth curling into a smile as she moved her head down and brushed my lips with hers.

A shiver ran through me, as was Rachel's affect on me. "Promises, promises," I replied.

"But what I was actually thinking for today — after you get your delicious bum in the shower — is we can do our interview for the show, and then maybe head out and do some shopping." She moved her head towards my side of the bed. "Get you a new bedside table. Perhaps even matching ones." She held up a hand. "And before you explode, yes, I know this is laden with emotions for you, but honestly, don't you want somewhere to put your rings, rather than on the floor?"

I stared at her, this woman who'd waltzed into my life and turned it upside down.

And now she wanted to buy bedside tables.

But this time, I didn't hesitate.

This time, there was no angst, and I was all-in. I wanted nothing more than to buy a bedside table with her and *everything* that meant.

She kissed me again, and then stared, waiting for an answer.

"I'd love to go bedside table shopping with you. And I promise not to have a meltdown and break up with you in the shop."

"We're not going to Ikea, I'm not tempting fate that much," she said, jumping off me and grabbing her towel again. "So we're good? Shower, interview, shopping, dinner, sex? A Tuesday sorted?"

I grinned. "So long as I'm spending it with you, it sounds like the best Tuesday ever."

THE END

Want more from me? Sign up to join my VIP Readers'
Group and get a FREE lesbian romance,
It Had To Be You! *Claim your free book here:*
www.clarelydon.co.uk/it had-to-be-you

Leaving A Review Makes You More Attractive!

Breaking news! Did you know there was a recent survey done and it found that leaving reviews on Amazon, Kobo, iTunes or wherever you bought this book makes you 77% more attractive? It's all to do with the increased brain power used to write the review which makes you more intelligent and therefore far more of a catch; plus, all that typing on the keyboard leaves you with strong hands, along with firm, lean fingers. I don't need to say anymore, do I? *wink*

Reviews are hugely important as they encourage new readers to take a chance on me — if my book's got some reviews, they're far more likely to give me a try. So if you'd like more books from me, please take a moment to leave your thoughts. And it doesn't have to be a novel — even a few lines makes a difference and every review means so much!

And if you need any further encouragement, just remember: ladies love bigger brains + firmer fingers.

If you fancy getting in touch, you can do so using one of the methods below — I'm most active on Twitter, Facebook or Instagram.

Twitter: @ClareLydon
Facebook: www.facebook.com/clare.lydon
Instagram: @clarefic
Find out more at: www.clarelydon.co.uk
Contact: mail@clarelydon.co.uk

THANK YOU SO MUCH FOR READING!

Also by Clare

London Romance Series
London Calling (Book 1)
This London Love (Book 2)
A Girl Called London (Book 3)
London, Actually (Book 5)
Made In London (Book 6)

Other Novels
The Long Weekend
Nothing To Lose: A Lesbian Romance
Twice In A Lifetime
Once Upon A Princess
You're My Kind

All I Want Series
All I Want For Christmas (Book 1)
All I Want For Valentine's (Book 2)
All I Want For Spring (Book 3)
All I Want For Summer (Book 4)
All I Want For Autumn (Book 5)
All I Want Forever (Book 6)

Boxsets
All I Want Series Boxset, Books 1-3
All I Want Series Boxset, Books 4-6
All I Want Series Boxset, Books 1-6
London Romance Series Boxset, Books 1-3

Made in the USA
Monee, IL
21 July 2021

74041007R00194